UNTAMED

A DARK FORCED MARRIAGE BRATVA ROMANCE

BRATVA KINGS

JANE HENRY

Untamed: A Dark Forced Marriage Bratva Romance

Copyright © 2025 by Jane Henry

All rights reserved.

This is a literary work of fiction. Any names, places or incidents are the product of the author's imagination. Similarities or resemblance to actual persons, living or dead, events or establishments, are solely coincidental.

No part of this book may be reproduced, scanned or distributed in any form or by any electronic or mechanical means, including information storage and retrieval systems, without written permission from the author, except for the use of brief quotations in a book review.

The unauthorized reproduction, transmission, distribution of, or use of the copyrighted work in the training of Artificial Intelligences (AI) is illegal and a violation of US copyright law.

ISBN: 978-1-961866-27-0

Acknowledgments

A huge thanks for the invaluable beta feedback I got from influencers Catherine @glavreads and Sierra @boundtoread. Thank you, thank you, thank you!

I also want to thank Michelle Lancaster for the awesome face mask paint job and pic, The Book Brander Boutique for bringing my vision of Rodion Kopolov to life, to my amazing editor Steph at KLS Literary Services for your humor, feedback, and patience helping me work through this story and my endless questions. And as always, thank you to Jessie and Michael for having my back and doing all the things so I can focus on what I love to do most of all — tell the stories.

TRIGGER WARNING

Readers please note: *Untamed: A Dark Forced Marriage Bratva Romance* contains graphic violence and heavy mention of SA.

SYNOPSIS

When fiction meets fantasy it's not all fun and games..

I don't just dream about possessive anti-heroes.

I crave them.

The dark, dangerous ones dripping with Bratva energy, the ones who claim you with a single look and make the world kneel at your feet just to keep you safe.

"Touch her and die..."? I live for it.

"My wife..."? My favorite.

It's all a harmless fantasy.

Until it's not.

I've built an online following fan-girling over book boyfriends just like him.

And he knows it.

The only problem? Rodion Kopolev doesn't just embody the dark anti-heroes I love...he is one.

So when his obsessive focus lands on me, I feel like the heroine in one of my books.

His possessive words claim me.

His dominant touch brands me.

And when I try to run, he chases...

But when the threats of my past creep closer and I need protection from a dangerous stalker, Rodion is the devil willing to protect me... for a price.

Turns out, when the fantasy becomes reality, it's not so harmless after all...

CHAPTER 1

RODION

The low thrum of dance music beats steadily, like the heartbeat of California's underbelly. Neon lights slash across the dance floor, throwing jagged shadows over the dancing forms of women. I lazily watch them. I love women of all shapes and sizes. I don't care about the color of their skin or their hair, if they're short or tall, curvy or slender, or if they have glasses or freckles or whatever. Women are god's gift to men, and fuck, I miss having one in my bed. It's been way too long.

I've tried to be good. Responsible. *Mature.*

God.

California might glitter, but I miss the familiarity of home. Here, under these neon lights, I feel untouchable and detached—like a tiger prowling, watching the world from behind the bars of a cage.

I want out.

I nurse my glass of the bar's sorry excuse for vodka—some cheap, local crap that doesn't hold a candle to what we drink at home for any excuse to cheer a victory—and glance at my hands.

Fuck. For a second, I swear I see flecks of blood from the job I wrapped up earlier. But no, it's just the lights messing with me. I washed my hands in the penthouse bathroom so many times under steaming water that they're half-scalded.

Not that it matters. Rafail, my oldest brother and the pakhan of our family, rules with an iron fist and expects every job to be wrapped up neat, tied with a bow. Me? I like the reminders of what I'm capable of.

Maybe it makes me a sociopath. I like to think it keeps me human.

Got one more job to do here.

A burst of laughter gets my attention. I look over to see a table of giggling women. I shift closer to the bar, slinking into the shadows so I can watch unnoticed. Six of them, dressed in low-cut tops and short skirts, sit at a table cluttered with empty glasses. A young brunette with waist-length glossy hair shoves her phone under the nose of another woman. The second one's wearing something across her shoulders. A sash?

I squint.

Bride to Be, the gold lettering reads. Ah. A bachelorette party.

How cute.

"I'm telling you, it's the possessive ones! Like, 'I own you' energy!" A blonde giggles over her drink. Her friend rolls her eyes but doesn't argue.

My ears perk up. *"I own you energy."* What are they talking about?

I've got better things to do than eavesdrop, but I'm bored as hell and need to get laid. Rafail would fucking kill me for not sticking to the plan.

I fucked up, big time, and he sent me here to lay low while he manages the fallout. Turned out I could utilize my skills while here for the greater good of my family, so I can't lose focus now.

I look away from them.

My phone buzzes with a text.

> **Rafail**
> Heads up. Semyon got fucked over…
> instead of wedding bells, looks like he'll be
> playing clean-up crew and teaching some
> lessons.

Shit. It's been a year since Rafail married his wife, Polina, which meant it was time for one of us to get married. We had to. Taking the position of leadership after my father's death, Rafail wasted no time in establishing himself as the married eldest because, in the old-fashioned, cutthroat world of the Russian Bratva, a married man had more power. Respect. A man like *me*—wild and free, untamed by the love of a woman—was unfettered but unpredictable... *and* wielded less power.

We don't have time to date casually and don't have the luxury of playing around. Marriage, children, the stability of vows are a must.

Semyon was ready to marry before the ink was dry on Rafail and Polina's marriage certificate. He didn't have the time or patience for anything less.

What *was* it about our luck, anyway? Rafail's first attempt at marriage was an epic fail, and now Semyon...

> **Rafail**
> So maybe... if you happen to find a wife in California, make it happen. At least for now. The Romanov gala is in a month, and we need a show of strength when we attend

Of fucking course. Rafail didn't "joke." Semyon's fucked-up nuptials left us with few choices, and one of them was up to *me*.

God.

Find a wife, he says. Like it's that simple. I already play his enforcer, his pawn. Now he wants me to play groom too? God forbid I don't bow to the family legacy.

I roll my eyes and lift my hand, about to order another drink, but the bartender beats me to it, sliding a glass into my outstretched palm. "Here," she says, smiling. "This is better than the vodka here. Do me a favor? You seem like a decent guy."

Little does she know. Still, I flash her the grin that melts panties and throw in a wink. Her neck flushes with heat, but she schools her expression fast, tilting her head toward the end of the bar.

I take a sip of bourbon—strong, potent, now we're getting somewhere—and follow her gesture.

"I'm not supposed to intervene unless customers cross the line," she says, her voice low. "But that asshole's been buying drinks for that table of women, even though they're clearly trying to avoid him. I don't like it. You seem...scary-looking enough. Not my business, but that guy's bad news. Maybe just park yourself down there?"

I nod. Playing silent bodyguard for a stranger isn't on my agenda, but I push off the bar anyway, drink in hand, and head down the row.

The bar thrums with a low bass. The air reeks of expensive cologne, tequila, and cheap sex. I shake my head. I hate California. Too many rules, too many people who thought money made them untouchable.

But tonight isn't about me—it never is. I'm here for the Bratva, for my family. For Rafail's newly born son, so small he can't even hold his little head up yet. For my parents, who were buried way too young, with their lives still ahead of them.

I'm here because Rafail and family honor demanded it.

One target's an arrogant little bastard who thought he could cheat the Russian mafia and walk away. And I came here to remind him how far loyalty went when it was wrapped in barbed wire.

I know immediately who the bartender's talking about. I give the businessman in a wrinkled suit a once-over. He's got one of those comb-over hairstyles to mask his receding hairline and a gold chain around his neck. I glance at his hand, where the indentation on his finger indicates a wedding band recently removed.

Sigh. So predictable.

I'm not a hero. Hell, I'm barely human some days. But I know the lines a man doesn't cross. And when I see this guy crowding her, all I can think is *I've crossed too many lines already. This one? Not tonight.*

He leans across the table and pushes a drink to one of the women.

She shakes her head. "No, thank you."

"I bought it for you," the chubby douchebag says, pushing it over to her again. Oh, for the love of... Rafail would get on a plane just to throat punch me if he knew I was getting involved, but I can't help it.

There's nothing I like more than helping a damsel in distress. *And* it's gotten me laid more times than I can count.

My voice is low when I meet his eyes and push the drink back. "Hey, buddy. She said no. Drink it yourself. Better yet, why don't you leave her the fuck alone and don't come back?" I feel their eyes on me but focus on this guy and this guy alone.

Beady eyes narrow on me as he draws himself up to his full height. *Aww.* He thinks he can get away with it. I almost feel sorry for the poor bastard.

I'm easily a head taller than him, with one more tool in my kit he probably doesn't have: *I* don't care if I spill another man's blood tonight.

"Who the fuck asked you to get involved?" the businessman asshole says. "I bought her a drink. She wanted one."

"I did *not!*" I turn to look at her and narrowly miss getting coldcocked by this asshole. I swivel, grab his wrist just in time, and shake my head with a little *tsk.*

"You really shouldn't have done that," I say in a whisper, twisting his hand back until pain dances in his eyes and he grits his teeth. "I promise you. You're going to regret that. Why don't we take a little walk."

Still gripping his wrist, I drag him toward me and discreetly shove him in front of me.

"I'm-I'm sorry," he begins, but I shake my head.

"Too late for apologies, my man," I say, my temper rising. "You disrespected a woman."

I follow few laws, but *never disrespect a woman* is one of them.

As we head toward the exit, I can hear the table of giggling bachelorettes.

"Oh my god, he's like one of the book guys."

"Did you see those muscles?"

"He looks like the video mafia queen posted!"

Mafia... what? I catch a glimpse at the screen. What the fuck is *that?* I try to take another look, but my friend, the predator, tries to use my distraction to his advantage and wheedle out of my grip.

Nah.

I wrap my hands around the back of his neck and help him focus on doing what the fuck I say. The neon *Exit* sign flashes in the center of the doorway above a dark hall.

"This is what you're gonna do," I tell him as we near the door. "You're gonna get the fuck out of here and pretend tonight never happened. You'll pretend we never talked, that you never tried to push yourself on a woman who said no."

Blood thrums in my veins, molten lava teeming with destruction.

"You can't—"

I lean in close. He's half a breath away from meeting my fist. "I have a knife in my pocket and a gun in a holster at my back. I can and will." I hold him in my right hand so I can discreetly flash the sign of the Bratva, a universal tat that every man of our family gets when he's sixteen years old.

I watch his eyes widen in recognition. Good. I kick open the door. "Good riddance," I mutter as I shove him out and slam the door behind him.

The bartender catches my attention and gives me a thumbs-up. The women giggle and wave at me, but I only jerk my head and sit back down at the other end of the bar. I shoot my younger cousin and best friend Matvei a text.

Dude, you see these mafia posts these girls online are raving about? Tf? I just scared away some guy that wouldn't leave them alone and they were GIGGLING. I heard something about mafia books.

The response comes immediately.

> **Matvei**
> Got your head up your ass again? You that clueless what these romance girls are reading these days? Serial killers, masked men, stalkers… I got fucking tagged in a post. This is amazing

I snort and shake my head. I don't know if I'd say it's *amazing,* but it's amusing, definitely.

I tap the screen as I sit back at the bar and drink. He sends a group text.

Jesus, Matvei. Leave Raf out of it. We leave him out of anything remotely fun.

> **Matvei**
> You guys see this shit online?

I roll my eyes and play dumb.

> I'm swimming in shitbags in California. My brain is fried. Maybe I need to find one of those oxygen bars they have or something. The fuck are you talking about?

> **Matvei**
> All those girls online are drooling over mafia men.

Ice hits my teeth, and I shove the glass back on the bar while I glance at the girls who are whispering to each other and casting discreet glances my way.

> **Semyon**
> What the fuck are you going on about now?

I pop an ice cube in my mouth like I'm eating a bowl of popcorn. This is entertaining, but I need real food that's not in the form of liquid and ninety proof. My gaze falls on the table of scantily clad, giggling women.

This time, I take a closer look.

It's some video with a masked man holding an ax. He's swinging it with force, cutting wood in the dead of winter. Bare-chested. Fuck. Who *does* that? Wear a coat, fuckwit. Even my nips ache just thinking about that frozen hellscape.

Americans romanticize the strangest shit.

My phone buzzes again, and I consider flushing it in the nearest bathroom when a video pops up from Matvei.

I click the triangle. I have to download a fucking app just to see the damn thing and immediately have to turn the volume down on my phone when some stupid dance music blares on the screen.

It's a girl—no, a woman—talking about her fantasies of dark, possessive mafia men. It should be absurd, laughable. But there's something about the way she says it, her tone laced with teasing vulnerability. Like she wants to be swept away but can't trust anyone enough to let it happen.

And she's... crying. I know it's staged. I know it's just for show, but something in me cracks at the sight of a woman in tears. My hands clench into fists.

Who do I need to punish?

Her caption reads: *"Who else dreams of being kidnapped and 'tortured' by a hot, billionaire, masked mafia man? Asking for a friend."*

My lips curve into a smirk. No tall order, lady. Though... I mean... I tick off all *those* boxes.

I just need a mask. That's easy enough.

Matvei sends another video.

Matvei
This shit's gone viral

Semyon
Is this a bad joke?

Rafail
What the fuck is this?

Matvei:
You guys need to listen up. There are MAFIA THIRST TRAPS. They want us. Like, really want us.

> Rafail, you're not keeping him busy enough.

But just for the fuck of it, I click the link.

And I watch. A gorgeous blonde with wide blue eyes and thick lashes licks her lips while the right side of her screen shows a masked man with tats and muscles.

I roll my eyes. He's fucking scrawny compared to *my* brothers, and did she really think those pecs were real? Nah. I can tell from here he used a filter like a goddamn fucking pussy.

I almost shut the thing and get another drink when she starts fanning herself with her phone—no, it wasn't a phone, it's much too big for a phone. I look closer. Is that an e-reader?

That's when I notice the wall of books behind her, like some sort of fucking shrine to a bookstore, but it isn't just any bookshelf. They're color-coordinated in a rainbow, twinkling pink lights entangled with greenery, making it look festive.

"This is all I want, girls," she says, wiping a fat tear from her cheek. "I work sixty-hour weeks at a thankless job, and when I come home? I want *this guy* waiting for me." She lowers her voice. "Is that too much to ask?"

Huh.

I scroll.

And I scroll.

And I scroll.

I feel my lips curve into a smirk, the kind that typically makes my enemies rethink their decisions.

They want... *us?*

They don't. No, they really, *really* don't.

They think they want us—the barbed-wire promises, the wolves lurking just beyond the storybook light. But what they want is the illusion of us, not the raw, vicious truth. No woman wants my calloused, bloodstained hand in her hair —or, more accurately, wrapped around her throat, pinning her to my headboard, or—heh. Maybe that *was* a good drink.

I tap my finger against my jaw. I still have a job to do before I go back home, but January in Moscow is frigid as fuck, and if I'm honest, I might not want to move here, but this weather feels downright balmy. And it's nice not having to put up with the daily discerning eye and constant criticism of my eldest brother.

I look back over at the giggling party girls. They're glued to their screens, their expressions dreamy as they giggle over obviously fake videos with posers— men wearing masks from a goddamn party store, their weapons a sham. It's like some sort of cosplay gone bad.

I can't help but snort when a few of the videos have *three* men, ropes in hand, masks hiding fuck knows what, with a low growl of a man's voice. *"We're coming for you. And when we find you, beware..."*

It's so damn *fake.*

Obviously, a real man didn't fucking *share.* This is the stupidest shit I ever—

My hand hovers over the *x* at the top of the page, ready to shut it down, when I see... *her.*

Fiery red hair tied back in a thick ponytail, a mischievous spark in her jade-green eyes.

She's so different from the other videos I've seen, so authentic. Unlike the fake thirst traps or heavily edited videos, she looks candid and excited, as if she can't wait to talk about her latest book.

She looks... *real*. Strong. And even though she's wearing a plain white top and a pair of jeans, the girl fills them *out*. She has the body of a gymnast, tightly wound and powerful. My breath slows as I take her in—sparkling green eyes, a strength in her every movement that makes my fingers itch to touch her, to feel if she's as real as she looks.

"Girls," she says, shaking her head.

Girls? Was she completely unaware of the absolute magnetic pull a woman like her had on a man like me?

I'm instantly, irrationally filled with rage toward any other man who sets eyes on her. She's unlike anyone I've ever seen before.

"Stop what you're doing *right now* and read this book." She holds up a black and gold book with raised lettering, the edges sprayed gold, as she flips through it. "You've never heard of it before. No one has. It's unlike anything I've ever read before. And this book." She shakes her head and bites her lip.

That single motion—her teeth grazing her lip—ignites something primal. It's the smallest tell. I've honed my observation skills, and I know how to read body language. It's part of my job description, and partly why I can so easily spot lies. She really *does* want what she's reading about.

This girl *wants* to surrender, even if she doesn't know it yet. I'd make damn sure she learned what that meant.

I swallow hard and watch.

She lowers her voice to a whisper. I hold my breath, mesmerized by her voice, the way she talks, even the way her fingers grip around the book in her hand. I imagine what it would be like to have those hands splayed over my body or pinned in one hand while I fisted her gorgeous hair in the other. I'd fuck her right against that bookshelf until she screamed for mercy... until she knew the difference between fiction and reality and never again fell for a goddamn book boyfriend when she belonged to *me*.

"This looks tame, doesn't it? A poor school teacher on holiday in the wild Scottish moors. A single father, mourning the loss of his wife while navigating the world alone..." Her voice drops. "Only *this* guy's in the mafia, and he'll stop at *nothing*..." Her voice drops even lower. "*Nothing* to claim her."

She shakes her head. I hold my breath. She fingers the golden edges, and my dick comes to *life*.

"When I tell you there's *no line* this man won't cross for her..." She shakes her head as if completely overcome with emotion. "Chases her in the woods... kidnaps her in the back of his car... fucks her blindfolded in an abandoned warehouse while suspending her from—"

She covers her mouth as if she's said too much.

"You'll have to take my word for it."

My mouth is dry. This woman is *completely* unaware of what she's playing with. She doesn't realize the line she's walking—romanticizing the very thing that could destroy her.

"Careful what you wish for," I mutter under my breath before I down the rest of my bourbon.

The bartender slides me another without being asked. I raise the glass in silent thanks before my gaze flicks back to my mark, the reason I'm here.

Still busy with the blonde, still oblivious.

All I have to do tonight is case him and confirm he's cheating on his wife before I blackmail the fuck out of him and extort him for ten times what he owes us.

Easy.

I exhale and stare back at my phone as if rewarding myself for a job well done. My mouth dry, I click the *follow* button at the top of the page.

I check the messages that have been buzzing in my pocket like an angry swarm of bees. There's a new notification in our group chat.

<text>

Rafail: I don't know what stupid nonsense you're spending your time watching, but if you don't do what I fucking tell you, I'll show you exactly where I'll shove your goddamn phone

Rafail is impatient on a good day. Sleep-deprived, daddy of a newborn Rafail is a fucking animal.

Well, he can get mad at us all he wants. The reality is, *he* is happily married while Semyon nurses his wounds and plans for option B, and I'm thinking of—

No. I am thinking nothing.

I slip my phone in my pocket. I can't afford distractions, least of all ones wrapped in unrealistic, staged internet fantasies. This is my job, my duty, and—

My phone buzzes.

With a growl of annoyance, I pull it out again. My heart flips over.

It's a notification. I follow exactly one person online, and here she is, and—oh my god. She's in her pajamas.

I swallow hard.

She's in *bed*, a bed with a sturdy headboard and a thick comforter while she playfully bites her lip while holding a paperback book.

She's so damn cute. If only she knew how far-removed real life was from her stories. Princes don't exist in our world— only wolves and their prey.

Still, my fingers hover over the screen. A stupid idea creeps into my mind, one that Rafail would probably punch me for.

What if I... I polish off my drink and look around. Dim lighting. It's perfect.

I open my camera, position the phone to catch the glint of my pistol holster under my suit jacket, and hit record.

The video's quick—just enough to show the weapon and a flash of stubble and a smirk. I add a caption:

> **Careful what you wish for,**
> **@dreammafiaqueen.**

It's a reckless, dangerous game. One that could unravel everything. But as the video uploads, I feel like I've stepped off the edge, daring her to follow.

And yet, as I hit *post* and slide the phone away, I can't help the laugh that rumbles in my chest. Self-deprecating, bitter, but amused all the same. She likes Bratva? I'll call her bluff.

"I am going to regret that," I mutter.

I don't do distractions. Not when blood is on the line. But as I slip through the crowd, heading back to the hotel, my hand brushes the cold steel of the knife strapped to my hip, and I find myself wondering.

What would a woman like her taste like—innocence or fire?

And what would she do if she really met her fantasy man in real life?

My phone dings with a notification. I frown at the screen then click it as a slow, wicked grin spreads across my face.

Reply from @dreammafiaqueen

CHAPTER 2

EMBER

THE HIGH FROM today's photoshoot still hums through me. My arms ache from holding my equipment, my knees from crouching for the perfect angles. I can't remember the last time I ate, and the California sun left my skin warm and tight. I'm probably going to be sore tomorrow, but it's worth it.

There's nothing like nailing the perfect shot to remind me why I do this—why I've fought so hard to build something that's mine. It's the only time I'm untouchable.

And tonight? I've got a delicious book waiting for me. I need it after today.

"Hey, Ember!" I look up to see Victoria, one of the other photographers, hurrying across the parking lot with my phone in her hand. "You forgot this!"

"Oh god, thanks!" I take it from her with a grateful smile,

though my stomach knots. The phone buzzes in my palm like a live wire.

No one in my real life knows about my side gig.

She hesitates. "Uh... you might want to check it. Your phone's been buzzing nonstop. You've got fans or something?"

Crap. I keep my work and my personal life separate for a reason, and the thought of someone stumbling across the latter? It's enough to make me sweat.

I laugh it off. "Oh, probably just a group chat exploding. You know how it is."

"I do. Later!" She grins, waves, and jogs off to her car. Innocent as hell.

I sigh, tucking my phone into my back pocket as I head to my car. I toss my camera bag onto the passenger seat and glance at my hands. The scabs on my knuckles from last week's shoot have just started to heal. It had been a gritty urban portrait session with a graffiti artist, and I'd spent half the day gripping the sharp edges of scaffolding for the perfect rooftop shot.

It's worth it though. Every bruise, every ache, every risk. Being a freelance photographer is unpredictable, feast-or-famine, but I love it. I love telling stories with my camera, crafting something permanent out of fleeting moments.

This is what I control, what I can really and truly lean into.

The influencer work? That's another story. For some reason, that's taken *off*, so I'm fully planning on making hay while the sun shines because who knows how long this will last.

I've somehow landed myself a super fan, and I can't get him out of my mind, no matter how hard I try.

I toss my duffel on the passenger seat of my car and peel off my gloves, trying not to wince at the new scrape across my knuckles. How'd I even get that one?

I glance at my phone.

I give myself the brief luxury of scrolling through notifications and reading comments. It's fun, an escape from reality into the safe bubble of my book world where book boyfriends can do no wrong. Or, no wrong we can't forgive easily, knowing there's a happy ending coming.

Sigh.

When I get home, the apartment is quiet, just the way I like it after a day full of coordinated chaos. I kick off my boots, head to the kitchen, and pop open a cold one, already thinking about the video I'll post tonight.

I kinda wish I had a sweet little fluffy pup to greet me at the door, but my hours are too unpredictable, and if I'm honest —*I'm* too unpredictable and not ready for the responsibility of another living being to care for. Doesn't mean I don't have a whole folder of puppy videos saved to smile at when I'm stressed. It's just not time.

I've survived too much—*no.* I won't let my mind go there. I read romance for a reason, to remember there's softness in the world. After hours, I step into that role, not to forget, but to reclaim what was taken.

To dream a little.

Sliding onto the couch, I pull my laptop closer and start scrolling for inspiration.

Victoria wasn't kidding. The notifications are on fire, and it isn't just the comments and likes on my posts. I have to disable those so I can save my battery during a shoot, but I still get private messages.

Tonight, my timeline is full of familiar faces—friends. Other girls like me who've mastered the art of blending their real lives with their fictional fantasies. We collectively drool over all of them—mafia men, billionaire bodyguards, forbidden romances, sexy vampires. And then something catches my eye.

I've got twenty private messages, and they're all my friends sending me the video. *The guy from last night.*

I wondered if my messages scared him off. I had a little fun telling him posers like him were a dime a dozen.

But no.

The thumbnail alone catches my attention: this time, he's wearing a mask, and his eyes meet mine on-screen. He's stroking a gun like it's his personal talisman. I swallow hard. There's something... sensual about it. It breaks the rules of social media, and he'll be banned for it... eventually.

He lifts his mask just enough to smirk and stroke his chin. The stubble along his jaw promises a delicious scrape, and the smirk? Not just cocky—it's predatory, like he's already imagined exactly what he'd do to you if you got too close.

But something about him seems... dangerous.

Too dangerous.

My finger hovers over the play button.

What can it hurt?

I press it.

The video is quick. Like last night, just a few seconds of him adjusting his jacket to show the weapon. Then the caption appears.

You've been a bad girl, @dreammafiaqueen.

My breath catches. Somehow, my body's decided it's both a thrill *and* a threat.

Is this a joke?

My stomach twists. The profile name is simple, generic, but it's the implication that has my heart racing. Does he *know* me? No. He couldn't.

I post a comment.

Dreammafiaqueen
This is so staged it isn't even funny, girls.
Let's stick with the book boyfriends.

Still, my finger trembles as I scroll to his profile. There's nothing else posted. Just two videos, and somehow, it already has thousands of likes. The comments are a mess of thirsty replies.

Marry me!

Daddy vibes, omg!

> Where do I sign up to be kidnapped?
> Asking for a friend.

> Weird way to propose, but I accept.

I swallow hard, my drink forgotten on the table.

Who is this guy?

Is he mocking me?

I've had trolls before. It comes with the territory, but this feels different. My brain tells me it's probably just some douche trying to cash in on the latest craze. Plenty of guys do it. They slap on a leather jacket, pull on a mask, post a thirst trap, and suddenly they're the fantasy du jour and raking it in, especially the guys with the manly voices. Jesus, some of them are probably still in high school, and yet here we are.

But my gut says this one... this one is different.

Something about his muscles, the way he handles his weapons...seems different. Something about the way he moves, the comfortable look of him with the gun—it feels *real*.

I laugh to myself for even entertaining the thought that any of these men are any more real than the last, but it's shaky, the kind of laugh that betrays how tightly wound I am. I take another sip of my beer and tell myself this is absurd— but some part of me, the part that revels in fantasy and happy endings—wonders.

I have to keep in mind there's a difference between fantasy and reality, and there's no reason whatsoever to believe this guy is legit.

I shake my head, trying to snap myself out of it. It's ridiculous. I don't believe in this stuff. Not really. Sure, I love the stories, the tension, the escape they bring, but I know better than to think men like this actually exist. Men like this don't stalk women online. They don't care enough to play games. They're too... busy... doing... illegal things.

Right?

My phone buzzes, breaking the spell. I glance at the screen. It's a DM from one of my friends, Bookbabe, who always seems to catch everything before I do.

> **Bookbabe**
> Girl. This guy tagged you. He's insane. 😳
> 🔥

> Yeah. What the hell?

> **Bookbabe**
> Are you freaking out? Because I'm freaking
> out FOR you. What if he's legit? Do you
> think he's real??

I pause, staring at her question.

Do I think he's real?

The videos replay in my head, and I realize I don't have an answer. Of course he's *real*. There's no telltale watery abs that indicate AI, no whispery hint of a fake. But I know what she means.

Be careful what you wish for.

I open his profile again, my heart in my throat as I watch his follower count climb like a silent army. Thousands of strangers are seeing my name next to his threat, and every second that passes makes it feel more... real. My name, *dreammafiaqueen*, is still in the caption like a goddamn beacon, drawing even more attention. I note that his likes are all public, and every one of them are all *my* videos.

And even as his follower numbers soar, who *he* follows remains...one.

Me.

My chest tightens, my fight-or-flight instincts kicking in.

There's only one way to find out if this is a joke.

I click the message button, and my thumbs hover over the keyboard. For a moment, I hesitate. My rational brain screams at me to close the app, to forget his smirk and the promise in his words. But the part of me that craves excitement and the attention of a man just like him—the part that reads the books I do—whispers, *just one more message. It's fiction. It's harmless.*

I type the words before I can stop myself.

But before I can hit send, the app pings with another tag. My breath stalls as another video fills the screen.

No. This can't be happening.

Oh my *god*. It's him again, but this time, there's no leather jacket, nothing but his bare chest, and *what a bare chest it is*. Unlike the other men who cover shit up with leather jackets or hoodies, he's *ripped*. Strong, powerful hands anchored on his hips, jeans just low enough to show the hint of dark hair.

My mouth is dry. I swallow, but it doesn't help. The other videos hinted at how built he was, but...

I choke on a strangled scream as comment after comment pours in.

> Do you need a baby mama? Do we need to keep your line of DNA open for the sake of populating the earth? I'm single. 🫰

> Do you come with an instruction manual, or do we just wing it? Asking for a friend. 😊

> Sir, respectfully, HOW DARE YOU? 😵

> Who gave you permission to ruin my entire day with this? 😩 🔥

> Jeans low, jaw high, confidence THROUGH THE ROOF. If he puts on a pair of gray sweats, I'm going to spontaneously combust. I'm not okay. 😵

> I don't care if this is staged, I am HERE FOR IT and so are my ovarieeesss!!!

I roll my eyes and barely refrain from gently reminding some of these girls that he tagged *me* and me alone, and they can keep their thirsty little mitts off him, but that feels so grade school.

Oh.

Oh, wait. *Mine* is the only comment he replied to. Holding my breath, I scroll down.

> Not staged.

Oh *sure,* he's a hot made man looking for some attention. And I've got a bridge to sell you, ironically not far from here... I roll my eyes when my phone dings with a notification.

It's a... *message?*

Bratvabloodline
What makes you think this is staged?

God, his username is Bratvabloodline.

My pulse racing, I tap out a quick message.

Because I would imagine men like...
supposedly you... have better things to do
than post thirst traps?

Bratvabloodline
Better things to do than get your attention?

I roll my eyes. My skin feels strangely hot and prickly. We can't get off the subject.

But this whole staged mafia thing...

Bratvabloodline
Like I said, not staged. Obviously, I can't
talk.

Ooh. Well played.

I can't not ask questions. If you're REALLY
mafia (LOL) which kind are you?

I'm disappointed when he doesn't respond right away. Maybe he *is* chatting with other women, and why does that make me feel jealous? Maybe he's—

My cheeks color as I go back to his screen, only to realize he's posted another video.

He stands in what looks like... a penthouse? He's wearing jeans hung low on his waist, his eyes riveted on the screen.

You've been a naughty girl, @dreammafiaqueen. You should know by now what happens to bad girls.

Wait. He said I've... been a bad girl? My breathing hitches.

Slowly, his eyes staring straight at me through the screen, he begins to unfasten his belt. I'm absolutely fucking mesmerized; my mouth is dry as he pulls the leather through the loops with an audible *snap*.

Ahhhhhhh!

Walking over to a gorgeous couch, he arranges pillows in the shape of... oh god. No. Is he really?

With practiced ease, he doubles the belt over in his large, very manly hand, and snaps it across the fullest part of the pillow.

I let out a little *squeak*.

I plan a quick internet search of the tats he has, only to be drawn deep into the meanings behind his tattoos. A crowned skull, inked on his forearm, signifies authority earned through ruthless power. Stars etched on his collarbones—prison tattoos—mark him as someone who bows to no one. The spiderweb ink over his elbow, a symbol of time served. And the one that has me most intrigued— intricate script on his knuckles spells out a phrase in Russian that translates to "Loyalty Until Death."

If he's faking, he's gone to astonishing lengths to make it real.

Okay, let's be rational here.

Either those are fake tattoos, or...

I go back to his screen and stare. I click the little triangle when I realize he's *talking*.

"Come a little closer," he whispers, gesturing to the camera and, *oh my god, his voice*. Rough and raspy, low and manly, and *tinged with a Russian accent*.

That's it. Tomorrow, I'm quitting my day job and going full-time influencer.

> So what, you're a Bratva boss now? Should I start practicing my Russian?

> **Bratvabloodline**
> You tell me, kitten.

Ugh, why do *I looooove thaaat?*

> I call bullshit.

> **Bratvabloodline**
> Careful.

My skin prickles. The word lands like a spark on dry kindling. There's a warning in his tone I feel in my spine.

> Why are you harassing me?

> **Bratvabloodline**
> You said you liked made men, kitten.

Kitten again. My fingers hover over the screen, poised to type an appropriately scathing reply, but nothing feels sharp enough.

You make it sound like I swiped you on a dating app. I was only…intrigued. Curious.

Bratvabloodline
Curiosity doesn't have to be fatal. Not if you're careful.

The audacity. My heart's racing, but I'm not about to let him know that.

Oh, please. Are you trying to be mysterious, or is it just a side effect of all the brooding in your pics?

Bratvabloodline
Brooding? You wound me.

You'll survive.

Bratvabloodline
You sound confident about that. Makes me wonder what else you think you know about me.

I can practically hear his voice in my head—low, teasing, infuriatingly smooth. This is just banter. Nothing more. Right?

I know you're probably not as intimidating as you want everyone to believe.

Bratvabloodline
Bold assumption. Ready to test it?

Test it? What does that even mean? My pulse stumbles, and for a moment, I just stare at the words.

Hard pass. I don't do alpha male posturing.

> **Bratvabloodline**
> Is that what you think this is? Cute.

Cute. Like I'm some naïve little thing he can toy with. My cheeks flame, and I'm about to type something sharp when another message pops up.

> **Bratvabloodline**
> Tell me something, Ember.

I freeze. He used my name. My real name. My heart pounds in my chest, fingers hovering above the screen.

> How do you know my name?

> **Bratvabloodline**
> It's in your profile. Relax, kitten. I'm not stalking you.

Kitten, again. The word slips through my defenses, a deliberate stroke that feels both possessive and unsettling.

> **Bratvabloodline**
> Unless you'd like me to.

My stomach tightens. Is he joking? He has to be.

> What's wrong with you?

> **Bratvabloodline**
> Plenty. But we're not talking about me. Yet.

The confidence in his words makes my skin tingle.

> I'm just trying to figure out why a guy like
> you is wasting his time chatting with me.

Bratvabloodline
Because I'm intrigued. And trust me, I don't
waste my time.

It feels like a warning as much as a compliment. A thrill works its way through me despite my better judgment.

> You don't even know me.

Bratvabloodline
Not yet. But I'm a fast learner.

There's a pause, long enough for my heart rate to settle, then spike again when his next message arrives.

Bratvabloodline
I'd enjoy learning you, Ember. Thoroughly.

My breath hitches. My hands tremble as I read and reread the words, heat rushing to my face.

I swallow hard, my mind racing, my nerves alive.

Bratvabloodline
Keep talking. Or better yet, stop talking and
let me tell you what happens next.

I shouldn't reply.

What am I doing?

Every instinct screams at me to stop, to delete the conversation and forget this ever happened. When I don't respond, he sends me another message.

Bratvabloodline
Behave yourself or you'll find out in vivid
detail.

And just like that, I'm not just hooked.

I'm trapped.

Nope. I will not reply. I have to get ahold of myself and be reasonable here.

I grab myself another beer, even as every instinct in me warns me to stop.

There is one of two options here: He's lying, and I shouldn't have any interaction with a man who lies. I don't do relationships, but I most especially don't do relationships with unreliable, self-centered liars.

Or two. He's *not*, which means... I should stay far, far away.

An hour passes.

Two.

My phone buzzes when I'm tagged in another video. I stare at my phone in the corner of the couch, as I dutifully try to ignore it and stare at my book instead.

But the real-life story is so much more interesting than the one I'm reading. I finally can't resist anymore and pick up the phone again.

He tagged me in another video.

CHAPTER 3

RODION

I WAKE UP DETERMINED. Today, I'll make choices my brothers can respect—choices that prove I'm more than the reckless, impulsive wildcard they expect.

This is the day I turn things around.

Last night, when she wouldn't reply to my messages anymore, I tagged her in another video. And even though I get the notification that she watched it, she still didn't reply to me.

I roll over, and something cold hits my chest. My phone. I shake my head at it and push it under a pillow near my head.

Nope.

Get away from me.

I spent all night flirting with a woman I've never met and

never will, letting her words slip into places they have no business being.

Reckless. Stupid.

Addictive.

It's my fault I'm all the way in California while the rest of my family's in Russia.

I can still hear Rafail, the disappointment in his voice worse than any punishment he could've levied.

You have to keep a handle on your anger, Rodion. You're not a child anymore.

He was right, of course. I didn't have to make a public spectacle of punishing the fucking traitor.

I scrub a hand across my brow and blow out a breath.

I can do this.

And I won't fuck this up by flirting and risking it all by putting myself out there on stupid *social media.*

I shake my head and get to my feet when another buzz from my phone sounds.

I stare at the pillow, vibrating with message after message.

If it were Rafail and I ignored him...

I scratch at my bicep and roll my eyes heavenward. Everyone has to take a piss or make a fucking cup of coffee... right? Wrong, when it comes to my brother. I can hear him now. "You only need one hand to take a leak. Use the other to check my messages."

I am going to get on Rafail's good side no matter what it takes. I *will* prove to him I'm not the tagalong he thinks I am.

I reach for my phone and check my messages.

Good thing.

> **Rafail**
> Saw the work you did yesterday, read the files and your report. Well done, Rodion. Talk's died down, people are starting to forget.

Pride blossoms in my chest. I was still a child when my parents died, and Rafail became guardian of my family. He's like a father to me and pleasing him matters. Semyon, four years younger than Rafail but still older, is colder, more detached, but that's just his personality. He's as faithful to my family as any of us, and I fucking hate that he got screwed over.

I have to make this right.

All of it.

> One down, two to go. Trailed Dovinksy last night and he's on par for being predictable as fuck once more. Anything else you need to share?

The little dots next to Rafail's name pop up, but instead of a text message, an image of his newborn son comes onto the screen.

My god.

A lump actually rises in my throat. I haven't cried since we got news of my parents' death. I didn't even cry the day we buried them. Semyon, Rafail, and I, along with two of my cousins, were the pallbearers. As is tradition, we tossed the dirt on the casket first. My baby sister Zoya openly wept as I hugged her, the only one of us who did. Yana wasn't close with my father and had her own struggles she kept close to the vest. Semyon was damn near stoic, and I would've sworn carved of ice if I hadn't seen the way he melted toward little Zoya, and Rafail was a statue.

But something about seeing that baby... that precious little bundle, wrapped in a swaddled blanket, his little fist to his mouth, white-blond hair like his mama's crowning his perfectly round little head... it moves something in me. I swallow the lump in my throat.

> **Rafail**
> **This little champ slept for five hours**
> **straight. We're feeling half-human again.**
> **He's eating up a storm and outgrew the**
> **newborn sleepers already**

I stifle a snort. Rafail Kopolov, Moscow's most feared, chatting about newborn sleepers and his little champ of a son. My eyes are a little blurry. I've always had a soft spot for the vulnerable. I can't help it.

> He's got your eyes, brother. He looks so
> much like you, except for the hair

> **Rafail**
> All I see is my wife when I look at him, but I
> couldn't be more proud

> **Semyon**
> Lucky him. That could've worked out pretty fucking bad for him

> Give it time. Still might get his daddy's take-no-prisoners attitude and chip on the shoulder. Too soon to tell

We ease from conversation about the baby to our sisters. Yana's in Cape Town with her husband Danila, Zoya's started her first year at university, Grandfather's taken up golf despite pushing eighty-two, and my uncle and aunt have taken what Rafail calls a "much-needed vacation to the Mediterranean." In other words, he wanted them out of his fucking hair.

I miss my family. I miss home. I miss my little sister Zoya's cooking and Rafail's hardass ways. I miss lifting with Semyon and drinking vodka with Matvei.

I will not fuck this up.

Guilt plagues me. If they knew what I did... that I put myself out there for the whole world to see... that I was flirting with an influencer and using my identity as Bratva to take advantage of the situation...

But no. No one can really tell I'm Bratva, unless they know the meaning of my tats.

I have to delete this account. It's stupid as fuck, and logical, sober me in the light of day, realizes what an idiotic thing I've done.

I have to delete this before anyone finds out.

But it's my only link to her.

I head to the shower when my phone buzzes again. I pick it up to see what one of my brothers forgot to tell me when I see... it isn't a text notification.

I frown. I thought I shut off notifications to my account, which is growing by leaps and bounds. It's only been a week, and I already have tens of thousands of followers. My video with the belt and the goddamn pillows has over 2.5 million views already.

What can I say? The dopamine hit is real.

And so's my growing attraction to Ember.

I frown at my phone. If she were mine, I'd punish the shit out of her for making her real name so easy to find. Rookie mistake, maybe. But what if some asshole decided to stalk her?

I stroke my chin.

Not a bad idea, really—

God. I can't do this. I CANNOT.

The little notification begs to me on-screen. I shake my head.

I won't do it. I can't. I'm a grown man, for Christ's sake, not some teen who needs the online fawning of thirsty women to stroke his fucking ego. My finger hovers over the button that reads *delete account.*

It's the right thing to do.

I shouldn't be here. It's dangerous and reckless and juvenile as fuck.

Still, before I go... I could take one more peek at those gorgeous green eyes of hers. Just one more before I shut this shit down for good and do something responsible with my life.

I walk to the kitchenette in the penthouse as if doing something practical with my time will somehow make it all better and erase my guilt.

Coffee. I need coffee.

I catch a glimpse of myself in the microwave reflection. My hair's askew, but just yesterday, I saw a video of a guy making coffee in boxers, and the women went wild. If I—

No.

No, *no, no, no,* NO.

I have better things to do than post videos vying for Ember's attention.

Still, I'm all alone here, totally *womanless,* dying for a good fucking lay. Who could blame me if I want another mild hit of dopamine? I don't care as much about the random flirtatious comments I get from the women online, but my notifications tell me every time *she* sees me, and so far this week, she's seen every one of my videos.

It's harmless.

I'm not *fucking* her.

I mean, not that I wouldn't if I had the—

No. STOP.

My mind circumvents the lame attempt at maturity.

Who is she?

What does she like?

What makes her happy or sad?

Is she outgoing, or does she keep to herself? Does she have any pets?

Is she vanilla?

I groan at the instant hard-on I get imagining her tied up and begging for me, but maybe... maybe those videos are just for clicks. She can't... *really* be into that shit she talks about.

Can she?

It doesn't matter. I grab my inner voice by the throat and toss my lack of focus against the wall.

It needs a *stern* talking to.

GET YOUR SHIT TOGETHER, MAN.

I throw my phone across the counter and wince when it slides right past the coffee machine and cracks against the wall.

I didn't mean to throw it *that* hard. I sheepishly walk over, pick it up, and check. Thank fuck, these things are made from military-grade glass these days. No damage.

I blow out a breath and close my eyes, grounding myself in the scent of strong coffee.

Coffee.

Gym.

Food. Shake.

Work.

In that order, *period*.

I take my coffee cup and open the mini fridge, pour some creamer into it, and lean against the counter while I sip it, like a mature adult who has his shit together and is going to plan his day.

I put the camera on my phone and hit the filter app thing I found from a Google search when my eyes catch the corner of one of the masks I used to film a video last night. I'm not a one-mask guy like some of the broke losers I see who think shirtless is all it takes to satisfy the discriminating needs of these online women.

Nope.

They want a real man. A man with some bulk on him, some tats, who covers his face for the sake of a little tease, not because he's got a hairless baby face that belongs behind the screen of a video game monitor, instead of mature, respectful women like *my* followers.

I grab the first mask that comes to hand and slide it over my head.

One more for the sake of the memories.

I hold up my coffee.

My time here has come to an end, beautiful. I have work to do, and this is all too distracting.

I shake my head in mock sadness, though, honestly, it's not much for show. For the past few nights, interacting with Ember online, with her sharp wit and tongue, it felt a little less... lonely.

But I have to stop this before I get in real trouble. Before Rafail finds out.

I grab a quick soundtrack. I don't edit my videos. I like 'em raw and untamed. I post the video and toss my phone down.

I watch it come on the screen.

I sigh.

I already have fifty likes and half as many comments.

I smile to myself over them.

> So we're just ignoring the fact that you
> woke up looking like a Roman god, huh?

I shake my head bashfully. Well, I wouldn't go *that* far.

> This is illegal levels of fine. I'm calling the
> authorities (aka myself).
>
> That coffee is lucky. Wish I was that close
> to your lips.

Not Ember, so... down girl.

> Do you come with a warning label, or do
> we just combust silently over here?

I scratch my chest with a self-deprecating shrug. Well, thanks.

Still no Ember.

I don't care about them. It's cute and even sweet, but I don't care who these women are. Even if they were half as into me as they play-act behind the safety of a keyboard... they're not *her*.

I should be deleting this.

Still... she hasn't responded in hours.

Wait. Is she alright?

My heart rate spikes.

I quickly tap the messages on the app and open to the last chat we had. *Twelve hours ago.* There's nothing to indicate she's been online since then.

What the fuck?

I go to her page and see she uploaded a video just before messaging me and hasn't been online since.

Along the bottom of the video, little messages pop up with hearts and arrows and likes while I'm scrolling the latest comments.

> Don't listen to that asshole, Mafia Queen!
> Delete his ass and block him!

> No one should talk to my bestie like that.
> Let me at him, sister! 😠

Wait, I didn't—*no.*

They're talking about someone else?

I narrow my eyes at the screen. Here I am, wearing a

fucking mask in my kitchen while drinking my coffee, and someone's disrespected my girl?

Who the fuck did that?

I scroll until I see the comment.

Then the second one.

And the third.

My gaze grows instantly hazy, my knuckles turning white when I grip my phone so hard.

> Romance novels don't make up for the fact
> that you're basic as hell. Try a real hobby.
> 

I'll give him a real fucking hobby involving my fist and his fucking face. I click on his profile pic. Balding, middle-aged douchebag with a double chin.

My jaw drops when I see another comment. The fucking nerve?

Why hasn't she deleted this shit?

> All that fantasizing, and you still look like
> you'd bore a guy to death in five minutes.
> 

Five minutes? I'd end him in one. The fucking son of a goddamn—

> Reading about mafia guys won't make one
> want you. Stick to the fairytales,
> sweetheart.

Real mafia guys? I'll give him real mafia guys.

Davay posmotrim, kak tebe ponravitsya, suka blyad.

Let's see how the little bitch would like *this*.

My phone buzzes with text after text I ignore. Before I can stop myself, I type a response to the online douche.

> **Bratvabloodline**
> **You want to take that up with a real man, princess? Cute. Disrespect her again, and I'll remind you how much those keyboard warrior hands can hurt when they're broken.**

I stab at the screen.

Within seconds, my comment's liked, and the comments below it start flooding in.

> He's defending her! Like a real made man! Gahhhh, Be still my beating ovaries! 🍸

> "Ooooooh. Real men do exist, and here's one right here. On brand, sir. On. Brand. 😂 👏

I can't do this. *I shouldn't be doing this.*

I close my eyes and breathe in through my nose.

It's just an online comment. Relax.

That son of a bitch wouldn't have the nerve to say that to my face.

An online comment from a real guy who hurt a real girl who I actually—

No. I don't even know her.

I stare at my screen, willing her to reply to me, when I see another notification pop up.

It's her.

Heartbeats thundering, I click on her video.

There she is.

My girl.

Flaming red hair hanging down in waves, those vibrant green eyes boring straight into mine. I don't even hear what she says, and I don't read the caption. It's another book, but this time, I notice something in the background.

It's a tiny white cup in the corner of the screen with the words *Brookie Bites* in typewriter font letters.

I screenshot the video and zoom in. It's blurry, but I know exactly what that logo is because it belongs to the coffee shop *right down the street from me.*

No. There's no way.

I click on her profile, but she doesn't have her location on, just a general *Southern California.*

Good girl.

My heart races faster.

I *knew* I saw her before.

Where?

My phone dings and buzzes, and I practically drop it while

I ignore my brothers' messages and quickly google the coffee shop. Surely, there have to be—

No.

There's ONE, and it's right here in California.

It can't be.

She's right here in my city.

I close my eyes and pinch the bridge of my nose. I have to get it together, and *now*.

NOW.

With effort, I click on the screen and go to the messages from my brothers.

Thankfully, they're talking amongst themselves and haven't noticed my absence.

Rafail sent me specs on the third asshole I'm tracking down today. This one will be harder. The first, a middle-aged accountant with ties to multiple shell companies, folded like a cheap suit after a few broken bones. The second, a wannabe tough guy hiding behind a fake identity, couldn't last more than a few minutes under pressure.

But this guy? He's a slippery son of a bitch. Arnold Prokhorov, ex-Bratva turned freelance operator, knows how to disappear. Multiple aliases, offshore accounts, and a knack for slipping through cracks, even the best trackers struggle to follow. He's been playing cat and mouse with the family for years, leaving a trail of dirty deals and dead partners.

But hey, I like the challenge.

Slipping a knife onto the counter that I'll bring with me, I send a quick reply to Rafail: *On it.*

Gym first.

Prokhorov second.

Still... my mind is on Ember. The asshole who disrespected her, the fire in her eyes.

Is she feeling the pull between us? Is that why she hasn't responded to me?

I groan when my phone dings with another notification. I have to get my ass to the gym and ground myself in sweat and hard work so I stop this bullshit already.

But when I check my phone... it's her.

My heart tumbles in my chest. I click the message.

> **Dreammafiaqueen**
> **You don't need to fight my online battles with those self-serving comments, thank you very much. I can handle myself. I don't answer online pricks. I leave them because the more engagement my posts get, the more follows I have, and unlike some people, I'm not just doing this for attention.**

I stare at the screen and frown, my fingers flying over the screen.

> Excuse me for defending your honor. The prick deserved it. If I—

Her response comes before I finish mine.

Dreammafiaqueen
You don't have to threaten the guy. That's illegal and you could get kicked off here, you know.

Worth it. And it wasn't a threat.

Dreammafiaqueen
Oh, roll my fucking eyes. As if you're going to track down some anonymous loser and defend the honor of a woman you've never met over a stupid comment? Dude. Get a grip.

I narrow my eyes at the screen. I'll get a grip alright, a grip of the fiery red hair wrapped around my fist that would get her attention loud and clear.

I think you spelled 'thank you' wrong.

I hit send, shutting down the conversation before she has the chance to reply. Tossing my phone onto the couch, I let the words linger in the air. She thinks I'm bluffing. She thinks this is just some harmless back-and-forth online.

I guess I can't blame her.

She doesn't know me. *Yet.*

I grab the phone, heart hammering with something sharp and hungry. I scroll fast, zeroing in on a name that's proved useful: a fixer from my last job in L.A.

One call. One favor. Her location is mine before I hang up the phone.

Perfect. West side gym. My lip curls, adrenaline spiking as the address blinks on my screen, a live, pulsing dot. Like she's waiting for me.

She's *right there,* dangling within my reach like she was placed in my path on purpose.

I strip down, throw on workout gear, and slide my phone into my pocket.

The whole way there, I feel like I'm chasing something I'm meant to catch. Like if I don't make it there faster, she'll slip through my fingers.

When I walk into the gym, the scent of rubber mats and faintly metallic sweat fills my nose. A receptionist glances up, eyes widening slightly at my imposing figure. "Hello, sir! Are you here to sign up?"

I look around and don't see her yet. Thankfully, she wouldn't recognize me.

First, I'm not wearing a mask. I guess those masks serve a purpose. Second, I have a long-sleeved shirt on covering my tattoos. She's heard my voice by now, but I don't need to talk to her.

I nod, handing her my credit card without hesitation. "Yeah. Sign me up. I'll fill out whatever forms you need later." I lean in and flash her my most charming smile. "I'm pressed for time. Could you do that for me?"

Her cheeks redden, and she stammers out a quick, "O-of course. I'll have the paperwork for you to sign when you leave."

Card back in hand, I step past the desk, scanning the space until I find her. *Ember.* She's at the squat rack, barbell balanced across her shoulders as she powers through reps. Her fiery hair is tied up, but stray strands cling to her damp skin.

I don't linger. That would give me away. Instead, I head to the free weights nearby, grabbing weights and setting up a bench. From here, I can see her without making it obvious.

She finishes her set, resting for a moment and glancing around. I keep my focus on my chest press, pretending not to notice her. When her gaze passes over me, there's no flicker of recognition. Good.

The tension in the air shifts slightly when she moves closer, now at the rowing machine in the same section. Her focus is razor-sharp, every move precise and deliberate.

She's humble; I can tell that much. She often takes videos of herself in lounge clothes and sweats, cuddled in a blanket with a cup of tea and a book. Here? She's all business, and I'm fucking here for it.

Her hair's pulled back into a high ponytail, a few rebellious strands framing her face as she focuses on her next set. The flush on her cheeks isn't makeup—it's pure effort, earned with every lift and every bead of sweat that slides down the side of her neck.

She's not trying to impress anyone. That's the kicker. No fake smiles, no posturing for attention. Just pure, unfiltered focus on herself. It's intoxicating, the way she moves with quiet confidence, like she's in her own world. And for a moment, I let myself think how easy it would be to pull her into mine.

Her strength is magnetic, but it's the duality that gets me. She's lethal yet doesn't flaunt it. Beautiful, yet completely unaware of how much she commands the room without even trying. It's raw, it's real, and it's *impossible* to look away.

I keep my workout steady, timing my sets to hers, staying just close enough to keep her in my periphery.

She doesn't know it yet, but I've already made her my target.

And I never, ever miss.

CHAPTER 4

I STARE AT THE VIDEO. My laptop glows, my heart pounding when I click start. This one is...different.

The video begins with a blurry view of a man's face on a video call. He's sitting in a cluttered room, his face cast in shadow but the terrified whites of his eyes staring at the screen. His voice quivers.

"I—I'm sorry, okay? I didn't mean it. I didn't—"

"*Louder.* Don't fucking stop until you sound like you mean it and you're not just afraid of me tracking you down and beating your ass." Oh my god. It's...it's his voice.

The man flinches, looking anywhere but at the camera. "I—I'm sorry for what I said. I'm sorry I harassed her."

My masked man's voice is sharper, pressing. "Who?"

"Dream Mafia Queen," he says in a rush of words. "I'm sorry."

I stare, horror-stricken and somehow...warm with pleasure. He... did this... for me? It's like the online version of cornering my schoolyard bully with a fist under his nose.

"Good. I'll let that pass. Now delete the comments and delete your account. Everything."

He nods frantically, his fingers scrambling over the keyboard. I scroll back to my comments as fast as my fingers can move and see every one of the hateful comments on my posts are gone.

My hands shake, my breath coming in shallow gasps. He did this online. He can't threaten someone like this, he'll get—

Oh. Wait.

That's when I note that this video is only for my eyes.

I stare and blink, shaking my head. What has he done?

I put my phone down, my emotions all over the place.

This...this crosses a line, he has to know that. I'm shaking my head in disbelief, still trying to process how I feel about this, when my DM's ping.

Bratvabloodline
He won't bother you again.

I shut the app and stare at my wall.

I've never had anyone defend me before. I didn't know it would feel like this. I can't—

I really need to get my head in the game.

The gym is my church. This is where I worship.

I need to get my sweat on.

I toss on my gear and head to the gym, where I can control chaos and channel it into something tangible.

The weights don't lie. The pull-up bar doesn't judge. In here, I'm strong.

Untouchable.

I love plugging in my headphones, cranking my music, and zoning out. It's just me versus me.

It feels *good*. It feels *right*.

And I'm finally getting over the mixed emotions from the apology. So the prickling awareness at the back of my neck? It pisses me off.

At first, I ignore it. There are always eyes at the gym, fleeting glances I brush off like sweat on my forehead. But this? This feels different. It's heavier. More deliberate.

For fuck's sake.

Who's staring at me? Yes, I have a fine ass—thanks to endless squats and hip thrusts—but it's *my* ass, and I don't appreciate someone raking their unwanted gaze over it.

I drop from the pull-up bar like a cat, landing lightly on my feet with a soft thud. I turn toward the source of that invasive gaze, already bristling with annoyance.

I'm not wrong.

But I'm also completely unprepared.

He's leaning casually against the dumbbell rack, arms folded across his chest, a cocky smirk curving his lips. He's tall—ridiculously tall—with a face my grandma would've called "devil-may-care." His body? Built like he spends his life in places like this, all broad shoulders and carved muscles.

But it's not just the muscles. Not even the height. It's the way he looks at me—sharp, knowing, like he's already two steps ahead. Like he knows me.

Wait... maybe he *does*. He looks oddly familiar. Do I know him from somewhere?

Still, he shouldn't be looking at me like that, like he—no, my romance conditioning is getting ahead of me again.

"Is there something you need?" I snap, my voice sharp enough to cut.

His smirk deepens, his cheek dimpling just enough to make me furious. And yeah, fine, he's hot. Too hot. And by the way he carries himself, he knows it.

"You're cheating," he says, his tone maddeningly smooth.

I blink. "Excuse me?"

"Your hands," he says, gesturing lazily toward the pull-up bar. "They're too close. It makes it easier."

That voice...

No. It can't be.

I roll my neck with exaggerated patience. "Oh, really? So, you've been watching me long enough to critique my form?" I narrow my eyes at him, the annoyance simmering into something sharper. "And how's my ass? Get a good look at that, too?"

The words are out before I can stop them.

"I haven't, actually," he says, pushing off the rack with an infuriatingly casual flex that makes every damn muscle in his body stand out. I swallow hard, hating myself for noticing. "But if you want to turn around..." He twirls his finger in the air, smirking like he owns the world.

"I'll turn around," I say sweetly, flipping him off instead. Then I face him fully, which—great—gives him a perfect view of my chest. My stupid, flimsy workout top does nothing to hide the outline of my nipples.

His eyes flick down for a fraction of a second, just enough to make me want to throw a dumbbell at him. His smirk grows, and he shakes his head like I've just confirmed everything he already assumed.

"Figures you've got a mouth on you," he says, sighing like he's already resigned himself to some cosmic truth. "Figures I love a woman with a mouth on her."

And I hate how much that makes me want to smile.

"Are you going to do a real set, or are you done already?"

My lips part in disbelief. "Excuse me?" I repeat.

He gestures lazily to the pull-up bar, his smirk widening. That isn't just one dimple, but *two*. The rugged appeal of this man is hard to resist—scruff on his jaw, and even though he wore a long-sleeve shirt, I could see the outline of strong muscles beneath the fabric. His voice is smooth and deep and does all sorts of things to my body.

"I thought with the way you were doing those, you were maybe pacing yourself."

Pacing myself?

I press my lips together. If he's trying to get a rise out of me... it's working.

"So you're the resident expert here? Funny, you don't have a badge, and I don't recall ever seeing you here before."

When he takes another step closer, my first thought is... *god* he's tall. Intimidatingly tall. But his presence feels... predatory, but in a way that makes me want more.

I really, *really* need to stop spending every waking hour reading dark romance.

"Not an expert," he says with a shrug. "I know my way around a pull-up bar though. And you look like a woman who likes to challenge herself." He winks, and my belly does a flip.

I like to challenge myself, alright. Right now, I want to challenge myself to grow the fuck up and get out of here before I let Mr. Flirt get to me.

I tilt my head. Couldn't hurt to get a little view, could it?

"Prove it."

He doesn't hesitate. He steps under the bar, jumps, and grasps it with practiced ease. His muscles flex as he hoists himself up, slow and deliberate, his form infuriatingly perfect. Each movement is controlled and smooth, like an Olympic gymnast's. By the time he hits fifteen, my jaw's tight.

"Show-off," I mutter.

He drops down, rolling his shoulders as he faces me. "We should have a contest. I'd love to see you try to overpower me."

I snort. "There's no contest. You're predisposed for greater upper body strength." I jerk my chin over to the leg machines. "Though I could crush your skull with my thighs."

His gaze grows predatory as it travels down the length of my body. "If that's a threat, I can live with it. If it's a promise..."

The thought of his head between my legs makes my cheeks heat instantly.

I should be furious at the audacity, but honestly... I walked right into that.

"Ladies first," he says, stepping back with a smirk.

I grab the bar again, ignoring the way my palms are slick with sweat. My muscles protest, but I push through, matching his pace with stubborn determination. I feel his eyes on me—heavy, like a weight of their own. They trace the line of my arms, linger on my shoulders, and sweep down the curve of my back.

By the time I hit ten, my body is screaming at me to stop, but I don't give in. Not with him watching. I drop to the ground, landing lightly despite the burn in my legs, and turn to face him, a little out of breath. "Your turn," I say, tilting my chin up in challenge.

He steps up, his grin widening as his eyes lock on mine. There's something unspoken in his gaze, a spark that feels electric. "Try not to be too disappointed," he murmurs, his voice low and smooth. It sends an unexpected shiver racing down my spine.

He grabs the bar with a casual confidence that makes me grit my teeth. His movements are fast but controlled, playful in a way that feels infuriatingly deliberate. By the time he hits thirteen, he slows down, lets go with his right hand and drags out the last pull with his left like he's savoring the moment. When he finally drops to the ground, he's barely winded, wiping his hands on his shorts with maddening ease.

"I could've gone higher," he says, his voice dripping with smugness. "But I didn't want to embarrass you."

I laugh, sharp and short, masking the heat rising in my chest. "Oh, trust me. You didn't."

Our eyes lock, and for a moment, it's like the rest of the gym disappears. The hum of machines fades, the clinking weights vanish. It's just him, his gaze sweeping over me, staying a fraction too long on my lips. My pulse drums in my ears, louder than it should be.

I hop up and once more... crash out at twelve. It's hard as fuck, *ugh*.

Then the clang of weights in the distance cuts through the spell. He steps back, his lips curling up like he knows exactly what he's done.

"Not bad," he says, his tone full of teasing arrogance. "For a beginner."

I scoff, crossing my arms. "Beginner? You've got a lot of nerve."

His grin deepens, and his eyes spark with something wicked. "I've got a lot of things," he says, his voice dipping into something that makes my breath hitch. "See you around, beautiful."

And just like that, he turns and walks away, leaving me standing there, my heart pounding against my ribcage. I'm not sure if I want to roll my eyes or chase after him.

Something about him feels dangerous. Familiar, even...

Where the hell is my head at? It's like I've met two men straight out of my books these days, and I need to focus back on *reality*.

My phone pings, vibrating on the floor next to my water bottle. I freeze mid-reach, unsure why the sudden sound sends a prickle of unease crawling up my spine. It's just a notification, another dopamine hit waiting to be claimed. But something stops me, a stubborn refusal to let my curiosity win.

I count to ten before finally checking, keeping my breathing steady. It's probably just another—

The sight of the name on the screen punches the air from my lungs. The phone slips from my hand, clattering to the ground, and I bite back a scream that threatens to claw its way out of my throat.

No. Not now. Not here.

Shawn
Hey, little sis. Back in town. Want to grab a drink?

Back in town.

Back in town.

The message is short. Innocent, even. But from him, it's a bombshell, a ghost I've spent years running from finally catching up to me. The stepbrother who turned my childhood into a nightmare is back, and suddenly, I'm a trembling little girl again.

I wish I hadn't read it. I don't want to remember.

I force the phone into my pocket like that will bury the past along with it. My reflection in the mirror catches my eye—steady, fiery, and strong. I repeat the lie in my head like a mantra: *You're not her anymore. You're not weak. You're not helpless.*

But the trembling in my hands says otherwise.

On autopilot, I head back to my apartment.

I have to get out of here. It's hard leaving a place that's familiar, that's home, and venturing into the wide world of newness and unfamiliarity.

But my job can be anywhere now. Well, relatively speaking. And now that my influencer gig's taking off...

I grab a book from my nightstand, clinging to its weight like a lifeline. Tonight, I'll lose myself in a fantasy—because that's all I can afford to trust. A world where women like me can find safety in surrender, even if it's to someone dark, dangerous, and entirely unreal.

I can still see his predatory grin. I can still feel the way he held me in his clutches, terrified and cowering...

I whisper a quiet plea to the universe: *Don't let him drag me back there.*

I can't.

Before I can help myself, I check my messages. My heart thumps.

He tagged me in another video.

I scrutinize every detail. I can't help it. I'm looking for a clue, something,...but there's nothing.

Again, I don't comment and hours later, my phone's on silent.

I'm being good. Sensible. Diligent.

I'm tucked under a blanket, the heft of a new book in the palm of my hand. My huge mug of hot cocoa sits beside me, the fragrance lifting heavenward and warming the interior of my teeny, tiny, cramped apartment.

I left twinkling white fairy lights around the window after Christmas because I liked how they looked. I've spent every last penny building this book sanctuary in my shitty little apartment, and now it's time to do what I love best—escape into my fantasy world.

Three chapters in, I'm drumming my fingers on the back of the book, waiting for things to pick up. I'm an impatient reader. I don't like slow-moving plots or info dumping. I want action, and I want it now. Yes, I get that she's a school teacher with dumb luck and a shitty past. Yes, I get that he's a single dad in need of a nanny. They should be kissing by now.

Frowning, I put my book in my lap and wonder if there's something wrong with me. I haven't been able to get into a good book in weeks, and I *need* to. I have videos to post, goddammit.

I sip the tepid dregs of my cocoa and heave a sigh when I glance at my phone. My skin prickles the same way it did when Mr. Hottie ogled my ass at the gym.

I know what my real problem is though. I want another look at hot Mr. Fake Mafia, the one who's been posting thirst traps and tagging me mercilessly. I have to stay focused though; I want to escape in my fantasy world—but wait.

Isn't my online presence my fantasy world? There, where I have friends who share the same passion for romance and happily ever after, and where we can collectively drool over the mafia bad boys and tattooed heartthrobs, like modern-day heroines of Regency novels and their dashing scoundrels.

I'll take one little break. Just a quickie.

I open the app on my phone and stare at the unending list of notifications. I've starred one, though, and his are at the top of the list. The little triangle on the top of the notifications that indicates my private messages.

I haven't responded to his videos since yesterday.

Bratvabloodline
You ghosting me, kitten?

I roll my eyes even as heat rises in my chest I try to ignore.

I can't help myself and post a comment.

> Ghosting you? That would require a relationship, methinks.

Bratvabloodline
Touché. It's been twenty-four hours since you responded to me and your last message said BRB

> I was unaware you were counting. I have a day job, you know. Sadly, as fun as reading romance books and posting videos is, it's not the most reliable source of income.

Bratvabloodline
Of course. Understood. But the next time you say, 'be right back,' I expect you to be right back

Oh *does* he?

My pulse spikes. I can imagine those words in his dark voice, touched with that accent... masked up and tatted, those muscles flexing while he grabs my chin and makes me look him in the eyes.

My hands shake when I reply.

> Meh

Bratvabloodline
Ah. The bratty type.

Listen, buddy. I know your type. Dark,
broody anti-hero with a superiority complex
posing with his arsenal of weapons about
power. I've read your whole vibe on every
bookshelf in America. And while that's all
fun and games for fantasy, this is the real
world here, not one built on happily ever
afters

Bratvabloodline
You have a lot of opinions about me for
someone who doesn't know me, little
queen

Why do my cheeks heat at that? I swallow hard and roll my eyes again.

Aww. You're like a mafia fangirl's dream
come to life. But real? Nah. You're all
smoke and mirrors

Bratvabloodline
And yet, you haven't tested that theory,
have you? You haven't blocked me either

The breath catches in my throat.

I swallow.

You must be bored. You really have nothing
better to do than try to get my attention?

Bratvabloodline
You have no idea the lengths I'd go for you

I swallow hard and bite my lip.

Maybe I think this whole shtick is
kinda cute

I wait for his response. I wonder if I've gone too far. I wonder—

A quick notification pops up:

@bratvabloodline has posted a new video.

I click it like my next breath hinges on watching it. The clip is short but... intoxicating. He's damn good at this.

Bathed in shadows, the gleam of steel catches the light as he assembles a weapon with precision. His movements are fluid and sure, every shift of muscle deliberate. I watch, mesmerized, as his large, powerful hands move with such brutal efficiency. It's clear: he's a master at this.

Uuugh. What else would he do with those hands?

The faint hum of Russian music fills the background, setting a mood that's both primal and sophisticated. Though his face is masked, his eyes burn with an intensity I can't help but be drawn to. He's smirking. I know he is.

I watch, unable to look away, as the camera lingers on the veins running along his muscled, tattooed forearms, sleeves rolled up to show the curve of muscle. I imagine what it would be like being pinned beneath those arms, helpless to move his weight off of me...

His movements are deliberate, sensual, as he snaps pieces into place. I get it...this is anything but *cute*.

God, he's playing with fire. He'll get banned so damn fast for this.

A knife flashes next—a deadly contrast to the smooth lines of the gun—its edge catching the dim light. He lazily twirls it between his fingers like a baton before he fists the handle and slams it, blade first, into the table. The camera pans up slowly, where the mask has gone slightly askew—I catch a glimpse of a stubbled jaw, tilted just enough.

Finally, he leans into the light and strokes the stubble on his jaw.

The video ends with him running his thumb over the edge of the knife and glancing straight at the lens.

Intimate.

Predatory.

He's looking at... *me.*

The screen fades to black, leaving only one caption.

Still think this is cute, @dreammafiaqueen?

Oh my god.

I stare. I gulp. Thank fuck he can't see me right now because I'm incapable of rational thought or speaking intelligible English.

This is better than any book I've ever read, and I'm not the only one who notices. The post already has hundreds of likes and as many comments. I read them with interest.

> Plot Shmot. Who needs plot when we have THIS? !?

> Alexa, play 'Toxic' on repeat

> He's giving me morally gray vibes and I'm... morally compromised. ⚠

Happily ever afters are overrated, girls. I don't need an HEA. I just need HIM. Preferably on top of me. 🙏

Roses are red, violets are blue, a five-finger necklace if the giver is you 🥀 😈

Wait, WAIT. Do they know each other in real life?? @dreammafiaqueen hasn't said anything. GIRL!? 😮 🙀

Uh oh.

I click back to my messages, my heart hammering.

You, sir, are ridiculous.

Bratvabloodline
Sir. That's a start. Good girl.

That shouldn't make me all kinds of hot and bothered. *It shouldn't.*

You're making a mockery of me.

Bratvabloodline
I'm not.

Really? What's next, a moody black-and-white photo of you in a trench coat in a dark alley? Puh-lease.

Bratvabloodline
I don't need props to prove a point.

Yet you're parading props all over social media as if begging to get banned

Bratvabloodline
Not props. Tools.

You think you're scary?

Bratvabloodline
Little queen, you wouldn't last five seconds
if I really wanted to make you beg.

The room feels hotter suddenly, the air too thick. I should laugh this off, but... my thighs clench involuntarily.

You're all big talk for someone hiding
behind a screen

His response is immediate.

Bratvabloodline
What if I weren't? What if none of these
were props and I wasn't hiding?

This stops me cold.

The image of him stepping out of the shadows, commanding the space around him, is so vivid it makes me shiver.

God help me. I think I want him to prove it.

You're overconfident. Arrogant. Guys like
you are all the same

His reply comes so fast that I barely have time to breathe.

> **Bratvabloodline**
> And girls like you always pretend they don't want to submit, that it's all just a fantasy, until they're on their knees, shaking, begging… it's only arrogance if you can't back it up, beautiful.

Oh god.

My breath catches. *Damn him.*

> You've got quite the ego. Shame you don't have the balls to prove it.

What am I doingggggggg? My mouth is dry, and my hands are shaking.

> **Bratvabloodline**
> Careful, little queen. That's not a challenge you want to make. You're making me very eager to prove how serious I am

There's an ache between my legs I *refuse* to acknowledge as my fingers fly over the screen.

> Oh, I'm shaking, I'm so scared. You, behind your phone, hiding in the shadows? Going to stop me? Please.

That's it. I'm leaving him on read. I refuse to let him win this little… game, or whatever it is he's playing. I grab my phone, pick up the book I'm reading without showing the cover, and do a quick little video asking my readers if they are as impatient as I am to get to the real meat of the story, or is it just my mood?

I don't even edit it this time. I usually like to edit the hell out of them.

I post, comment on the responses I got from my last post, and, against my wildly better judgment, make a few comments on the thirst trap he's trying to bait me with.

> Little do you know what I really wish for.
> But nice start. Color me intrigued...

I grin to myself and throw caution to the wind like an idiot, baiting him publicly.

> How much of this is posing and how much could you actually deliver? Are you into the "touch her and die" vibes or is that only for fiction. "My wife?" or meh? Would you actually put your woman on a pedestal and treat her like a queen, or are you just here for the attention?

I bite my lip, toss my phone down, and go to make another cup of hot cocoa. My phone buzzes and buzzes, notification after notification coming through.

I really need to change those settings.

I hesitate. I know I should stop. Block him. Shut this down. But instead, I press deeper, unable to resist the pull.

I can't help it. I click his last message.

Bratvabloodline
Do you really want to find out how wrong you are?

> Maybe I do.

The pause stretches long enough to make my chest tighten, anticipation building like a live wire. Then his response lands, lethal and dripping with dominance.

> **Bratvabloodline**
> Good. Because when I'm done with you, you won't remember what it felt like to ever be in control.

My heart thunders in my chest. I know I'm walking a dangerous line, but the way his words sink into me makes me crave what's on the other side.

No. I'm going to find out this is all fake, he'll reveal his endgame, and I'll feel all dejected and bereft.

Whatever. I am so over posers who think they can flirt with a needy woman online and stroke their own ego. He's probably banging one off in his mother's basement while he—

In our message line, another post pops up, directly embedded in our conversation.

I stare, my eyes narrowing. It's... I know this place. Cold washes over me as I recognize a shadowy corner of my latest shoot and the caption beneath it. He hasn't posted it though... this is only for my eyes.

> ***Caught the little photographer queen dreaming of her own anti-hero.***

I recognize myself immediately, camera in hand, pointed at fading poinsettias outside a local cathedral after they discarded them at the end of the Christmas season.

He's... this is... that's *me.*

I should block him.

I should call the cops and report stalking like a reasonable, *rational* person… like I should have long ago when my stepbrother hurt me. I know what happens when you ignore your instincts.

But I don't trust cops. I don't trust *men*.

I'm suddenly filled with a blinding rage. My fingers shake on the screen.

> Who the fuck are you and what are you doing?

Bratvabloodline
I'm calling your bluff, little queen. And I already told you who I am.

> My bluff? Dude you've got one thick head if you think for one minute that I'm actually entertaining any of this. It's for show. In real life, you can fuck off

Bratvabloodline
Is that so? After everything, you're upset now? I told you what my life is, and you kept playing your little games. What did you think this was?

> What I think is that you are out of your goddamn mind

Bratvabloodline
Maybe. But I think you'll love your little present, little queen

My jaw drops. He did *not*.

The buzzer to my apartment building makes me jump a mile. What the actual *fuck* is going on? My heart is racing.

With shaky hands, I hit the buzzer, half expecting his deep voice and the Russian accent on the other end.

"Hel-lo?" I stammer.

"Hey, Ember. There's a delivery here for you. Would you like me to bring it up? I'm heading to your floor to do a security sweep anyway."

I blow out a breath and glare. "Who's it from? What is it?"

"I can't tell. It's all wrapped up, and there's no card."

It could be a bomb. Could be a weapon. Could be—

Okay, alright, I'm getting way ahead of myself here.

"Bring it up. Please," I tack on.

I pace my apartment for the two whole minutes it takes for him to get there. It's not out of the ordinary for me to get packages. In the past year, since my job as an influencer has taken off, I've gotten branded merch, books from authors, and sponsored deals. It's been sweet, really. Who knew?

But the message he left... it's just so... *personal*.

I hold my phone in hand when I realize he's replied to my comment on his post.

"Touch her and die" isn't a vibe... it's a promise. A real man doesn't need to make speeches about his devotion. He shows it. As far as "my wife" – My wife wouldn't need to wonder where she stands because she'd feel it every second of the day—in the way I protect her, the way I'd learn every part of her.

Well then. My mouth is dry, my heart hammering. I can't help it.

I'm melting a little.

You don't put a woman on a pedestal to admire her from a distance. You put here there as a reminder of how much she's worth, so she knows she's the one calling the shots—even when it might feel like she isn't.

I swallow hard.

He's good.

Too good.

But god help me... I think I'm starting to believe him.

The knock sounds at my door so loudly I jump.

"Who is it?"

"Reggie. At the door, Ember. Did you forget already?"

I laugh nervously. "Just force of habit, Reg. Thanks." I open the door to find Reggie with a box. This place is cheap, and Reggie likely makes minimum wage, but he takes his job seriously, and I'm thankful he does.

"Thanks," I say confidently. I still have no idea who this is from, though I wonder...

Reggie salutes me then turns to leave as I discreetly begin opening the box. I stare at the contents, my cheeks coloring, as I quickly slide the top on the box and feign normalcy.

"Ember, you expecting a guest?"

I shake my head. "No, why?"

He frowns. "Thought I heard someone moving around up on the roof. Figured maybe you had company. I know that's one of your favorite places to go." He scratches his nose and shrugs. "Call me if you need anything."

My heart beats so fast I feel dizzy. It *is* one of my favorite places to go. The roof is private, locked off. No one should be up there.

"Probably just a bird," I say, even though the excuse sounds lame as fuck even to my own ears. That's no fucking bird, but if this man is really who he says he is, poor Reggie doesn't stand a chance. I can't take that risk.

My heart is hammering, and I feel a little shaky. I wish I could be reasonable about this, but a part of me... the dangerous side of me, the part of me that's drawn to anti-heroes... wonders.

Surely, my imagination has gotten the better of me.

Hasn't it?

"Could be. Sounded heavier than that. Want me to check it out?"

I shake my head. "No, no, I'm sure it's nothing." My grip tightens on the box. He nods and walks off, waving his fingers at me, leaving me alone with the weight of unease on my chest and the box in my hand.

Now that he's gone, I open the box again, my mind whirring. I stare. This... it can't be.

One of the most gorgeous, still-functioning vintage cameras on the market, the *exact* one I've been eying for months. Way out of my price range.

I drop the box as if it's on fire when the lights go out.

My heart beats faster.

It's just the lights.

Just lights.

It happens all the time. We don't have a generator here, and wind speeds get out of control sometimes.

I swing my flashlight beam from my phone around the apartment. A smart, logical person would call the cops, but the last time I did that, I lived to regret it.

It's why I work out so hard. It's why I carry pepper spray in my bag and have memorized every self-defense move on the planet.

I don't need someone to come and rescue me. I can do that for my own damn self.

I look at my phone, but there's no new message from my stalker poser—*whatever* he is—so I toss it on the coffee table and stare at the stairs to the roof.

There's no fucking *way* I'm going up there. Nope. Not gonna do it. Either this is all coincidence, or something's gone terribly wrong. In either case, I'll call a lawyer or whatever, but I need to have an actual story to tell them.

An online stranger flirted with me?

Someone I don't know sent me a gift, when I get gifts daily from various sources, often not identifying the sender?

My security guy heard someone on the roof earlier?

Every fear is legitimate but sounds stupid. I need more to go on; I really do.

But isn't this the type of logic that talks people out of making logical, reasonable decisions?

I send my online stalker a message.

> What did you do?

No response.

I think about calling Reggie again, but I feel like a wuss. I can't do that. I roll my eyes to myself and look back at my phone.

Still no response.

I will him to answer as my anger rises. How dare he play around with me like this?

Is he?

Now I'm furious. I open the door to the roof and holler up the stairs. "Hello? Who the hell is up there?"

Nothing.

I take the stairs two at a time and anchor my hands on my hips at the top. The light isn't that great up here unless there's a full moon, but right now, there's a waxing crescent, the little sliver of moon casting hardly any light, so it's dark.

I grip the phone tighter, my chest heaving. My mind screams at me to stop, to just call Reggie or leave it alone. But my body, my stupid, traitorous body, propels me forward.

I mentally go through self-defense moves if I need them.

"Who the hell is up here?" I bark into the darkness as I swing the light beam across the roof.

Silence. Then, as I take a step closer to the corner, a deep, low chuckle cuts through the night.

"That's cute, little queen," a voice says, smooth and unhurried, with just enough of an accent to make my knees weak.

Oh god.

Oh god, oh god, oh god.

My stomach drops, and I whip around, shining the beam where the sound came from. The flashlight shakes in my hand as the figure steps forward into the dim light.

I wasn't imagining things. I wasn't making shit up. He's here, in the flesh, and I—I can't breathe. I can't talk. I'm frozen in place like he's waved a magic wand and incapacitated me.

He's wearing the same black shirt from his videos, the tattoos winding down his forearms visible as he tucks his hands into his pockets. His mask is firmly in place, the black hollows of his gaze fixed straight on me.

"You," I hiss, my voice trembling with anger and... something else. "You followed me," I snap, trying to sound braver than I feel.

He cocks his head. "You invited me, little queen."

"You and I have very different interpretations of what 'invitation' means. I did not invite you."

"Didn't you?" His voice lowers as he takes a step closer. "All those messages, all those taunts. Testing me. Begging me to prove you wrong. Did you think I wouldn't call your bluff?"

I backpedal, but he matches my movements, his steps slow and deliberate.

"You're insane," I breathe out, but my voice has lost its bite. "If you hurt me—"

His words come in a rush, sincere and full of meaning, his hands splayed out in front of him like a gesture of peace. "I'm not here to hurt you. I told you that."

Did he? His words are quiet, but they slice through me like the edge of his knife.

My back hits the wall, and I realize I've run out of space. He prowls toward me, and god help me—either I've watched way too many masked men videos, or he knows exactly how to play this because this feels like the most delicious foreplay I've ever experienced. There's an electric current under my skin, a thrum of anticipation echoing in my chest as heat floods my core.

He moves with predatory, fluid grace, all muscles and sinew. Those videos didn't do him justice—he's strength and power personified, so much taller than I imagined, so much bigger, his shoulders blocking my view, and the mystery of the man behind the mask has my heart beating so fast I'm a little dizzy.

I stifle a squeak when he reaches me. His arms cage me in, the heat of his body seeping into mine, but he doesn't touch me. Not yet. One arm pressed against the wall, his gaze bores into mine. I lick my lips, my mouth dry.

"Go on," he murmurs, his lips close to my ear. "Tell me to leave. Tell me you don't want this, and I'll go."

I open my mouth, ready to shout, to shove him away, to say something—anything—but nothing comes out.

I imagine he's smirking as if he knows my answer already. One of his hands lifts, and his knuckles brush my cheek, the touch barely there but enough to send a shiver down my spine.

"You like being in control, don't you?" he whispers. "But what if, just for a moment, you let go? What if you let someone else take the weight for once?" He bends his mouth to my ear, his words a heated whisper that makes my bones feel like rubber. "What if you *gave in* to that fantasy, little queen?"

I open my mouth to tell him to stop, but nothing comes out.

"You could've blocked me the first time I tagged you, but you didn't. Deep down, this isn't a fantasy for you, is it?"

When I don't respond, he continues.

"Tell me to go, Ember." His voice is low and molten. "Say the word, and I'll vanish."

He pulls back slightly, just enough to meet my eyes. "The choice is yours. Always. But make no mistake—I don't bluff."

His words hang in the air, thick with promise, as he steps back, giving me space. My knees nearly buckle as the heat between us dissipates like smoke.

I stare at him, my pulse pounding in my ears. I should tell him to leave, to get the hell out of my life before he burns it all down.

But the words won't come.

He chuckles softly, shaking his head. "That's what I thought, little queen," he says before disappearing into the shadows. "I'll be waiting."

And then he's… gone, like Batman. *Poof.*

I'm left alone on the roof, my body trembling and my mind spinning.

God help me, I think I want him to come back.

CHAPTER 5

RODION

I shouldn't be doing this.

I really, *really* shouldn't be doing this. Rafail is going to have my fucking head.

But what he doesn't know...

I don't want to terrify the girl. I'm not that kind of a guy. But I *do* want to call her bluff, and I couldn't help myself. She has post after post about being tied up and blindfolded, about how she fantasizes about being taken in the dark and manhandled.

I would know. I've pored over every post with glee, taking clear notes.

She can lie all she wants. I know better. She wants this. I could tell by the way her breathing hitched, and she didn't tell me to go.

I pried myself away from her with difficulty.

She was even more beautiful than I remembered.

I lean against the edge of the rooftop, watching the faint glow of light filtering through the windows below. I put the lights back on so I can see her again. She's back inside, pacing like a caged lioness, her hair catching the soft glow of those fairy lights she loves so much. I can see her outline clearly enough to know she's furious. Confused. But she didn't tell me to go.

And that's the only reason I walked away.

I'm not the monster she imagines me to be. Not yet.

Still, my blood sings from the memory of her—her wide green eyes flashing with fire and fear, the way she anchored her hands on her hips and tried to stand her ground against me. She was trembling, sure, but not from terror. I've seen terror before. This wasn't it. This was something else.

Excitement.

Even as I left her, I could feel it, a live current connecting us, sparking every time her lips curled in defiance or her voice rose to challenge me. She wanted to fight, and I wanted to let her win just to see how far she'd push.

But I can't. I can't fucking get involved.

She's innocent—wrapped in her soft blankets and fairy lights, her books and dreams. And my world? It's drenched in violence and lies, blood under every nail. She doesn't know what she's playing with. She doesn't know what I am.

I clench my fists, my knuckles aching from how tightly I grip the edge of the roof. I should leave her alone, let her think this was some strange fever dream, a flirtation gone too far. She deserves to live her life in peace, untouched by men like me.

But when I closed the distance between us earlier, when her breath hitched, and her pupils dilated as I leaned closer...

Fuck.

She can lie to herself all she wants. I know better.

She wants this. I've seen it in every word she's typed, in every post she's shared. The way she threads her fantasies with raw longing, the way her voice breaks just a little when she talks about surrendering control.

She wants this, even if she doesn't realize it yet.

And now I can't stop.

My phone vibrates in my pocket. I pull it out, already knowing it's her. A message lights up the screen.

Dreammafiaqueen
What did you do?

I smirk to myself, my thumb hovering over the reply. I should ignore her. Walk away. Hell, run before this goes further.

But I've never been good at ignoring temptation.

I left you a small present, little queen.

I press send, slip the phone back into my pocket, and step away from the rooftop edge. It's better this way—for her, at least. She thinks I'm gone. She thinks I've let her go.

But I'll be watching.

Just to make sure she's safe, I tell myself.

And maybe—just maybe—to see if she'll come looking for me.

> **Dreammafiaqueen**
> You shouldn't have come here. I didn't invite you.

Her message flashes on my screen, her defiance practically dripping through the text. I smirk, shaking my head. She's trying to play the game, trying to keep control, but she doesn't realize how much she's already surrendered.

> Didn't you, though?

I send the reply and pocket my phone, pacing the rooftop as adrenaline courses through me. I shouldn't have come here, and yet... I can't stay away. Not when I've seen the way she responds, her breaths quickening, her eyes flaring when I step close.

I can't do this. I won't. I shouldn't.

But the word *shouldn't* has never stopped me before.

Pulling out my phone again, I tap into the feed from the camera I had discreetly installed in her apartment. Her face fills the screen, beautiful and furious as she paces. The light from her fairy lights softens her edges, but it doesn't hide the fire in her movements. She's muttering to herself, running her fingers through her hair, biting her lip in frustration.

The way she bites her lip... my fingers flex at my sides, imagining them tracing the delicate curve of her jaw, tilting her face up so she can't look anywhere but at me.

I check the biometric data monitor I installed earlier. Her heart rate is elevated, her breathing quick and shallow. She's angry, sure, but there's something else there too. Excitement. Anticipation.

She wants this, even if she won't admit it yet.

And that's why I'm here—not to scare her, but to remind her that the fantasies she hides behind her screen can be real if she lets them. If she lets me.

But I can't push too hard. Not yet. I've spent years mastering control, and this is no different. I'll take my time, unraveling her defenses piece by piece until she doesn't just trust me—she craves me.

Her phone lights up on the camera feed, and I watch her glance at it, her thumb hesitating over the screen. My response must've shaken her more than she expected.

Good.

I close the feed, my pulse steady and calm despite the way my blood burns for her. For now, I'll stay in the shadows, watching, waiting. She'll come to me when she's ready.

Because deep down, she knows what I know.

She's mine already.

Get some sleep, little queen. I'll be back

Dreammafiaqueen
Are you watching me?

Good night, beautiful

Her pacing slows as her phone lights up again on the camera feed. I watch as her brows furrow, her lips pressing into a tight line. She picks up the device hesitantly, and when she reads whatever message just came through, her whole body stiffens.

Her hands shake as she types back furiously, then stops. Her face twists into something I can't quite place—fear, anger, maybe both.

I flip to the biometrics. Her heart rate spikes off the charts, and her breathing grows shallow. Whatever that message was, it hit her hard.

A second later, her phone buzzes again, and I catch the flicker of panic on her face before she slams it down on the table.

Who the fuck was that?

I access the feed again, zooming in to catch the name on the screen.

Shawn Steele

My stomach tightens, the way it always does when something doesn't sit right. Who is this asshole? She looked rattled, and Ember doesn't rattle easily. I've been watching her long enough to know that much.

I switch to my own phone, pulling up every scrap of information I can find on Shawn Steele. Not much turns up—a few social media accounts, a sparse LinkedIn page, and an address in the Midwest that doesn't seem to fit with Ember's life here. He's marked as "stepbrother" in some public records, which makes my stomach churn.

I dig further, scanning the few photos I can find. There's a smarmy grin, the kind that makes my fist itch to connect with his face. But what catches my attention is the absence of her. No pictures, no posts, no shared mentions.

I look harder, cross-referencing where I can, and I finally find a link—a mention in an old blog post she wrote years ago before she built her following.

"Family is supposed to protect you. When they don't, it's up to you to protect yourself."

The words hit like a bullet, sharp and damning.

What did he do?

It doesn't take a genius to put the pieces together. Ember hates him. And whatever he just sent her has her spiraling.

I watch as she paces again, grabbing her phone only to put it back down, running her hands through her hair. She's muttering to herself, the words too low for me to make out.

My chest tightens as I lean back against the rooftop wall, staring down at the quiet hum of her apartment. Shawn Steele. I don't know what kind of hold he thinks he has on her, but if he's the reason she's so guarded, so defensive...

He'll learn very quickly that she's not alone anymore.

And if he's stupid enough to try and hurt her again, I'll make sure the only thing people remember about Shawn Steele is the name on his gravestone.

CHAPTER 6

EMBER

THE SOFT GLOW of my laptop screen bathes the room in pale light as I curl up on my couch, knees pulled to my chest. I shouldn't be doing this—not after everything that's happened. Not after the man with the sharp gray eyes, the knowing smirk, and the audacity to *watch* me had the nerve to leave a gift.

But here I am.

Scrolling through my messages, my pulse skitters when I see his name pop up again. I know it's him—I don't even have to check. His replies are always short, sharp, and smug as hell.

> **Bratvabloodline**
> I never asked. Enjoy the present, little queen?

My breath catches, and heat prickles up my neck. I narrow my eyes at the screen, hating that I can practically hear his voice—low, rough, dangerously calm—when I read those words.

I type out my response with a little too much aggression, my fingers flying across the keys.

> You think leaving a creepy camera at my door makes you charming?

The dots appear immediately. *Of course* he's waiting. He always is.

Bratvabloodline
I'm nothing if not resourceful.

I groan and slump back against the cushions, biting my lip to keep from smiling. He's infuriating. Maddening. And yet, I can't bring myself to block him.

> You sound so proud of yourself. Stalker goals unlocked. Congrats.

Bratvabloodline
Careful, Ember. I might start thinking you like my attention.

The nerve. My heart slams against my ribs, and I sit up straighter, my fingers trembling slightly as I type.

> I don't.

Bratvabloodline
Liar. If you were mine, I'd punish you for that.

I blink at the screen, my throat going dry. It's just one message, but it hits like a punch—cutting through my thin defenses, forcing me to confront the truth I don't want to admit. I *do* like the attention. I shouldn't, but I do.

And the worst part? He knows it.

You're full of shit.

Bratvabloodline
Maybe. But I'm also right.

I let out a soft growl, the sound echoing in the quiet of my apartment. Of all the arrogant, self-righteous—*god*, he's infuriating. I shouldn't reply. I should shut the laptop and go to bed, pretend this conversation never happened.

Of course I don't. Instead, I type out a reply, my fingers hesitating before I hit send.

What is it you want, anyway?

The dots blink in and out again, taking longer this time. For a second, I think maybe he's backed off. Maybe he's realized this whole thing is ridiculous and crossed a line.

Then his response comes through.

Bratvabloodline
What I want? I want you to admit the truth.
That you like the attention. That you want a
man who sees you—not just your camera,
not just your posts. YOU.

I swallow hard, my cheeks heating as the words sink in.

You're delusional.

> **Bratvabloodline**
> Am I? Tell me, when you post about men who tie you up, blindfold you, who take what's theirs—are you thinking about someone specific?

My chest tightens, my pulse stuttering as I stare at the words on the screen.

> I gotta go.

I slam my laptop shut as if that could sever the connection, but it's too late. The words are already in my head, echoing in his voice, lingering in the spaces where I don't want them.

The worst part is, I can't stop the thought that creeps in, unbidden and unwanted.

Is it him I think about?

CHAPTER 7

RODION

I SMIRK as her message goes dead, the little notification telling me she's offline.

She'll come back. She always does.

Leaning back in my chair, I tap my thumb on the screen, scrolling through her posts—words she thought she shared for strangers to see but were maybe actually meant for someone like *me*.

She can lie to me all she wants. I know the truth.

And I'll wait.

For now.

CHAPTER 8

EMBER

I SLEPT LIKE SHIT.

First, the messages from... whoever he is.

The hot, tattooed badass with the mark of the Bratva on him. It's... starting to feel more and more like he's telling the truth.

He was on my roof.

But he didn't hurt me. He didn't even touch me. So far, all he's done is shamelessly flirt, give me an insanely expensive camera I've been researching online, like he's hacked into my search history.

Oh, god. If he looked into my search history... my cheeks flame.

No, wait. I shake my head and drop my forearm across my face. He *came to my home*, which means he looked me up and found my address.

I blink my eyes open, my vision blurry, and blink again.

This is...different. Shawn never leaves me alone. Shawn finds every one of my locations and even though he leaves me for months at a time, he always resurfaces like a relentless weed, immune to being plucked and destroyed.

But this guy...

I sit up in bed, staring at my phone plugged into the bedside table like it's a snake coiled to bite me.

I'm kind of embarrassed he knows where I live. I don't even know the guy, but there's a reason I film all of my videos in front of the bookshelf or on the rooftop.

There's a reason that one hundred percent of my friends are fellow influencers who share a mutual love of reading and bad boys.

In real life, I don't make friends easily. I don't trust anyone.

This apartment is a study in contradictions, a ridiculous blend of hope tangled with despair. The kind of place that clings to the smell of mildew no matter how hard I scrub or how many candles I burn. The walls are thin, the once-white paint now an uneven patchwork of peeling corners and smudges that won't scrub out. At night, the soft glow of the fairy lights I hang disguises the cracks spidering across the ceiling.

I've thrown down thrifted rugs to cover the worst spots of the cheap laminate flooring, little splashes of color I hoped would lend a vintage edge but sort of scream "flea market finds."

My bed is crammed into the far corner of the studio, tucked beneath a window that rattles in its frame every time the wind kicks up. The bedspread is soft and inviting, though, my one splurge after a recent shoot—a pricy comforter I bought on sale, the bright crimson fabric a rebellion against the drab apartment.

I pinned a sweet little string of lights made of tiny romance book covers on the wall above it, one of my favorite little bonuses from a sponsored ad. I love the little gallery of escapism and reminder of a world that's fully within my control.

Unlike this one.

Sigh.

Before I get out of bed, my phone pings. My heart surges and I reach for the phone, only to realize... it' s Shawn.

I close my eyes and will him to just *go away*. I don't want to deal with him, with the memories he dredges up and the way he makes me feel.

> **Shawn**
> I want to visit dad's grave together.

Of freaking *course* he's tugging at my heartstrings. Just because he's back in town, he wants to play nice. Wants to pretend that nothing ever happened, that I've forgiven him for what he did.

His dad wasn't my father, but my mother's husband. We buried him a decade ago, and I did love the guy. He was good to me—good to us.

Except for the day he moved his son into our home after his ex-wife gave up custody.

I toss the covers aside and head to the kitchen for a cup of coffee. It feels as if my phone has eyes on it, boring into mine.

Is he watching me?

Does he have cameras set up here, after all?

Why would he go through that much trouble for *me?*

I take the camera with me and prop it on the kitchen table, staring at it for a moment as if it'll reach out and bite me.

My god, it's a beauty.

I look away from it. It doesn't belong in a place like this.

The kitchenette, if it can even be called that, sits on the other side of the room. A single-burner hot plate balances precariously on the edge of the tiny counter, and the mini fridge hums loudly, drowning out the faint murmurs of my neighbor's all-day TV fest. I tried to dress it up with dried lavender and baby's breath from a farmer's market, but it didn't really help.

I really hate this place.

I should pack up and move.

But here's where I have my connections. I can get a gig in a matter of hours, and I've finally started making a name for myself, booking clients. Now that the influencer gig is picking up, that's less of a pressing need, though. I can, for once, be a bit more discriminating.

I have goals and aspirations, not the least of which is to sock away every penny I can so that I can move into a place of my own. Suffer for a bit, then buy my own place.

Wherever I want.

I look back at the camera. It rests on my kitchen table like a coiled snake—beautiful, dangerous, and impossible to ignore. Its black leather casing, weathered and soft, contrasts with the sharp glint of its brass accents. An antique. A collector's dream.

A note, handwritten on textured paper, lies beside it: "Use it wisely."

My stomach churns. It's not signed, but it doesn't need to be.

What's his name?

"Um, excuse me." I'm talking to dead air like a psycho, but I can't shake the feeling that he's watching me. "Who the hell do you think you are?"

It's ridiculous. But this feeling, the same one I got at the gym, is prickling the back of my neck and won't go away.

My eyes flick to the corners of the room, to the window, even to the tiny blinking light on my laptop.

He's been watching me. I know he has.

"Do you think this is a game?" I say out loud, again to no one.

What am I doing? I rub my temples. I'm losing it.

I pace the small space of my apartment, my steps muffled by the worn rug. He's been watching me—closely enough to know my weak spots, to anticipate that I'd be drawn to the camera like a moth to a flame.

I should call the police. I should burn the thing and be done with him.

Instead, my fingers itch for the leather strap.

The thought makes me nauseous, and I push the chair back violently, sending it scraping across the floor. The sound jolts me, grounding me, and I take a shaky breath. This isn't normal. This isn't okay.

But damn it, if there isn't a part of me—small, treacherous— that feels seen.

I stare at the camera, daring it to reveal the secrets it carries. What's on the film? What has he captured?

Some modern photographers don't use a dark room anymore, fully embracing the lure of digital art and eschewing the older methods. But me... I love it.

It takes less than five minutes to load the film into the developing tank, my hands working on autopilot, movements honed from years of practice.

Until the first image appears.

It's me.

Walking down Melrose, oblivious that I'm being watched.

Me, sitting on a park bench, scrolling through my phone, completely exposed.

Me, entering my apartment building, keys in hand, shadowed by the late afternoon light.

I slam my fists against the table, the developing solution splashing over my hands as I head to use the bathroom. Surely he hasn't set up a camera in *there*.

But when I get to the bathroom, the glaring, flickering fluorescent lighting reminds me that this is the worst part of this apartment. A cramped space with tiles that perpetually feel damp and a shower curtain that clings to my skin no matter how hard I try to avoid it. It's a good thing I'm barely five feet tall because anyone bigger than me wouldn't even fit in that shower.

I hung up a framed print of a sunlit forest on the wall, a hopeful touch, but even that can't mask the reality of rust-stained fixtures and a cracked mirror.

God, I hate this place.

I flick off the light and march back to my room, coffee in hand, and check my messages.

I have a few choice things to say.

Sure enough, Shawn's back at it again, and there are... wait. I blink. I look again.

That's *four times as many* notifications as I normally get on one of my posts.

I stare, my eyes wide, as I flick open the app. My jaw unhinges.

Overnight, three different follower badges are tacked next to my name, thanks in no small part to the videos my stalker's account tags me in.

My mouth goes dry as I quickly do the math. This is... this is going to bring in money. *Good* money, ten times faster than any photography gig I could bring in, all while sitting in the privacy of my home.

I could... if this keeps up, I could move out of this shithole and into a place of my own—

No.

NO!

I can't allow myself to fall for this... *I can't.*

There has to be another way.

My notifications tell me that he posted another video.

Last week, I was happily immersed in my fictional worlds, where it was...safe. And now...

My hands are shaking, and I can't look away. I click the button.

I exhale. Now that I've seen him in person, the sight of him on-screen makes my heart slam so hard against my rib cage I hold onto the bed for support. The camera shows his best angles, yes, but I know what it's like to be next to him, to see those veins along his neck when he leans against the wall, to hear his low, dark voice in my ear, to see his broad shoulders and powerful frame, knowing he could and would have his way with me and I'd never be the same.

Also? *He smelled so good.*

Sigh.

My god. I'm wet and bothered—and he didn't even touch me.

I swallow hard and let myself watch the video.

This one's new, shot in the early morning light I am oh-so-familiar with on the rooftop. I narrow my eyes and look closer—no, he isn't on *my* rooftop. Instead of the industrial pipes and sea of gray, I can tell this rooftop's different. Higher end.

Of *course* it is.

The video's both mesmerizing and unsettling, shot with the raw precision of someone who knows exactly what they're aiming for. He stands in the frame, his broad shoulders filling the screen. This time, he's not posed or polished—his stance is casual, almost lazy, though, like before, it's somehow *drenched* in Bratva energy.

Maybe because he *isn't* posing. Maybe because he *is* the real thing.

I can *feel* the undercurrent of tightly coiled power in the way he leans against the wall, his arms crossed loosely over his chest.

The camera catches every detail: the veins along his forearms, the latent power and ink that scream *danger*.

I once read somewhere that a woman is naturally drawn to a man with ink because she *knows*... he won't pussyfoot around. He's a man well acquainted with pain and risks, a man who is willing to take her to new heights.

I have no idea if it's true.

I want to see his jaw again. I want to see that stubble, that smirk, but most of all... I want to see his eyes. I can tell by the way his lips are moving he's talking.

I swallow hard, start it over, and turn the volume up on my phone.

"You want a man to protect you," he whispers, his voice low and rough and so sexy a pulse of need throbs between my thighs. I swallow. That subtle Russian lilt turns every word into a threat wrapped in velvet, and I could listen to him talk all day long. I'm not the only one—comment after comment comes in, flirting with him, begging for more, offering him their first-born children and hands in marriage.

His gaze is unflinching as if he's addressing *me* directly.

Maybe he is...

"You don't want a gentleman, little queen."

I gulp.

There's no maybe about this. He *is* talking to me.

The camera pans in slightly, framing his masked face, those eyes growing so serious my breath catches. "A gentleman does what's right. Plays by the rules." He's shaking his head, then leans in closer, the movement deliberate. I watch the veins in his neck stand out slightly as he speaks with quiet intensity. "I would break every rule, every law to keep you safe." The pause that follows is intentional, almost cruel, the tension crackling through the screen as he holds his breath.

"I would stop at nothing. No one..." His voice drops to a lower register, rougher. "And I mean, *no one* would ever harm a hair on your head."

He doesn't say it, but I hear his words loud and clear...

Except me.

Still, the thought of Shawn in town and all that entails reminds me how nice it would be to have exactly this.

No.

He stalked me. I don't know him.

I can't trust him.

For a moment, the silence lingers, heavy and charged. The video ends abruptly, leaving behind the sound of my own shallow breathing and the thunderous pounding of my heart.

With trembling fingers, I click my message as text after text comes in. I don't want to look at those. They're Shawn, I know it.

Instead I pull up *his*.

> **Bratvabloodline**
> Morning, little queen. Did you sleep well?

I need to take back some control here, so I don't answer and instead click the message from my friend.

> **Bookbabe**
> OMG. Ember. EMBER. This guy is so
> into you!

> Into me or stalking me?

I can't tell her the truth. I don't want to. It's... too personal, somehow.

Bookbabe
What if he's LEGIT? What if he really is
this...sexy af guy who's super into you?

How do I break this to her?

Strange way to flirt, no?

Bookbabe
Well, not really. He knows what you're into.
You're basically like hey, so role playing a
book girl into a masked man is my thing
and he's all, lemme show you the fantasy
RIGHT HERE AND I LOVE YOU

He didn't say he loves me

Bookbabe
Pfft. Girl. He's posting videos directed at
you four times a day. Some of the thirstier
girls are a little jealous that he only ever
responds to YOUR comments.

I blink. Wait. What? He does?

My head pounds. I should've made that stupid coffee.

I swallow hard. This feels... alright, okay. So color me
intrigued.

What if I could play this right?

What if... what if I could make this work for me?

What would you do if you were me?

Bookbabe
I would do exactly what you're doing. Give him shit online. Tease him. Milk this for all it's worth. Your notifications have shot up overnight, your followers are climbing by the second… and maybe suss him out a bit. Has he slid into your DM's yet, or…

Um. Yeah.

Bookbabe
NO FUCKING WAY. Annnnnddddd???

He's even flirtier in the DM's than he is publicly.

Bookbabe
SEEEE?!??! He's into you. Like really into you

That's what I'm afraid of.

Bookbabe
Well has he stepped out of line?

Is stalking me, taking pictures of me, then giving me the vintage camera of my dreams with the pictures on it stepping out of line?

Is looking up my home address and…

Yes. Yes, it is.

The question is… Is it worth it?

Do I care?

I'm not sure…

Liar, liar, pants on fire.

Bookbabe

Okay. So do what I said. Have some fun.
Suss him out.

What if he's really BRATVA?

I *know* he is. He has to be.

Bookbabe
Oh c'mon, he can't be really…

He has a Bratva tattoo and a Russian
accent.

Bookbabe
You mean… they really exist? They're real?

I laugh out loud.

Well yes, obviously.

Bookbabe
**I thought they were made up for the book
world!**

I smile at that.

Some are, some aren't

Bookbabe

I smirk.

Bookbabe
**Okay, I gotta go to class. Ugggh,
responsibility rearing its ugly head once
more. Le sigh. Keep me posted!**

She's a teacher by day, one of the reasons why she *smartly* kept *all* her identifying information off her socials. Meanwhile, I might as well have hung a neon sign around my neck that says *Stalk Me*.

Freud would have a field day with this.

I go back to my messages.

> I saw the pictures…

He responds immediately. My heart beats so fast that I'm a little dizzy.

> **Bratvabloodline**
> And my latest video, I see. I promise you, Ember. I'm not bluffing. I meant every word.

> Yes

I pinch the bridge of my nose, unsure of how to respond because honestly? A part of me… *wants* this. There's a reason why I spend so much time reading the books. There's a reason I started this account. And sure, while I keep telling myself that this is fantasy, that I don't really want this, it would be a lie to say there isn't a part of me—a small, hidden, quiet part of me I don't share with anyone else—that fantasizes about what's directly in front of me.

I swallow hard and don't respond. I quickly check my texts, and my blood runs cold.

Shawn has sent me twelve messages since last night.

> **Shawn**
> Hey, sis. I really want to see you. It's been
> so long, and I'm only back in town for a
> while. How's breakfast?

When I didn't respond, the messages grew increasingly urgent and pushy.

> **Shawn**
> Why are you ignoring me? I'm waiting.

> **Shawn**
> Hello? Are you up? I know where you live,
> Ember. If you don't respond to me, I'm
> coming by in person.

I don't know how to play this. If I tell him off, he *will* retaliate and make my life a living hell.

But I can't play nice, not with this asshole who made my childhood a living nightmare.

> **Shawn**
> Please. Things are different. I'm not the
> same person I was. I'm sorry. Please
> forgive me. I want to see you.

I shake my head when a brilliant idea crosses my mind.

A crazy, brilliant, terrible idea.

Fury races through my veins as I type a message to my masked stalker. My hands are shaking.

> Hey. Stalker boy.

> **Bratvabloodline**
> Ouch. I'm not a boy.

I smile to myself. He didn't deny stalker.

> **Bratvabloodline**
> What is it?

My heart thunders in my chest so hard I'm a little dizzy.

You said you're not bluffing.

> **Bratvabloodline**
> I'm not

> You also said you're not going to hurt me.

> **Bratvabloodline**
> I would never hurt you.

Talk is cheap, but... but...

If he were going to hurt me, he... he would have already.

Right?

No, Ember, you stupid bitch—my inner voice warns me before I shut that shit down and continue my conversation.

> Can we meet for coffee?

Some place public, out in the open, where he can't do anything to me.

My pulse races as the dots on the other side of the phone appear then disappear, come back again, then disappear.

I wait and wait, but nothing.

CHAPTER 9

EMBER

THE COLD ROOFTOP air bites at my skin, but it's not what sends a shiver rippling down my spine.

He's here.

Again.

So the guy is local. On the one hand, that should terrify me.

On the other...

I'm not gonna lie. I feel like I'm living in the pages of a romance book.

Towering over me, his presence is oppressive, magnetic. I tilt my chin up to meet his gaze. The black mask covering his face doesn't give much away, but his body radiates tension. Every inch of him screams predator.

And mother of god, I'm here for it.

"Your posts," he whispers in that accent that makes my body sing, begging for more, like verbal foreplay. I swallow hard. "All these fantasies. You have no idea how close you are to living them."

I need to push a little. "What makes you think I want to live them out with you?"

Do I?

Feels a bit strange addressing someone wearing a mask, but the anonymity, the mystery... my heart's beating a million times a minute.

I remind myself that the books I've read... they're... *fantasy.*

I look into his eyes, brooding and intense. He's so big, he blocks the sun. I shiver.

When his hand reaches out to me, I'm holding my breath. His fingers graze my chin, ensuring my gaze doesn't leave his. "Maybe I'll let you test me—see how far you can push me before I let you see whose queen you are."

"But you... you don't even know me," I whisper.

"Don't I?" He leans in closer, and it sets my nerves on edge. I don't like feeling like he's prying into my mind, like he knows more than I want him to. I turn away, and when he takes a step toward me, I try to push past him.

He catches my wrist and twists gently but firmly until I'm facing him again. My breathing's hitched, and his is labored through the mask.

"Take it off," I say, my voice steadier than I feel. "The mask."

For a moment, he doesn't move. The stillness unnerves me. Then, slowly, his hands rise. He pulls at the edges of the mask with deliberate care, like he's revealing a weapon instead of his face.

My hands still over his. "Let me," I whisper.

A thrill races through me when he drops his hands and nods. I feel as if I'm lifting a curtain because we both know —once that mask is off, there's no going back. It's a step toward each other we can't undo.

My heart races as I slowly lift the fabric. It catches on stubble. When I slide my hand beneath it, he stifles a shiver of his own, a groan trapped in his throat. His big hand spans my waist.

I can't help the grin that spreads across my face.

That strong, masculine cut of his jaw. Olive skin. Wicked, full lips slightly parted.

Just before I lift the mask completely, he uses one of his hands to help me and pulls the mask off the rest of the way.

And when he does, it hits me like a punch to the gut.

I know him.

Not from his voice or the way he moves. No, it's that face— sharp jawline, those dark, brooding eyes, and the faint scar that cuts across his brow. He's been at my gym. Watching me. He's the guy who challenged me, who watched me, his intensity making my stomach churn with something between fear and fascination.

I pride myself on noting details. I can't believe I didn't figure this out sooner.

I pull back.

"You," I whisper, the word escaping before I can stop it. My pulse thunders in my ears, and my hands tighten around the forgotten coffee cup like it's my only lifeline.

His smirk, slight but unmistakable, curls at the corner of his mouth. "I've been watching you," he admits, his voice a low rumble that feels more intimate than it should. "And you noticed. Didn't you?"

I want to argue, to deny it, but I can't. Of course I noticed. You don't forget someone who looks like him—especially not when they watch you like you're the most fascinating thing they've ever seen. But it doesn't explain why. Why hide? Why now?

"Why the mask?" I ask, shaking my head, forcing my voice to stay calm, controlled. "Why all the games?"

His smirk fades, replaced by something darker, heavier. "Because I didn't lie, little queen," he says simply like it's a fact as immovable as gravity. "My name is Rodion Kopolov. Third in command to the Kopolov family Bratva. I could be put away or killed if I put my face online." He shrugs. "Also? You like it."

And yet... it's like the reality of it is so out of the ordinary that I can't quite make sense of it all. I'm torn. The audacity makes my blood boil, and yet I can't ignore the pull of his words. He's not entirely wrong. Intrigue has always been my drug of choice.

But I'm hung up on... *Bratva.*

He's real, dangerous, and standing too damn close. Sure, he could be lying, but somehow I know he isn't. There's a sort of cognitive dissonance. He's standing before me, the mark of the Bratva on him. He says *he is Bratva*.

"I don't like this," I snap, stepping back.

Now *I'm* the one lying.

I am definitely the one lying.

"Yes, you do," he says with that wicked grin that makes my brain short-circuit. "I've read your posts, Ember. I know what you want, what you dream about when no one else is watching. I've watched every one of your videos on repeat. I've looked at the books you read. I know every fantasy you've imagined, and I know if you really had a problem with me, you would've blocked me a long time ago. And you haven't. I took risks making those videos, because I know... *I'm* the one that can give you what you really want."

My heart slams against my ribcage. I should be angry. Hell, I am angry. But beneath it, there's something else—something I don't want to name. Something dangerous.

"You don't know me," I repeat, the words coming out weaker than I intended.

When he leans in, his breath brushing against my cheek as he speaks. His voice is a promise, dark and electric. He bends so his lips brush my cheeks, and the next thing he says makes me shudder.

"You know as well as I do that's a lie, and I told you if you were mine, that wouldn't fly, didn't I? We're going inside, little queen. Someone needs a lesson."

CHAPTER 10

RODION

SHE DIDN'T LIKE IT, but I put the mask back on.

I like how she acts when I wear it.

"This is not what I had in mind," she says with an adorable frown. I stifle a smirk.

When I told her there was a lesson I had to teach her, I could tell exactly what she had in mind by the way her eyes lit up. It made me almost pull her over my knee right then and there because I know she craves it. I've watched the videos. I've seen her reactions. I've hacked into her e-reader and read every section she's highlighted and recommended since I found her. I've seen the stitches incoming where she talks about being overpowered and punished by a strong, preferably masked man.

I know that some of this is only fantasy, but I also want to make sure she's prepared. It's important that we know how to defend ourselves.

"So tell me. Who's Shawn?"

I know what I found out, but I want to hear what she has to say in her own words. Her whole body freezes. Just for a second. Just enough for me to see the truth in her eyes before she schools her face into something defiant.

"How do you know that name?"

"I asked a question first." My voice drops, low and calm, the kind of calm that precedes a storm. She hates it—I can see the flash of anger in her face—but I don't care. Not when I've seen the texts. Not when I know something isn't right.

"It's none of your business," she snaps, wrapping her arms around herself like it'll protect her.

"Wrong." I take a step toward her, closing the space between us, the mask making me feel sharper, colder—like a weapon. "he won't leave you alone, and you're mine, so he's *making* it my business."

Her chin tilts up stubbornly, but her voice trembles when she speaks. "And what exactly are you going to do about it? Beat him up? Kill him?"

"If I need to." The words hang between us, heavy and unshakable. I mean it, and she knows it.

She scoffs, even as her cheeks color, turning on her heel and pacing to the other side of the room. "I don't need your hero complex. I can handle him, you know."

I love hearing her say my name, even when she's angry.

I want to hear it again.

"Maybe you can, maybe you can't," I snap, sharper than I intended. She flinches, and I force myself to breathe, to pull back from the edge. "Not yet." My voice softens, though the mask keeps it cold. "But I'm going to teach you."

She spins to face me, her green eyes blazing. I want to grab her chin and force her eyes to mine before I claim her mouth and teach her manners. "Teach me *what*, exactly?"

"To fight. This is why we're having your first lesson in self-defense."

Her laugh is sharp, almost self-deprecating, but there's an edge of something—self-doubt maybe—underneath. "You're crazy."

"And you're reckless," I bite back, closing the distance between us again. She doesn't back away this time, her gaze darting between my mask and my eyes. When her pupils dilate and she visibly swallows, it only confirms what I already know. Ember's fucking turned on. "You don't know what you're up against, little queen. You don't even know how to defend yourself. I'm not always going to be there to stop someone from touching you."

"Oh yeah?" she challenges. "I've studied self-defense. I work out, hard." Her voice is husky as she licks her lips and meets my gaze. I step forward before she can react, crowding her space. Her breath catches, and she raises her small hand as if on instinct to warn me off, but her movement is slow and wide. With barely an effort, I grab her wrist without hurting her, just enough to immobilize.

Her body stiffens, her eyes locking onto mine. "What the hell are you doing?"

"Proving a point," I murmur. I twist her wrist slightly more, shifting her balance so she stumbles forward, her chest brushing against mine. When her free hand hovers between us, it's as if she's unsure whether she wants to fight or flee.

I know what I fucking want. I'm holding myself back, but I want to prove this point.

"Let me go," she demands, but the tremor in her voice gives her away. A stray strand of hair crosses her face, and she blows her breath at it to get it out of her mouth with an angry frown.

"Break the grip. Don't pull," I command, guiding her wrist out of my hold before releasing her. She stumbles back, rubbing her arms, her cheeks flushed. Even though she glares at me, I can tell her confidence is shaken. "You didn't give me a chance—"

"Exactly my point." When I step closer, this time, she doesn't retreat. "In a real fight, there *are* no chances. You get one move. If you don't make it count... you lose."

Her lips part, but she doesn't speak, just stands there, her chest rising and falling, the frustration in her gaze evident.

"Still think you know self-defense?"

"Fuck you."

"Careful, little queen." I shake my head, holding her gaze. "You're treading deep water."

She swallows hard, her throat bobbing as she looks up at me. "And what makes you think I'll let you teach me anything?"

I lean in closer, the mask making my words feel darker, heavier. "Because you know I'm right."

"My god, you're arrogant."

"I know your favorite coffee order and your favorite books. It took all my self-restraint not to go to the house of the bastard who bullied you online—and yeah, I got his address, but I held myself back—to teach him a lesson in respecting you. And you thought I wouldn't check out a real-life threat to you?"

I shake my head. Silence follows, broken only by her sharp inhale. Then, finally, she sighs, biting her bottom lip as she considers.

"Fine. But no weird power-trip bullshit, okay? Just show me what to do. Please," she amends.

I give her a half smile. "Whatever you say, little queen."

We clear a space in her tiny living room—not that there's much room to clear. I shrug off my jacket, toss it onto her couch, and roll up my sleeves. I don't miss the way she watches me warily, her hands twitching like she's ready to defend herself already.

When I point to the space in front of me, a shadow crosses her features. "Come here."

"I don't trust you."

"Good," I say, my voice taut. "Trusting me would be stupid."

"You make no sense."

"You're a walking contradiction yourself, and I don't have time for games. Now come *here*."

Jesus, my palm itches to smack her ass.

Reluctantly, she steps into my space, standing stiff as a board. "Now what?"

"First lesson: confidence," I say, moving behind her. She jumps slightly when my hands settle on her hips—not tight, but firm enough to reposition her. I love the way her hips feel under my touch, warm and supple.

Christ. I bring myself back to our lesson with effort.

"Never look vulnerable. Stand up straight."

She exhales sharply, her shoulders rising. "Like this?"

"Better," I murmur, my voice quieter now. I step back to study her stance. "Relax."

"Hard to relax when you're supposed to be trusting yet not trusting your fake Bratva boyfriend while being confident and not vulnerable yet relaxed. Am I supposed to be turned on? Angry? On edge?"

I huff out a quiet laugh while I walk in front of her. "Yes. Now. Hit me."

Her head snaps up, eyes wide. "What?"

"Hit me," I repeat, spreading my arms. "Come on, Ember. You want to fight? Show me what you've got."

"You're ridiculous."

"Crazy, ridiculous, insane. I've heard worse. You need to learn." When she doesn't, I egg her on. "You afraid of me? You can't do it?"

Before she can argue, I grab her wrist—not hard, just enough to startle her. She gasps, her body stiffening as I hold her still.

"What do you do now?" I ask, my voice a low rumble.

Her lips part, but no words come. She pulls at her wrist, trying to yank free, but I don't let go.

"Wrong," I say softly, loosening my grip just enough to guide her. "Remember what I said before. You don't pull. You *break*." I twist her hand sharply, showing her how to free herself. "Quick, sharp. Then go for the weak spots—wrists, elbows, knees."

She nods, biting her lip as she tries again. This time, she gets it, breaking free with a triumphant huff.

"Good girl," I murmur before I can stop myself. Praise wells in my chest.

Her smile falters, her cheeks flushing. "Don't call me that."

"Why not?" I tilt my head. "You like it."

Her chin in the air, she holds my gaze. "I do not."

I step closer, towering over her, my voice dropping to a dangerous whisper. "Liar."

Her breath hitches. I love to see the fight in her, the war between fear and something else—something she doesn't want to admit. I trace a finger down the side of her face. "Are you really telling me you don't like it?" I shake my head. "I've watched your videos, little queen. I know for a fact you fangirl hard over praise kink." I lift my mask for a moment, lean in, and kiss her cheek. "You're doing so well, baby. I'm so proud of you." I nibble her ear and span my hands over her hips. "You're learning so quickly."

"Ugh," she says in a heated whisper. "Mayyyybe..."

I stand up. "Mhm." I give her ass a sharp slap. "Back to business."

An hour later, we're both exhausted, and Ember has shown that she's a very good student. I feel a little better about the entire situation.

"You hungry?" I ask her, sitting gingerly on the edge of her couch so that I don't break the damn thing. I'm really not made for an apartment like this. I feel as if I'm walking in a fucking dollhouse. I can barely get through the doorways.

"I don't usually eat breakfast," she says, nodding toward her coffee cup. "Coffee is enough."

"Don't eat breakfast? Jesus. You have to eat breakfast."

"But what if I don't want to?" she snaps, crossing her arms.

"Cut it out, little brat. What if I tell you to?"

"Don't remember telling you that was your call?"

I roll my eyes. "Keep it up. You're giving me a good reason to tease our online followers."

Ember shakes her head. "No way. I think we need to keep up the façade. Keep them guessing. I think we're both in danger if we start hinting that we're actually in a relationship with each other because obviously—" She holds up a finger. "We're still not. Right? Do you get that?"

Oh, I got that. I also saw the way her cheeks flushed when she backtracked, making damn sure I know we're not a thing.

Ha.

"Whatever."

We sit back on her couch. More accurately, *she* sits on her couch, and I teeter on the edge, trying not to break it. I feel like a dad at a parent-teacher conference trying to squeeze his legs under an elementary school desk. It's ridiculous.

Ember leans back on the couch. "Do you cook, *Bratva boy?*"

I narrow my eyes at her. "Call me *Bratva boy* one more time and see where that lands you."

The way her eyes light up and her cheeks flush—my dick is totally in favor of this next move.

"I just asked a simple question," she says in a low, seductive voice. "*Bratva boy.*"

I grab her wrists easily with my left hand, engulfing them, and bend her over my lap with no effort. She squeals, but I'm here for it, and she's so easy to overpower. I grab my phone with no problem whatsoever, flip the video camera on, hit record, and prop it up on one of her little book-shelves. I'm careful to make sure you can't tell we're in her place.

"Oh my god!" she says, trying to squirm out of my grip. "Are you recording? What the hell?"

She protests right before I crack my palm across her ass. My palm covers her entire ass. It's satisfying as fuck.

When she squirms and scissors her legs, my dick approves.

"This is what happens to bad girls who don't do what they're told," I whisper before I lift my palm and crack it across her ass again. "You say you want to be overpowered, and then at the first opportunity, you talk back to me. This is where it's going to get you. But I think you knew that."

I spank her again and again until the wriggling slows and her breathing grows heavy. She's draped over my knee, utterly pliant.

"Didn't you, little queen?"

"Didn't I—didn't I what?" she says in a breathy whisper.

"Know this is where you'd end up?"

"I—" A knock sounds at the door, so loud and sharp the door rattles.

"Ember. I know you're in there. Open up!"

I wanted to kill Shawn before. Now, I want to make the death slow and painful for his shitty timing, since I still don't even know what the fucker did to her.

"What perfect timing," I mutter, sliding her off my lap. I tilt her chin with my finger. "We're not done here. I'm gonna go get that door."

"With your mask on?"

I blow out a breath.

The knock sounds again. I reach for the edge of my mask and tug it off in one swoop. I watch as her eyes go wide. She likes when I take it off.

Reaching her hand out to me, she traces my cheek with her index finger. I close my eyes and brace against a well of emotions I wasn't ready for. "Don't ever get rid of that mask."

Fuccck.

I reach for her hand and kiss her palm. "I'm going to get that door."

I do a mental check of the weapons I have on me but know if this guy is the douchebag I suspect he is, I won't need anything more than my hands. I'm already a dead man walking with my brother, and I don't need to push this envelope.

I stride to the door with deliberate slowness, cracking my neck as I reach for the handle. When I swing it open, there's no mistaking the guy standing there. Shawn looks just as smug and self-satisfied as his texts suggested, tall but shorter than me, blond, clean-shaven, arrogant as fuck.

His confidence falters the second he sees me filling the doorway though. I watch as his brow furrows, and he glances past me, trying to look into the apartment. "Uh, who the hell are you?"

I lean casually against the doorframe, letting him see exactly how much bigger I am. "The better question is, do you typically bang down the door of someone when you're uninvited?" I cross my arms and shake my head before I cluck my tongue. "Those are terrible manners."

"Excuse me?" He laughs nervously, attempting to step closer. "I'm here to talk to Ember. This is her place, isn't it?" Placing his hands on his hips, he tries to stand taller and fails. "What are you, her security or something?"

"Or something."

I don't move, keeping my stance loose but unmistakably commanding. Douchebags like him are easily intimidated. "Let me make this simple. She doesn't want to see you.

Turn around, and we can pretend that this never happened."

Lies, but I know he won't buy it.

"Hey." Ember's voice rings out behind me. I glance over my shoulder to find her standing there, arms crossed, a flush still high on her cheeks. She's clearly trying to pull herself together, but there's steel in her voice. "Shawn, leave. I don't want to talk to you."

Shawn's face falls into a wounded mask, but I catch the glint of manipulation in his eyes. He edges closer, trying to peer around me. "Ember, come on. Don't let this guy speak for you. We've got history. I just want to talk."

"You heard her," I growl, straightening to my full height. "She said to leave."

I'm not sure decking this guy, whoever the fuck he is, is the best way to earn Ember's favor, but he's pushing the damn envelope.

Shawn's mask cracks, and his voice turns sharp. "Who the hell do you think you are? This is between me and her—"

I step forward, forcing him to stumble back into the hallway. My voice drops into a dangerous calm. "I'm the man who will happily remind you what 'no' means. Try me."

Don't kill him. Do. Not. Kill. Him. I conjure up the faces of my brothers, ready to murder *me* if I misstep here.

For a moment, Shawn's bravado wars with his self-preservation. His jaw tightens, but the size difference—and my unflinching stare—seals the deal. He throws his hands up in mock surrender, stepping back with a scowl.

"Fine. I'm going," he mutters, shooting a pointed look at Ember over my shoulder. "But we're not done, Ember."

"Yes, we are," she calls out, her voice steady despite the tension in her frame. "Don't come back."

He glares at me one last time before turning on his heel and stalking off. Footsteps sound on the stairs. The slamming of a door. I watch until he's fully out of sight, then close the door, locking it firmly behind me.

When I turn, Ember's watching me, her arms still crossed but her posture softer now. Her lips part, but no words come out. Instead, she steps closer to me.

"That was hot," she whispers. "The uh... difference between reality and fantasy? That one right there? Checks out on both fronts."

I can't help it. I need to kiss her. *I have* to.

We lean into each other. When her lips meet mine, I stifle a groan. *Fuuuck.*

I slide my hands to her waist, pulling her flush against me as she presses up onto her toes, her fingers tangling in my hair. There's no hesitation, no doubt—only heat and want, and I'm matching that fucking energy.

Her nails scrape against my scalp as she tilts her head, deepening the kiss. My hands tighten on her hips, and I steer her backward until her back hits the wall. She gasps into my mouth, and I take the opportunity to nip at her bottom lip, drawing a soft moan that sends a jolt of electricity through me.

"You're tempting the devil," I warn her, my voice rough with restraint.

"Maybe I hope he bites," she whispers back, her voice breathless. Heated. She's living up to her fucking name.

I don't give her a chance to second-guess. I capture her mouth again, my hands sliding up her sides to anchor her in place. She arches into me, and I'm seconds away from losing all fucking control.

But this time, she pulls back, her lips swollen and her breath coming in shallow gasps. Her green eyes blaze as she meets my gaze. "Let's get this clear. Just because I let you intimidate Shawn doesn't mean I'm letting you boss me around."

I smirk, brushing a stray lock of hair from her face. "We'll see about that, little queen."

Glancing at her phone, she groans. "Shit! I have to get to a shoot. I promised."

"And I've got to check in with my brothers." I pull away from her with reluctance. I know I need to leave. I have to make sure she learns to trust me, and right now, I've pushed far. "Tonight, Ember."

CHAPTER 11

IT's a strange way to date someone, but here I am, outside her building, coffee in hand and mask in place.

Last night, I made my decision. My contact here in LA, a detective who works well enough for cash and discretion, dug up what I needed on Ember—and her fucking step-brother, Shawn.

The way she flinched at his name, froze at his texts... I'd seen enough. The messages he's been sending her?

Screw discretion. My brothers will get over it.

I'll fucking kill him.

This morning, the texts from Rafail came in, each one sharper than the last.

Rafail
The Romanovs' Gala next week. You must
bring a woman, Rodion. Everyone is
watching. Jesus. If only it were your wife.

I can't focus on this, not yet. She barely knows me, definitely doesn't trust me, and there's no fucking way I'm taking anyone else.

So I table the conversation and mute our messages.

For now.

But god, what I wouldn't want to do to make her an offer. An escape from that shitty apartment, from the reckless "starving artist" routine, wandering through alleys unarmed. She didn't see the danger she courted.

Ember Steele. Fierce but blind to the way men looked at her.

The thought of Shawn ignites something dark in my chest. That bastard won't touch her again.

She deserves a reckoning for her carelessness—walking around the city as if she weren't a target, a temptation. If I had my way, I'd bend her over my knee for that alone. A good spanking to remind her who the hell she belongs to.

For now, I wait.

I have plans for her, shit I want to do... if I could make this all work *and* appease my brother at the same time.

But I can't get ahead of myself.

What if in the light of day she's come to her senses and tells me to fuck off?

I shift my weight, gripping the coffee cups tighter as her front door creaks open.

I need to confront this woman about her fucking recklessness and vulnerability, so when she asked if I wanted to swing by today, I didn't even hesitate.

The door opens, and for a few seconds, my thoughts come to a screeching halt.

She's here.

I just saw her, but it feels like seeing her for the first time all over again.

Never in my life would I have agreed to allow her to stay alone after Shawn's fucking display; never would I have imagined she'd be on her own, but she won't come to my place, and she won't let me stay at hers.

I guess in her world, that makes sense. In mine, I'm making fucking accommodations, and my patience is drawing to a close.

I hold my breath when she steps outside. Her lips, slightly parted, draw my gaze like a goddamn magnet, the morning sun catching the copper in her hair. Her emerald-green eyes widen in recognition as they meet mine, her breath catching momentarily. In an instant, the widening fades, replaced by a sharp, narrowed glare.

Though she shifts nervously, and her cheeks turn pink, her voice is conversational.

Interesting.

"Hey. So we're really keeping up with the mask thing?"

I don't respond right away, letting the words settle between us as I extend one of the coffee cups toward her. She doesn't take it at first, her gaze flicking between me and the drink like she's weighing whether or not to throw it in my face.

Finally, she snatches it, takes a tentative sip, and then narrows her eyes even further. "This is exactly the way I like it."

I love the way she sighs contentedly as she takes another sip. "Though I guess the fact that you know how I take my coffee should be the least of my worries.

"And yet," I say, my voice low and amused, "you drank it. As far as the mask... it's part of my identity at this point."

The blush deepens when she looks away. She doesn't know how to play this—how to deal with me.

Good. It means I've got her off balance.

"Walk with me," I say, already turning toward the street.

For a second, I think she won't follow, but then I hear her boots on the pavement behind me.

We walk in silence, the city waking up around us. She's clutching her coffee like it's a shield, glancing at me from the corner of her eye every few steps.

"We should go to the roof," I grumble, eying the entrance that will take us to the elevator.

With a nod, she agrees, turns a corner, and shows me a rusty metal door hidden in the shadows. I haven't been here before. We walk across the cracked pavement.

"Where the hell does this lead?" I ask her with a growl because the very thought of her here, alone...

"Upstairs. The roof? You said that's what we needed."

Her shoulder brushes mine, and I can feel the tension radiating off her body like static.

Like *fire*.

I've got Ember alone, I'm masked up, and I have a detailed recollection of every single one of her damn fantasies.

Maybe there is a god.

She doesn't know I've cataloged an entire list of every fucking fantasy she's ever posted online... and I have every intention of fulfilling these fantasies.

I'm holding back. Now isn't the time. She's got something to tell me, and I have to be patient.

I want to kiss her again.

I want to pin her up against this wall and claim her mouth. I want her to scream and fight me, clawing at my chest, unable to push me away until she finally melts into the kiss.

But right now, I'm focused on the fact that Ember takes risks she shouldn't, that she lives on the edge of danger, and the fact that literally *anyone* could take advantage of her in this alleyway.

My hands clench into fists.

"Why don't you—" The words freeze on her lips when she looks at me. "You're masked. I can't read your facial expressions, and yet I can tell you want to break something. What the hell?"

"What gave it away? Was it the clenched fists?"

"No," she says thoughtfully. With her arms crossed over her chest in an effort to self-protect, she looks little. Scared. "I think it's the way your body's as taut as a bowstring, and you're growling like an animal."

Am I?

Fuck.

"You walked over here as if this were second nature. Like you're going to get something to drink at a fucking coffee shop. You're obviously familiar with this entrance."

When I don't continue, she shakes her head and uncrosses her arm. "Sooooo... what? Your point?"

"My point is that you're vulnerable out here, in that shitty apartment with a lock I could break if I sneezed, and you think it's alright that you just waltz into this dark alleyway like someone couldn't just *take* you. Take advantage of you when you have a fucking predator breathing down your neck." I take in a cleansing breath. "And I'm not talking about *me*."

Rolling her eyes, she shakes her head. "Are you for real?"

"Excuse me?"

She's getting so fucking close to my hand across her ass—

"You say you're *Bratva*. The kind of men who break the law as a matter of routine?" She stares as if waiting for the connections to click before blowing out an exasperated breath. "It just doesn't make any sense that someone who *supposedly* flaunts the law gets his boxers all knotted over a dark alley?" Tipping her head to the side, she pins me in place with a stare. "Explain."

"My boxers all knotted?" The words come out like a growl.

Maybe we don't need to play out a scene.

Maybe she's walked herself right into a real-life one, right here, right now.

"Are you muttering under your breath?"

I clench my teeth and consider ripping off the fucking mask so I can breathe better. "Open the fucking door, Ember. Let's go upstairs. *Now.* Not one more word, or I swear to fuck—"

Her lips part in what I can only describe as humor-laced defiance, the little fucking *brat*, her brow arching like she's testing just how far she can push me. "Or you'll what?" A theatrical shiver completes the effect. "Scowl at me harder?"

The smirk curling at the corner of her mouth is a spark to dry kindling. I step closer, shortening the distance between us, the heat palpable now.

"Or I'll show you exactly what it means to walk into a scene you can't talk your way out of." My voice is low and measured but carries the weight of a promise. When she swallows, her throat bobs, the first real sign of fear.

About time. Now we're getting somewhere.

When she lifts her chin up, I nod toward the door. "Upstairs. *Now*," I repeat, my tone leaving no room for an argument. "You want an explanation, Ember? You'll get one. But not here. Not like this."

Seriously? I mention coffee and get ghosted by my online stalker?

I can't ask him to do this. I *can't,* but—

> **Bratvabloodline**
> I thought you'd never ask. Look out your window, beautiful. Meet me on the rooftop.

Oh god.

I freeze, my pulse thundering in my ears. My hand trembles as I pull the curtain aside—and there he is, leaning casually against a lamppost, two coffees in hand... all masked up, before he turns and heads toward my building.

Her hesitation stretches out as her eyes search mine as if looking to check the veracity of what I'm telling her. Finally, she exhales and turns toward the door before unlocking it with a sharp twist of her wrist.

I can't help myself. Before she can step through, my hand catches her, pulling her against me. My mouth is by her ear before she can protest.

"And when we're done, little queen," I whisper, "you'll understand why some lines aren't meant to be crossed. Not by *anyone.*"

Her shiver tells me she's heard every word... and that she just might be ready to test me anyway.

"Riiiight," she says with a tight smile before she ducks under my arm and disappears into the dark. She calls over her shoulder, "Be careful on the second stair. It wobbles."

I want to smack that perfectly taut little ass so goddamn hard—I stumble on the second step, and she sighs. I can't help that my feet hang off the edge of the damn things.

Flights and flights of stairs later, we're wheezing and out of breath when we make it to the rooftop.

She stops dead in her tracks, forcing me to turn back and face her. "So I—I've gathered you're... into me."

"I am. Obviously, yeah."

Her laugh is sharp, almost bitter. "You don't even know me."

I lean against the wall. "I know more than you think."

She crosses her arms, her coffee cup tucked into the crook of her elbow like a weapon. "If that's supposed to make me feel better, it doesn't."

"Maybe it's not supposed to."

Her lips press into a thin line, and for a moment, I think she's going to walk away. But then she sighs and looks up at me, her eyes full of something I can't quite name.

I lean in, close enough to feel the faint hitch in her breath. "Tell me, Ember, when you post those book scenes, do you ever imagine someone like me reading them?"

I watch her pupils dilate and her throat move as she swallows. "I always imagined a man like you'd have a better use for your time."

Ouch. My brother would agree. I blow out a breath. "Yeah."

She stands up taller. "Listen...you saw how problematic Shawn is."

I grunt in reply but don't interrupt.

"This is maybe the craziest idea in the world, but...the hate comments have all but stopped since you've been interacting with me. And I just think that... well, maybe if he won't accept a no from *me*, he might if he thinks you're my boyfriend."

Her cheeks flush.

I knew it. I won't hesitate, not when she's giving me exactly what I want. "First, you're going to tell me exactly who the fuck Shawn is and why I need to fuck him up. Second, you will *not* fuck around with your safety. If I'm going to pretend to be your fake boyfriend or whatever the fuck, then you're not gonna poke holes in the bucket by doing stupid shit."

"I didn't say you have to fuck him up—"

"As if I'd pretend to be your boyfriend and not take that step if I had to."

Her eyes widen, before she finally nods.

I pause, letting my words hold weight. "And I'll have a condition of my own."

Actually more like *twelve* conditions, but I'll ease her in.

Relief flickers across her face, but she quickly masks it, her walls slamming back into place. "There always is," she says with a sigh. "What?"

There always is? What the fuck?

"We do this on my terms," I begin, stepping closer until we're toe-to-toe. "We're doing this at my place, not yours. I wouldn't fit in your shower."

Her jaw drops slightly, a flush rising to her cheeks again. "I —*what?*"

"You heard me," I say, my smirk returning. "Your apartment is a hazard. I'm not letting you live there while some asshole's breathing down your neck."

She takes a step back, shaking her head. "I don't know about this."

"Then it's off." My temper flares. There's no way it's actually off. She's given me exactly what I want—a chance to protect her. But she isn't making it easy.

Ember plants her hands on her hips. "You think I'm asking you to protect me, to keep me away from an actual predator, and I'm going to do this by putting myself in the close proximity of a stranger who claims he's *Bratva*? How can you claim you want me to be safe and make good decisions, then make an offer like *that*?"

Fair point.

"Fine," I say, letting out an exaggerated sigh. I'll let her have her way. For now. "Stay in your place, but we're dating. Officially. *Publicly*. But if we're dating, I'm taking you on a date."

"Fake dating," she corrects, her voice firm. She glares at me, but there's a flicker of something else behind her eyes. Curiosity? Intrigue? I don't care what it is—it's enough to keep her standing here, enough to keep me in her orbit.

"Listen, Ember. I'll gladly keep you safe, but I want this clear. If we're pretending to date, you're getting the *full* Bratva experience."

She nods. "Alright, but another condition of mine?"

I grin at her and nod. Relief floods through me.

"No mask."

CHAPTER 12

AND THAT'S how I ended up agreeing to go on a *trip* with a badass, tattooed Bratva boy—erm, *man.*

I asked for epic? Turns out we're heading to New York next weekend.

I can still hear Shawn's question.

Are you her security?

Yes. Yes, he is, and I fucking love it.

Maybe I'm crazy. Maybe I've spent too much time dwelling on fantasy and fiction.

Or maybe every time I'm anywhere near him, every cell in my body comes to life.

"Wait." I'm lying on my bed, my knees propped up, my latest book calling to me, but I've got Rodion on the phone, and I have questions for him. Easing into this fake relationship thing is working out better than I thought.

"So you want me to go to this... gala, whatever that is. I'll need a fancy dress? And shoes and makeup..." My mind whirs with the details.

"Maybe give me a little credit. I already know all your sizes and sent them to the stylists, along with that style board you pinned."

I shake my head. Of course he did.

He's sliding into my fantasies the way he slid into my DMs, like a book boyfriend come to life, and I... am not really sure how I feel about this.

We've talked every single night since that run-in with Shawn and my self-defense lessons. I've had photo shoots, and he's been busy with "work."

I haven't asked him what that work entails, and he hasn't offered details. Maybe it's better that way.

I swallow hard. "Who will be there? Will this be like... you know... swimming in shark-infested waters, or..."

"It will be exactly that." He says something under his breath in Russian that sounds very much like a curse. "Which is why we need to make sure we're on the same page about you doing what the fuck you're told."

Right, right, we've been, uh... working on that.

I shiver.

The more I talk with him, the more we get to know each other, and the more I really do believe he's legit.

"Your followers are getting impatient, you know." I twirl my hair around my finger. They're so eager for an update from him they've been messaging *me* nonstop. "Are you going to post anything else?"

"I do have that video I could post..."

My cheeks heat as I remember being strewn over his lap, that massive palm of his across my ass. "Don't you dare!"

I'm unprepared for how his low, dark chuckle does *delicious* things to me.

"No one would know it was you."

"*I* would!"

"Listen, let them talk. You're the only one whose attention I wanted."

I swallow hard. "And now you have it?"

I hear him sigh on the other end of the line. "I do, but not in the way I want."

"I told you," I say in a whisper. "I'm not ready to go to your place yet."

Maybe I'm scared of what will happen if I do. But this weekend, we're heading to New York, and we'll share a room...

"I respect that." Three little words that somehow ease my worry. I wish more men got it.

"I've got a job to do," he says cryptically. "Check in before you go to bed?"

"Yes, sir," I say teasingly, just to hear the approving growl on the other end of the phone.

I can tell how hard he's working at holding himself back from absolutely smothering me. It's hard for me to know what part of the book boyfriend fantasy would actually be nice in real life.

So far, I've got a checklist.

Pinned up against the wall and kissed?

Five stars. Way better than anything my mind's conjured up.

Trapped against the wall, so close his breath warms your neck. His voice drops to that low, commanding tone, his hands hovering just shy of your hips, letting you decide if he can touch?

Get me a fire extinguisher.

The inescapable stare, his eyes on you *everywhere.* Realizing he's memorizing every detail about your day, down to where you get your coffee?

Uhm...

Letting himself into your home to leave a "thoughtful gift?"

Red flag!

My phone buzzes with a message. For a second, I fear that it's Shawn. I want to block him, but I'm afraid if I do, I might miss something crucial, and I need to be vigilant. Thankfully, it's just my book bestie.

Bookbabe
Hey, girl. Where've you been? Have you
been in touch with Bratvaboy?

Um yes

Bookbabe
Shut UP

Hahaha

Yes, we call him Bratva boy behind his back, and no, I haven't told anyone he's actually real, and I've seen him without the mask on. And no, I have absolutely not let *him* find out.

I strip down to my workout bra and panties and reach for a pair of PJs. I toss them onto my dresser as my fingers fly over the keys of my phone.

Bookbabe
WHAT'S HE LIKE?

What's he like? God. How do I answer that? Hot and magnetic, dominant and bossy as fuck. Funny, somehow sweet... *Intense.*

Literally? Like a book boyfriend come to
life.

In all the ways, sister. All the ways.

I feel kind of shy talking about him.

Bookbabe
OMGGGG but is he like legit Bratva? He
can't be, right?

My cheeks flush. I stare at the cozy jammies on my bed and think about it.

I'm not sure

It's a lie.

Deep down inside, I *know* he is. I obviously can't tell her, but I know now there's no other possibility.

I toss my phone down when a prickle of awareness skates down my spine.

For some reason, I feel like... I'm not alone anymore.

"Hello?"

I head into the hallway and stare, my heart racing. Rodion said he had a job to do...

I hear the door click open just before the lights shut off.

My pulse quickens. Oh god.

Please be Rodion, please be Rodion...

"Hello?" My voice is hoarse and barely audible. I quickly go over what he's taught me about self-defense, but why can't I remember it now? "Rodion?"

I stifle a scream when a hand comes over my mouth, and strong arms hold me. My pulse hammers for a split second before I recognize the scent of his body wash and the feel of his hand on my mouth.

"Quiet, little queen. *Fuck.* I didn't anticipate you'd be half-naked when I found you."

And now my pulse races for an entirely different reason.

"You scared me," I whisper as something soft and silky falls over my eyes.

My mind races with possibilities. We've talked about my videos, what gets me excited, and what he plans on doing, but...

His voice brushes against my ear, low and rough, igniting a spark that races down my spine. "Being a little scared, temporarily, is part of the whole appeal, isn't it? If you're going to fantasize about being blindfolded and kidnapped, Ember, you'd better be ready for the real thing."

My breath catches. I can't see him, but I can feel him—his presence looming, dominant, and inescapable. Silk ties firmly at the back of my head, leaving me blind but hyper-aware of every sound, every shift in the air.

"Rodion," I whisper, my voice trembling with a mix of excitement and apprehension.

He doesn't answer. Instead, I hear the faint rustle of fabric and the click of the door locking behind him. His footsteps are slow, deliberate, circling me like a predator sizing up his prey. My pulse pounds, a drumbeat of anticipation thrumming in my ears.

"You talk a lot about wanting someone who takes control," he murmurs, his voice moving closer. I feel his fingers trace the edge of my workout bra, a light, teasing touch that makes me shiver. "But talk is cheap, little queen. Let's see how much you really like it."

My mouth goes dry as his hands slide to my wrists, his grip firm but not harsh. He pulls my arms behind my back, and I hear a soft snap—what the hell? His laugh is low, dark, and wicked as he secures my wrists together.

"You make it too easy," he says, the heat of his breath brushing against my ear. "I thought you'd put up more of a fight."

"You didn't give me a chance," I manage to say, though my voice betrays me with its breathlessness. Heat floods me, and I mentally add *taken by surprise and blindfolded* to the super-hot list.

"You wouldn't win," he murmurs, his voice like velvet-wrapped steel. His hands trace a deliberate path down my sides, igniting a searing trail that makes my breath hitch. When his fingers settle firmly on my hips, he pulls me back, and I collide with the unyielding heat of his chest.

My thoughts dissolve, splintering into nothing but the aching anticipation of where his touch will land next.

"Now," he whispers, his voice laced with command, "you're going to stand here and take everything I give you."

Oh my god, what is he going to give me?

I can't help the soft whimper that escapes my throat. He hears it, of course. He leans in, his lips brushing against my neck, and I swear I feel his smirk against my skin.

"Good girl," he murmurs, and I'm undone.

He's right.

I love *good girl*.

Yes.

I stifle a giggle when I remember some fan art stickers an author sent me—black and white with handcuffed wrists, the words *Good Girls Love Dark Romance* across the bottom.

"Something funny, little queen?"

I shake my head and go to talk when he slides something across my lips and ties it securely.

"Go ahead, baby. Scream. Let me hear you."

I let out a little scream, but it's tentative and muffled.

"Do better." His palm slams across my ass, and I let out a louder scream on instinct.

"Better."

My heart races.

I'm leaning into this, yes, but... but do I trust him completely?

What happens if this isn't just a game to him?

I—

His hands roam, exploring every curve, every inch of me that he's claimed in his mind long before this moment. The contrast between his rough palms and the smooth fabric of my bra and panties is intoxicating. Every touch is a reminder that I'm not in control—that I've willingly given it to him.

And I don't want it back.

"You're trembling," he says, his voice almost amused as his hands slide to the hem of my leggings. "Is that fear, Ember?

Or something else? I watched that video you posted last night."

My cheeks flame. Of course he did.

Honestly? I posted it, hoping he would.

A convenient setup, really...

"You whined about not having a real-life book boyfriend come and kidnap you."

Maybe I shouldn't have been *that* obvious.

My heart rate spikes.

Kidnap me?

When I hesitate, he explores my body with the palms of his hands, pausing at the curve of my hips. "My god, you're gorgeous," he whispers in my ear before taking my earlobe between his teeth. "*Kakaya ty krasivaya, budto sochtili angely.*"

I want to know what it *means*.

His hands release the gag. I gasp in a breath.

"Tell me you don't want this as much as I do. Tell me exactly what you want. What you fantasize about. Tell me, or I'll fill in the gaps on my own, and I don't know if you want me to do that."

"First, tell me what you just said," I breathe out.

"You're so beautiful, it's as if angels created you."

My mouth is dry. "This is... this is a good start," I manage to eke out.

His smirk deepens, his grip tightening but not cruel. "Better," he whispers, his voice a dark promise. "But that's not enough. Tell me how."

I shiver under his intensity, my cheeks *flaming*. "I want you to take control." I hold his gaze. "Make me forget everything but... you."

"Good girl," he says again, his voice low and satisfied. Then his mouth crashes into mine, and I'm lost in the storm of him—his dominance, his obsession, his raw, unrelenting need, before the gag slides into place too soon.

I'm gasping, panting; my body's on *fire*.

This isn't just a fantasy anymore. It's real.

And I've never wanted anything more.

His mouth to my ear, he whispers, "Spread your legs for me." His harsh tone leaves no room for argument.

I hesitate for a split second, and his hand grips my thigh, fingers digging in just enough to make me gasp. "Now," he snaps, and my knees part instinctively, heat pooling low in my stomach as his control washes over me.

"That's better," he mutters, his voice laced with satisfaction. His hand moves higher, his touch slow and deliberate, teasing, as if he knows how badly I want more. "But don't think for a second I'll make this easy for you, Ember. You want me? You're going to earn it."

I'm already trembling, his words sinking into my skin like fire. I moan against the gag.

"Quiet," he bites out, cutting me off. Even blindfolded, I can feel his dark eyes on me, daring me to disobey. "You're not in charge here. I am. And I decide when you get what you want."

His hands slide to the inside of my thighs, his fingers brushing higher and higher until I'm biting my lip to keep from begging. He leans in, his breath hot against my skin.

"You've been running that smart mouth of yours for weeks," he murmurs darkly. "Posting your little fantasies. Talking about men like me. But now that I'm here, you don't have a fucking clue what to do, do you?"

I shudder, his words cutting through me like a blade. It's true.

"You want my mouth, don't you?" His voice is low and rough. "Nod if you want my mouth on you."

I nod, stifling a moan, thankful for the blindfold so I don't have to look into his eyes. I've never had a man do *that* before, and I—am not really sure if it's going to be as nice as I've imagined.

They sure do like it in the books...

I swallow hard, my pride warring with my desire. But he doesn't give me a choice. His grip tightens, his thumbs pressing into my thighs, spreading me wider.

He laughs, dark and almost cruel, and I'm here for it.

And then his mouth is on me.

It's not gentle. It's not teasing. It's raw, consuming, and merciless. His tongue moves with precision, claiming me the way his words have—completely and without apology. My head falls back against the wall, a muffled cry tearing from my throat as he devours me.

I can't see him but can only imagine his mouth moving like he's starving, like I'm the only thing that can satisfy him. It makes my entire body clench with need.

"You're mine," he snarls, his teeth scraping against my sensitive skin, sending jolts of electricity through me. "Give me that pussy. Spread your legs and lean on me."

When I do what he says, he grants me a reward. "Good girl," he says, his voice dripping with dark satisfaction. "Now keep your fucking hands where they are and take it."

I try to move, to shift under the overwhelming sensation, but his hands clamp down on my thighs, holding me in place. "Don't fucking move," he snaps, his tone a brutal warning.

Every stroke of his tongue, every flick and press, pushes me closer to the edge. He knows exactly what he's doing, exactly how to undo me. My breaths come in shallow gasps, my body tightening as the pressure builds to a breaking point.

"You don't come until I say," he growls, pulling back just enough to make me sob in frustration. "You'll come when I tell you to and not a fucking second before."

I whimper, my hands clenching into fists as I fight to hold back.

I'm trembling, teetering on the edge, and when he finally snarls, "Now," the word hits me like a command I can't ignore.

I don't know how to come on command. I don't know how—

"*Come*," he orders with a sharp slap to my hip, and something releases in me.

I fall apart, my body shattering under his relentless touch. He doesn't stop, doesn't let up, driving me through wave after wave until I'm wrecked, my legs shaking, my voice hoarse against the gag.

My body slumps against the wall, trembling, but all I can think is that I've never wanted him more. My breath comes in ragged gasps as I fight to collect myself. My legs are shaking, my throat raw from muffled cries, and still, all I can think about is him. How he pushes me to the edge and catches me every time. How I never knew surrender could feel this intoxicating, this safe.

His hands are on me again, firm yet careful, steadying me like he knows I can't stand on my own, as he removes the blindfold and gag. The gentleness of his touch is a stark contrast to the wreckage he's left behind, but it makes my chest tighten. When I glance up at him, his eyes are dark and unreadable, but his jaw is tight, his control ironclad.

"Why?" I manage, my voice a shaky rasp. "What do you want out of this? Out of me?"

His hands pause, and for a moment, I think he's going to answer. But then he mutters, "Not tonight," low and final, before untying my wrists and scooping me into his arms.

He carries me into the bathroom like I'm precious, not a trembling mess. The cool tile against my back when he sets me down feels grounding, but I can't take my eyes off him as he moves with quiet determination. He grabs a washcloth, wets it under the faucet, squeezes the water out, and kneels in front of me.

My chest tightens again when he smooths the cloth over my sweaty neck, his movements deliberate and tender. The warm cloth brushes over my skin, and I feel the tension in my muscles start to unravel with every pass. He doesn't rush. If anything, he takes his time, as though this moment matters just as much as the ones that came before it.

"If we were at my place," he murmurs, mostly to himself, his voice rough and almost wistful, "we'd both fit in the tub. I wouldn't have to do this like this."

I can't stop the small laugh that escapes me. "You really hate this place, don't you?"

His eyes flick up to meet mine, and the intensity in them steals the air from my lungs. "It's like having a diamond locked in a tin box," he says quietly, his fingers brushing over my arm as he wrings the cloth. "You don't belong here. It's not enough for you. Not nearly enough."

I swallow hard, the lump in my throat almost too much to bear. He doesn't linger on the weight of his words. Instead, he finishes cleaning me up with careful precision.

When he's done, he lifts me effortlessly, his strength making it seem like I weigh nothing. I wrap my arms around him instinctively, and the way he holds me makes my chest ache with something I don't want to name. He carries me to the bed and sets me down gently before disappearing into my closet.

When he returns, he's holding a set of pajamas I don't even recognize—soft, oversized, and nothing like my usual worn T-shirts. He dresses me in them, his hands careful but sure as he pulls the fabric over my skin. The intimacy of it hits me so hard that I don't realize I'm crying until his thumb brushes my cheek, catching the tear.

I expect him to leave. I hope he doesn't. But instead, he sits on the edge of the bed and grabs one of the books from my nightstand. He flips it open, his expression softening into amusement as he skims the first page.

He starts reading aloud, his deep voice with a hint of an accent wrapping around the words in a way that makes my cheeks flush.

"You're mine. Your orgasms belong to me. Your pussy belongs to me. Your body is mine to do with as I will. If I want to shave you, I will. If I want to spank your pussy red, I will. If I want to cuff you to my bed to wait for me, I will."

"This is what you read?" he asks, raising an eyebrow at me.

"Don't judge me," I mutter, but I can't help the small smile tugging at my lips.

"Judge you? Never, now that I know how to reap the benefits."

When he reads, his tone is teasing, dipping low on the dirtiest lines, but there's something warm and almost indulgent about the way he stays. He's still there when my eyes drift closed, my body sinking into the bed as exhaustion takes over.

When I wake, the bed is empty, the covers pulled neatly around me. The air feels colder without him, and the quiet ache in my chest surprises me.

I don't like it.

Reaching for my phone, I find it plugged in on the nightstand. I close my eyes against a rush of emotion, when I see a new message waiting for me. It's a video. My breath catches as I open it.

The screen fills with darkness at first, and for a moment, I think it's just audio—the faint sound of his breathing, steady and deliberate. Then the image sharpens. A blindfold rests in his hand, the silky fabric slipping between his fingers in slow, deliberate movements.

His face emerges next, masked, shadowed, and devastatingly calm. His eyes burn into the camera, filled with that lethal energy that always leaves me trembling. His voice is low and dangerous, a private caress meant only for me.

"Careful what you wish for, little queen," he murmurs, his fingers tightening around the blindfold before the screen cuts to black.

My breath catches, the silence that follows almost deafening. My heart pounds in my chest, my body warm with the memory of his touch and the promise of more. The video leaves me shaking, craving him in ways I don't fully understand.

Because it's not just the words or the way he looks at me like I'm his—it's the certainty in his voice that thrills and terrifies me.

I don't know if there's any going back from this.

CHAPTER 13

I FUCKING hate being apart from her. I've never been obsessed with a woman before, but everything about her, fucking everything, calls to me like the call of the siren. I only hope I don't crash myself on the fucking shore.

The phone buzzes in my hand. Again.

Rafail.

I should answer. He hates waiting, but my mind is stuck somewhere else. My thumb hovers over the video feed from her apartment. I ignore Rafail and click the button, an addict unable to stop himself from his next hit.

She's asleep, her breathing steady, her hair spilling across the pillow like some kind of goddamn halo. My shoulders tense as I check the biometrics again—heart rate, body temp —all steady. She's fine. Perfect.

And yet, something gnaws at me. Maybe it's because she didn't call back. Or because her name hasn't appeared in my notifications, no flirty comment under my video. Nothing.

I should know better than to post the fucking thirst traps, but I can't help it. It's the wildest of bait for the wildest of women, and I love the way she watches them the second I post them. I scroll through the comments on the latest upload directed at Ember.

> I really shouldn't have opened this. I have work to do and now I've forgotten my own name. Why is this man so hot???

> Sir, I will personally commit crimes for you. 🖤

> This energy could ruin my day, and I'd thank you for it. 😗

I scroll past, searching, searching… nothing from her.

I'm used to being in control. Planning. Acting. But with her, it's like every fucking second of silence feels like a failure.

The phone buzzes again, and this time, Rafail's name is flashing like a warning. He's gonna kill me.

"What?" I snap as I answer.

"*What?*" he echoes, sharp and biting. "What the fuck is wrong with you? I've been waiting for ten minutes."

I pinch the bridge of my nose, dragging my focus back. I don't talk to him this way and can't start now.

"I'm here. What do you want?"

"Watch it. You tell me. Are you bringing someone to this gala or not?" His tone is clipped, but there's a thread of something deeper—curiosity, maybe. Amusement.

"Yes," I say, jaw tightening.

"Who?"

I roll my eyes with a sigh. "You know who."

There are no real secrets in our family, though I've somehow miraculously been able to keep my masked online presence off their radar. He's seen footage of me with Ember and so has Semyon.

There's a beat of silence. Then he laughs, low and dark. "The pretty little redhead. Did you marry her yet?"

The teasing pisses me off more than it should. "No," I bite out. "Not yet."

He's silent again, but this time, there's no laugh, no follow-up. Just dead air. Rafail knows how to make his point with silence better than most men can with words.

I check the live feed again while I wait, watching the soft rise and fall of her chest. A faint shift, the way she tucks her hands closer under the covers. Something in me aches, sharp and... unfamiliar.

"You're distracted, Rodion," Rafail snaps, yanking me back.

"Just tired," I lie, biting back something harsher. I have to remember who I'm talking to.

"Bullshit," he fires back. "Focus. If you can't keep your head in the game, I'll pull you from the gala entirely and send Matvei."

No, he fucking won't.

"I'm focused," I say sharply, even as my eyes flick back to the video.

"Then prove it." His tone hardens. "We'll talk more about this weekend later. I have a job for you to do. Right now."

Here we go again. I straighten, already bracing. "What's the job?"

"Details are coming to your secure line. Handle it, and do not screw this up."

The line goes dead before I can respond. Typical Rafail.

A notification pings—encrypted instructions, just as promised. I scan the details quickly, forcing my mind to shift gears. It's a cleanup. A target with loose ties to a Bratva rival. Not messy work but work that requires my full attention.

Son of a bitch. I wanted to go see Ember. It's only been a few hours, but...

I clench my fist, pushing down the pull to check her video again. She's fine. *Safe*. I don't need to hover over every second.

But still, the idea of leaving her tonight twists something in my chest.

I grab my gear.

The distraction she's become... I've got to deal with it. With *her*.

The job will keep me busy for now, but it's not enough.

Not until I show her exactly what it means to be mine. Tonight, I'll handle Rafail's mess. But after?

I take a look at the tools I've set aside for her—the soft rope, the blindfold—and grin. Game on, little queen.

Then my phone buzzes again, and for a split second, I think it's Rafail, already breathing down my neck. But no—the notification is from her account.

@dreammafiaqueen has gone live

Live

My pulse spikes, and I swipe the notification open, the feed springing to life.

There she is. Her hair's still a mess from sleep, and her sweatshirt slides off one shoulder. The sight of her, disheveled but glowing, hits me like a punch. She's in her bedroom, the same one I've been watching all night, and she's staring into the camera with a look that's nothing short of fire.

"Morning, little queen," I whisper.

Her lips curl into a small, knowing smile, and then she speaks.

"This one's for you," she says, her voice low and teasing. She leans closer to the camera, her green eyes locking onto the lens like she knows exactly who's watching. *Me.*

My grin fades, replaced by something darker, sharper. The game just changed.

"Careful what *you* wish for," she whispers, echoing the words from my video. Then she sits back, brushing her hair out of her face with the kind of casual confidence that drives me insane before I realize—she's sitting in her panties on top of a pile of books, the leather strap of her camera hanging off the edge of her end table. She fingers the leather strap and wraps it around her chest, just under her breasts—the feed ends abruptly, leaving me staring at the blank screen.

Oh my fucking god.

Let the games begin.

CHAPTER 14

I DON'T HEAR from Rodion all day.

I hate it.

I find myself opening up the damn app every minute, checking to see if he posted a new video, or a new comment, *something*. Even though I have it set up to notify me when he posts, I manage to convince myself that I must've missed it.

I do my best to try to stay on task, but my mind isn't in the game.

The video showed he watched mine earlier, but...

I click the focus on my camera, adjusting the lens to center on the subject—a cluster of glossy city lights reflected in a puddle on the uneven pavement. It should be an easy shot, something I've done a thousand times before. But my hands aren't steady. The framing feels off, and no matter how I reposition myself, the composition doesn't click into place.

I blow out a frustrated breath and try again, crouching lower, angling the camera upward. The viewfinder blurs for a second, and I realize I'm not even looking at the scene anymore. My mind is somewhere else.

No. Not some*where*. Someone.

I shake my head and reset the focus, but my fingers stay on the buttons too long. A second passes. Then another. It's useless. The image in my head isn't the lights or the rain or the city's moody backdrop.

It's him.

His hands on me, the way they linger just long enough to leave an impression as hot as a brand. The low timbre of his voice when he murmurs something teasing and sharp, a challenge laced with a dare. The heat in his eyes when he looks at me—like I'm something rare, something he's already decided is... his.

The thought sends a shiver down my spine, and my hand slips, jarring the camera. "Shit," I whisper, cradling the lens as I try to reset the shot again. *Focus*, I tell myself. Just focus.

But the truth is, I've lost the thread completely. My eyes drift to my phone resting on the edge of my camera bag. I resist the urge to check it—for messages, notifications, anything. He hasn't called, hasn't texted, but I know he isn't far away.

Or is he?

The lights blur in the lens again, and this time, I don't even try to fix it. I set the camera down, my breath catching as my thoughts spiral back to him. I'm gonna give myself a minute to indulge the fantasy, to be as fucking obsessed about him as he is about me.

What's he doing right now? Thinking about me? Planning something?

My heart beats faster at the thought, and I press my hands to my thighs, willing the adrenaline to fade. But it doesn't. Not when every part of me is tuned to him like a live wire.

The camera sits forgotten on my lap as I stare out at the city, my pulse pounding in sync with his memory. I know then... it's hopeless. I've got a big, head-over-heels, heart-pounding crush for the guy.

I send him a message but it goes unreturned. I barely stifle the need to pout.

I need to talk with someone.

I pull up the app and message Bookbabe.

> I haven't heard from my stalker. 😔

Bookbabe
Nooooooo. He posted last night, though, didn't he?? Did you shamelessly flirt with him, or...?

> I did and he responded and then nothing

Bookbabe
Oooh. Does he…usually respond to you more often? Maybe he's… I dunno, like… offing someone or unaliving them or whatever tf mafia men do? What DO Bratva men do?

I don't want to know but I think it's more than that?

Jesus. I *hope* it's more than that.

Also? I'm not lying. I truly have no idea what he does because I would hazard a guess that nearly everything is… well, not exactly legal.

We joke in the romance community about these guys who are morally gray. But how gray *is* he? Are we talking a little bit of smoke mixed in with mostly white-gray? Or are we talking, like… charcoal gray?

Gunmetal gray?

Gah.

He did say he had a job to do before he broke into my apartment, and… my cheeks flush pink.

Bookbabe
Do you think something is wrong???

Oh god.

Oh *god.*

Why the hell has it never occurred to me that whatever he does for his family isn't just dangerous, it's probably *life-threatening?*

It's like I've never read any of the books that go into great detail about the risks and dangers, for crying out loud. This is partly my fault for dwelling so much in my fantasyland happy endings that I've forgotten his job is high-risk.

I do a quick search online. *Bratva jobs.*

What the hell am I doing? Like they're going to be listed in a classified section online or something.

But the hits come hard and fast, and I can't help but read them.

I hesitate for a moment, my fingers hovering over the keyboard. Then, like a reckless idiot, I type the words into the search bar: *Bratva deaths.*

The screen fills almost instantly. Headlines, articles, grim photos. It's a deluge of violence, and I should stop scrolling, but I can't. Each click pulls me deeper, the stories blurring together.

> *"High-ranking Bratva member found dead in Moscow alley."*

> *"Explosive car bombing tied to Russian organized crime."*

> *"Federal crackdown on Bratva operations leaves dozens arrested."*

I click one article. Then another. And another. Each one I read is more gruesome than the last.

A politician found shot execution-style in broad daylight. A businessman's body discovered weighted at the bottom of a river. A nightclub leveled in a firebombing.

Oh my fucking god.

Each story tightens the knot in my stomach. This isn't just some romanticized, book-boyfriend fantasy.

This is... this is his world.

Rodion's world.

I dig deeper. The arrests. Some of them make the news—sleek photos of men in tailored suits being led away in cuffs. Others... don't. They disappear, swallowed up by the system or something worse. The price of getting caught is isolation, surrendering any possibility of a relationship.

And the deaths? From what I'm reading? Those are the lucky ones.

My chest tightens as I read about men vanishing without a trace, rumors swirling that they were taken, interrogated, tortured for weeks. Families left to guess, their silence bought with fear.

I click off the screen.

What am I doing?

I sit back, pressing my hands against my face, trying to steady my breathing. He's reckless. Impulsive. Wild. And yet, somehow, he's survived this long. But how much longer can anyone survive in a life like this? What if a single mistake could bring it all crashing down?

And yet, here I am, tangled in the web he's spun around *me*.

I'm not usually neurotic or this nervous, but...

That's it. At the risk of playing the role of needy, wannabe girlfriend, I go to text him *again*.

> Hey. It's me. Remember me? The girl you were obsessed with and now you haven't even said good morning to??

No. Too toxic.

I delete it and try again.

> Hey. I know this might be over the top, but I haven't heard from you all day and I'm wondering if you're okay. I know the things you do are…er. Risky. Check in, okay?

I add a heart emoji and stare at it for a minute.

Too forward?

Then I remember the feel of his tongue between my legs and the way he made me come so hard I screamed.

Cheeks flushing, I sheepishly add two more hearts and send the message.

I drum my fingers on my thigh, waiting.

Nothing.

What do I even do with this nervous energy?

I could hit the gym… that might work. But even the gym has lost its appeal when I go alone and don't have my inked personal bodyguard by my side.

I could go home and eat dinner like a *sensible* person.

Or I could—

"Miss Steele?" A friendly-looking woman with silvery hair

tucked into a merciless bun smiles at me. "Mr. Kopolov sent me to fetch you."

Fetch me?

I blink. "What?"

She smiles broadly. "He sends his apologies, miss, and said he wanted to give you warning but had no time."

What the hell?

"Please. Come with me." Smiling, she gestures toward a sleek navy town car that purrs at the edge of the curb.

"Um. Who are you?"

Still smiling, she takes out a business card and shows it to me.

"Mr. Kopolov asked me to assist you in preparing for this weekend's gala?"

Oooohhh.

"Um. Yes?" I say hesitantly, though I feel the overwhelming need to verify what's happening. "Just a minute."

I pull out my phone to call Rodion, even though he's ignored every single one of my calls today. My stomach churns when I see he's not only ignored my messages but sent me one of his own:

Bratvabloodline
Go with Cindy and do what she says.

I'll fill you in later.

Oh, the fucking nerve.

I clench the phone, debating whether to call him again out of sheer spite. Instead, I take a deep breath and remind myself that his cryptic commands, as infuriating as they are, usually have some kind of purpose. Still, I'm not thrilled about being shoved into some mysterious agenda without so much as a heads-up.

The car is already waiting downstairs, Cindy standing patiently beside it, her hands folded neatly in front of her.

"Where are we going?" I ask, my tone wary as I approach her.

"Rodeo Drive, miss," she says, smiling with a hint of a sigh like she's anticipating the fun she's about to have. "One of my very favorite places to shop, and it's been a while."

I blink. Rodeo Drive? As in *the* Rodeo Drive? I've heard of it, of course—who hasn't? The stretch of boutiques that practically screams money, luxury, and exclusivity. A place so far out of my price range that it's laughable.

I hesitate, glancing at Cindy's polished appearance. Compared to her chic tailored blazer and heels, my casual skirt and top feel like a poor excuse for "effort." But at least I wore a skirt, I remind myself. It's better than the usual jeans and sneakers.

"Well," I mutter, sliding into the car, "I suppose if Rodion is otherwise occupied, I could handle something like this."

I think.

"Have you eaten?"

I shake my head warily. What does that have to do with anything?

"Ah. Mr. Kopolov instructed me to feed you first if you hadn't eaten yet." She smiles.

I open my mouth to protest because *how dare he*, but when my stomach growls, I remember how starving I am.

Fine, then. Apparently, the first stop is dinner. I suppose I'll make better decisions on a full belly, and I can assume he's paying, so...

Cindy ushers me into a sleek, minimalist restaurant with dark wood finishes and glowing pendant lights. The kind of place where the menu doesn't list prices, just descriptions so elaborate you'd need a dictionary to translate them. I order a gourmet burger and a side of truffle fries because I want to eat fast and get to the shopping.

What I *really* want is to get to *him*, and I think a part of me knows that doing what he planned for me is a good first step.

I'd be lying if I didn't like the way she swipes her card, and I don't have to pay for a thing though.

I'm starting to relax—right until I realize she's not just friendly. She's efficient. She's steering this whole outing like she's orchestrating an event.

When we pull up to Rodeo Drive, my jaw practically hits the ground. I knew it was fancy but seeing it in person is something else entirely.

Every storefront gleams with sleek displays of designer gowns, handbags, and glittering jewelry. I didn't think I was that into *things*, but seeing the gorgeous displays in front of me, I can't help but want to reach out and stroke the soft, buttery leather and gleaming diamonds.

Cindy leads the way with a confidence I can't even fake, gliding into a boutique where we're immediately greeted with smiles for her and a subtle once-over for me.

"This way, miss," the attendant says, ushering me toward a row of dresses displayed like works of art.

Cindy picks out a few, her discerning eye scanning me critically but kindly. "You've got wonderful proportions," she says, holding up a stunning deep emerald dress. "This color would bring out your eyes beautifully."

I almost snort. I'm not used to this kind of flattery, and I'm definitely not used to this level of attention. But I follow her lead, slipping into the dressing room with the kind of hesitation that makes the attendant tilt her head like she's trying to figure out how I got in here.

Well, she can fuck off. My Bratva boy book boyfriend got me here, so here I am.

The first dress fits like a dream, and I catch myself staring at my reflection, almost not recognizing the woman in the mirror. It makes my cheeks look flushed, my breasts fuller, my waist accentuated, and my curves... wow.

"Champagne?" the attendant asks as I step out to show Cindy. She doesn't wait for an answer, pressing a delicate flute into my hand before I can refuse. Not that I would. Free champagne?

The bubbles tickle my nose as I sip, letting Cindy fuss with the hem of the dress. I feel out of place, sure, but there's something undeniably thrilling about this—the attention, the indulgence, the way these clothes make me feel like I belong.

Even if I'm just Cinderella in a borrowed dress, I'm going to enjoy it for a little while.

I glance at my phone, hoping for some kind of update from Rodion, but there's nothing for the first hour of our trip. I finally send him an admittedly petulant little message.

> Thanks and all but WHERE are you? Are you alright?

My heart skips when I see a new message.

> **Bratvabloodline**
> Yes and I promise I'll make it up to you

It's simple, but it makes my chest tighten anyway. A promise. I'm drinking champagne, wearing a gorgeous gown I could never afford, and eying shoes fit for a princess and her rendezvous with Prince Charming, and he's telling me he'll make it up to me.

I take another sip of champagne, glancing around the boutique with its opulent decor and whispering sales staff. Rodion's world is nothing like mine. It's overwhelming and glamorous as fuck, but maybe, just maybe, I can navigate it.

If he's going to make it up to me, I might as well enjoy this strange ride while it lasts.

I'm sitting in the back of the car alone. Cindy's had all my purchases delivered to my apartment. We pull up to my building, and I see a shadow of a man but can't see details. From the distance in the dark I wonder if it's him but quickly decide it isn't because he doesn't walk like Rodion.

I stifle a sigh.

When he turns, horror dawns on me. Is it... *Shawn?*

Oh god. I can't handle the emotional rollercoaster from one thing to the next like this.

My mind races. The words are frozen on my lips. I'm trying to think of what to say. His messages have gone quiet for a few days, and I had almost convinced myself he was going to give up, but then—

I look again, and he's gone.

Was it my imagination? Did I conjure that up?

I shake my head and take my keys out when a low, dangerous voice whispers in my ear.

"Do exactly what I say, and I won't hurt you."

CHAPTER 15

EMBER

THE ROPES BITE into my wrists, but not hard enough to hurt. Just enough to hold me in place. The blindfold is soft, though it makes my world pitch black. My breathing echoes in the silence of the forest, shallow and sharp.

I know this isn't real. It can't be.

But the terrible memory whispers anyway, a ghost brushing my ear. Shawn's weight pressing me down, his hot breath sour as it chased me into every corner of my childhood. My stomach flips, bile and fear rising together until I hear it—a low chuckle, unmistakably his.

Rodion.

My lungs loosen enough to pull in air as relief floods me, shoving the past into the dark. He doesn't say my name, but he doesn't have to.

"Good." He hooks his thumbs into my leggings, dragging them down just enough to leave me exposed to his touch. His fingers brush against the bare skin of my hip, and I arch involuntarily, desperate for more. Blindfolded, my other senses are heightened.

"Patience," he chides, his grip tightening before his palm cups my ass. "I'll give you what you want when I'm ready. Not before."

I bite my lip to stifle the groan that rises in my throat. The combination of his dominance and the anticipation is maddening. I've never felt this out of control, this raw, this... alive.

He spins me suddenly, pressing me back against the wall. My bound hands press into the cool surface, the blindfold still firmly in place. His hands frame my face, his thumb brushing over my bottom lip.

"Say it," he demands, his voice dark and full of promise. "Tell me what you want."

I hesitate, the words catching in my throat. His grip on my jaw tightens just slightly, his lips a breath away from mine.

"Say it, Ember," he repeats on a growl.

"I want you to... do things to me." My cheeks flame at his low, dark chuckle. It feels like the most dangerous truth I've ever spoken.

"Not good enough. You post every day about your book fantasies? *Own* this, woman."

Oh my god I *love* that. My cheeks flush as I say it in a rush of words. "I want you to ruin me."

"I told you," he murmurs, footsteps circling me. "Careful what you wish for, little queen."

Relief floods me as heat races down my spine, battling the cold bite of the night air against my skin. He's doing this—exactly as I'd described it in the video I never thought he'd see. The timing, the details, even the pull of the ropes.

"You're sick," I say, though my voice is husky and affected, betraying me.

"And you like it." His words are a low growl, too close to my ear. I jerk instinctively, but he steps back, giving me space I don't want.

"Say stop if you want to." His tone turns softer, a question disguised as a dare. "I'll hear it, Ember. I'll stop everything."

I hate how much I don't want to say it. Hate how much I trust him, even now, bound and blindfolded and god knows where.

When I stay silent, his hand touches my arm, skimming down to my wrist where the rope holds me. "Good girl," he says, his voice thick with approval. "You're not afraid of me."

"I should be," I snap, but my voice trembles for an entirely different reason.

His fingers trail away, and the sound of his boots shifts, crunching leaves as he moves behind me. "Oh, I don't know. You might be safer with me than anyone else."

There's something dark in his voice, and I know it isn't a lie. If he knew what really made me scared... if I told him about Shawn.

I can't tell him.

Rodion pulls me back to the moment, brushing my hair away from my neck. His lips barely graze my skin, and I shiver. "I've thought about this," he admits, his hands tightening the ropes slightly as if to ground me. "Your little video —so proud of your words but so clueless who was watching."

"You were stalking me," I accuse, though the words sound faint, almost playful.

"You made it easy," he counters, and then his hand grips my hip, holding me firmly in place.

When he finally loosens the ropes, I let out a small gasp, though I'm not ready for the rough silk sliding from my eyes. I blink as the moon filters through the trees, and in front of me, he stands—bigger, broader than life. His face is unreadable, the sharp angles softened only by the ghost of a smirk tugging at his lips.

He takes my chin between his fingers, tilting my face up to meet his gaze. "I thought about tying you to a tree," he says casually. "But I have a better idea. For now."

I swallow; the reality of him is so much more than the fantasy. He takes my hand and gently but firmly pulls me along a narrow path. It's eerily quiet, the forest swallowing every sound but the rustle of our clothes and the occasional snap of a twig.

When the cabin looms into view, my knees nearly give out. It's old, the wood weathered but sturdy, the kind of place you'd find in a thriller or a dream.

Inside, the air is heavy with the scent of pine and cured wood. Firewood crackles faintly in the corner, though the flames are low, casting golden light across the room. A large but rustic bed sits in the center, draped in thick quilts.

Rodion's hand slides up my arm, his touch firm but never harsh. "Tell me to stop," he says again, his voice softer now. "Say it, Ember. Tell me to take you home."

I shake my head, my throat too tight to speak.

"Good girl," he murmurs. Then he pushes me back onto the bed, his weight pinning me down just enough to remind me I'm exactly where I want to be. His hands skim my wrists, binding them to the headboard with practiced ease.

Oh god.

When he leans down, his breath is warm against my ear. "Now, let's see how much you like this fantasy of yours."

I try to swallow but find it hard. I'm excited and nervous and so fucking turned on—I'd probably come if he dared to kiss me.

The ropes rub against my wrists, not enough to hurt but enough to remind me they're there—tight and unyielding, just like him. Firelight dances on the cabin walls, the only light in the room, and it paints Rodion in hues of molten gold and shadow. He prowls at the edge of the bed, his gaze devouring me, and I shiver despite the warmth of the room.

"Do you know what you've done, little queen? I've seen how many times you've packed up and moved. You're good at covering it up with the camera, pointing it at others instead of facing it yourself. But I see everything. The way you love to keep people at an arm's distance so you don't have to get too close..." His voice is a low growl, roughened with just enough heat and danger to make my stomach flip. "I want to hold you still so you stop running for a second. You don't trust me? Smart. I'm not here to promise you safety. I'm here to show you what those fantasies really feel like."

My body responds before my brain does, my thighs squeezing together in search of friction. He notices, of course, because Rodion misses nothing. A dark smirk pulls at his lips as he crawls onto the bed, his weight sinking into the mattress. He smells like woodsmoke and pine. The warmth of his body contrasts with the cold of the cabin. His eyes burn into me like lasers, focused and sharp.

I shiver.

I want *more.*

"You like this," he says, his hand brushing my bare thigh before gripping it hard, pinning me in place. "You like being tied up for me. You like being helpless under me, don't you, little queen?"

I hate how easily he pulls the truth out of me, even as I shake my head.

"Lying doesn't suit you," he whispers, leaning in until his breath skates across my ear. "But I don't mind. I'll make an honest woman out of you."

His hand leaves my thigh, and before I can process the loss, he flips me over and brings it down on my ass—hard.

Oh fuck.

The sound cracks through the cabin, sharp and punishing, and I gasp, my back arching involuntarily. The sting blossoms into heat, and I feel it everywhere, radiating through my body and settling deep in my core.

I want more.

"Rodion!" I gasp, but he shakes his head, his smirk turning into something darker.

"You know you love it, little queen," he says, his palm sliding over the spot he just spanked, soothing it before lifting his hand again.

The second slap lands harder, stealing my breath. It's the kind of pain that melts into pleasure too fast, too easily, leaving me trembling and aching for more.

"Do you understand now?" he asks, his voice velvet and steel. "You don't get to tease me with your fantasies and then squirm when I make them real."

"I wasn't squirming," I shoot back, the words leaving my mouth before I can stop them.

His laughter is dark and dangerous. "No?" He leans back, dragging his hand across my skin again before delivering another stinging blow. This time, I can't stop the whimper that slips from my lips.

"Say it, baby," he commands, his fingers tracing the curve of my hip, teasing and tormenting. "Say you're mine."

"You're insane," I manage, but my voice wavers, betraying me.

He shifts lower, his mouth pressing kisses along the sensitive skin of my thighs, each one hotter and closer to where I need him most. "You don't want me to stop, do you?" he asks, his lips brushing against the edge of my panties.

"No," I admit, the word barely a whisper.

"Good girl," he murmurs, his breath hot against me as he peels the fabric down. This time, I *love* the "good girl." His fingers slide between my thighs, and I can't stop the sharp cry that escapes when he finds how wet I am.

"You're dripping for me," he says, his voice heavy with approval. "My little queen, so fucking wet for her king."

I moan, arching into his touch, but he pulls away before I can chase the feeling.

"Oh no, you don't," he says, sitting back on his heels. "You're not getting what you want until I'm satisfied."

I writhe against the ropes, frustration building to a fever pitch as he trails his fingers up my stomach, between my breasts, and back to my jaw. He grips it, forcing me to meet his eyes.

"Do you know what happens to queens who disobey their king?" he asks, his tone deceptively soft.

I shake my head, too breathless to speak, and his smirk returns, wicked and knowing. "They get punished."

Before I can respond, he flips me over, the ropes twisting to hold me in place as he pushes me onto my stomach. His hand comes down on my ass again, the sharp sting sending a surprising jolt of pleasure through my entire body.

"*Count.*"

Oh my fucking god, he really is acting out every damn fantasy. But wait... I need a minute.

"Rodion—"

"I said *count*, little queen."

"One," I whisper, and he rewards me with another stinging slap.

"Louder," he demands, his free hand resting on the small of my back, holding me still.

"Two!" I cry, my voice breaking as the heat between my legs intensifies, the sting of his hand fueling a fire I can't control.

"That's it, that's my good girl," he murmurs, his voice laced with satisfaction. His hand soothes the burn with a slow, deliberate caress, but it's not enough. The ache inside me grows sharper, my body trembling with need. How could I have ever denied liking *good girl*?

It's everything.

The next strike lands harder, and I arch into it, the ropes digging into my wrists as I pull against them. "Three!" I gasp, the sound raw and desperate.

"Perfect," he growls, his free hand sliding between my thighs. His fingers find my slick heat, and I choke on a moan as he teases me, circling just enough to drive me mad but not enough to push me over.

"Rodion, please," I beg, unable to hold back anymore. "Please, I can't—"

"Shh," he interrupts, his fingers retreating just as I think he might finally give me what I need. "Relax, and I think you'll find you can take more than you think you can."

He flips me onto my back again with infuriating ease, his hands strong and unyielding. The ropes stretch and twist, holding me in place, and his eyes meet mine, molten and feral.

"You've been so good," he says, dragging a finger down the length of my body. "But I want to hear you beg properly."

"I am begging," I whisper, my voice shaking.

"Not enough," he says, leaning down until his mouth hovers just over mine. "Say it, Ember. Tell me you're mine."

"I'm yours," I breathe out, the words tumbling out before I can stop them.

But I like how it makes me feel.

Obsessive, possessive, jealous boyfriend?

Yup.

I watch as he slowly takes off his clothes. I'm mesmerized at the sight of the hard planes of muscles and ink, his sturdy thighs. He leans over me, kissing my cheek, grinding his hot, thick erection against my legs. Reaching to the side, he tears open a condom and slides it on.

I want him in me.

I moan and swallow as his hands move to my hips, gripping them hard enough to leave marks as he positions himself between my legs.

"Tell me you want this." His whole body trembles with the effort of holding himself back. Seeing his self-control breaks something in me, tearing down a wall I didn't know I'd constructed. My body arches into him, as I whisper a shuddering plea. "Yes. Rodion. *Please.*"

"That's it, baby," he whispers against my mouth. I'm holding my breath when he thrusts into me in one long, devastating motion.

I cry out, the sensation overwhelming as he fills me completely, his body pressing me into the mattress. The ropes hold me still, making every movement his to control, every inch of pleasure his to give.

"Mine," he growls, setting a brutal, relentless rhythm that steals my breath. "Say it again."

"Yours." I moan, my head falling back as the pleasure coils tighter, hotter, threatening to snap.

"Louder," he demands, one hand slipping to my throat, holding me in place as he drives into me. It's all I need. The pressure of his hand at my throat, knowing he could hurt me but isn't... the latent threat excites and unnerves me. At the feel of his hands on my throat, I *shatter*.

"Yours!" I scream as I break apart beneath him, the pleasure blinding and all-consuming.

He doesn't stop, chasing his own release as he growls my name like a prayer, his grip on my hips tightening. When he finally follows me with a groan of pure pleasure, his body shudders against mine, and he collapses onto me. I sigh, still shivering in the aftershocks of absolute ecstasy.

For a long moment, the only sound in the cabin is our ragged breathing, the ropes still holding me in place as he brushes a hand over my cheek, his touch surprisingly gentle.

"Little queen," he murmurs, his lips brushing against my temple. "Ember. You're *perfect*."

And as my body melts into his, spent and sated, I realize that in his arms, I don't just feel claimed—I feel safe.

This is nothing like my book fantasies and book boyfriends. Being with Rodion is so, *so* much better than anything I ever imagined.

CHAPTER 16

THE FIRE CRACKLES in the corner of the cabin, casting the room in a warm, flickering glow. I sit on the edge of the bed, my fingers tracing the rough rope that held her hours ago. It lies in a coiled heap now, harmless, but the memory of how her body strained against it—how she begged—lingers in my mind, stirring something deep and raw inside me.

She stirs beside me, her breath catching as she shifts against the mattress. Her hair's a wild tangle, sticking to her flushed cheeks, and when she shifts again, I see it—the faint red marks on her wrists and my handprint painting her ass.

Maybe I pushed too far. Maybe the line between fantasy and reality blurred too much.

She wakes with a small gasp, her green eyes fluttering open to meet mine. For a second, she looks disoriented, like she's not sure where she is, but then a small smile curves her lips. "Water," she murmurs, her voice hoarse.

Oh fuck. I worked her harder than I thought. Got a little carried away.

I reach for the glass on the nightstand, but before I hand it to her, I gently grab her wrist with my hand. My fingers move carefully, massaging the faint lines the rope left behind.

"Does it hurt?" I ask, my voice quieter than I expect.

She sits up slowly, taking the glass from me and sipping it before answering. "Not really," she says, her eyes narrowing as she studies me. "Why do you look guilty?"

I nod toward her body, the marks on her skin and her still-disheveled state. "I just—seeing you like this. The welts, your hair..." I trail off, shaking my head. "I don't know, Ember. Maybe I overdid it."

Not that it would be the first time. I was in constant shit with Rafail when I was younger for pushing too hard, taking too many risks, not listening to—

"God, no." She blinks at me, then her smile turns into something brighter, more playful. "Overdid it? Rodion, you've got to be kidding me." She leans closer, her voice soft but firm. "You didn't overdo anything. It was perfect. All of it." Her eyelids flutter closed as if she's still half-asleep.

I listen as her words sink in, cutting through the unease settling in my chest, and I let out a breath. "Good," I murmur, brushing her wild hair back from her face. "Because I'm not done with you yet."

She grins, but when her smile falters, I see a glimpse of something darker in her expression, enough to make me pause.

"What is it?" I ask, my voice sharper now.

She shakes her head, but I catch the flicker of hesitation in her eyes.

"Nothing."

"Liar," I say, shifting so I'm kneeling on the bed in front of her, forcing her to look at me. "You were afraid tonight, Ember. I didn't expect that. Why were you afraid when I took you? I mean, I expected a little fear, but I thought you'd know right away..."

Her breath catches, her throat working around a word she doesn't want to say. Finally, she nods.

"Yeah," she whispers. "For a second, I thought... I thought it might be him. You know."

The rage that surges in my chest is instant and white-hot, but I keep it contained, letting it simmer under my skin. "And now?" I ask.

She swallows hard, her eyes glinting with something like guilt. "Now I'm just afraid you'll think you went too far." But when she looks away, there's sadness in her gaze.

I clench my jaw, forcing myself to stay still. "I hate that you thought it was him. I hate he's in your head. This is what fucking sucks about people like him," I say, my voice low and rough. "They make the victim think it was their fault. Like they should be afraid of justice instead of him."

Her lips press together, and I see the tears gathering in her eyes, though she blinks them away before they can fall.

"We don't have to talk about it now," I say after a moment. "But you're going to tell me. You're not carrying this alone anymore, Ember." I give her a long look. "And I want you to admit there's nothing 'fake' about the two of us anymore."

She nods as her eyes light up, her fingers brushing mine, and the connection feels fragile yet solid enough to hold.

I stand, moving toward the fireplace. I stoke the fire to keep it warm.

"That's some delicious caveman porn, watching you tend a fire."

I give her a half smile and shake my head. "Is there anything you don't fantasize about?"

"Uhm. Amish romance. Vanilla sex?"

My shoulders shake with laughter.

"I'm sorry I don't cook, but I brought marshmallows. There's sandwich stuff in the fridge if you're hungry."

She laughs, the sound like a spark of light in the heavy quiet. "Marshmallows for dinner?"

"You're lucky I brought those," I tease, grabbing the bag.

She pulls on one of my shirts, the oversized fabric swallowing her, and pads barefoot to the kitchenette.

Fuck, that's a sight I'd give anything to see daily.

"I missed you today," she says over her shoulder, not looking at me. I wonder if she can admit it to my face. The words hit me harder than they should. She didn't say it like it was a casual comment. There's weight in her tone, a confession she's not ready to meet me head-on with.

Her head tilts slightly, and she glances over her shoulder at me. The cabin is so small, she doesn't have to move much to bridge the gap between us. "Want to tell me about it?"

I shake my head, my jaw tightening. "I can't."

Her gaze lingers, searching my face for something I can't give her.

I see the man's face again, pale and bloodied, in the back-room of the club. He'd tried to skim off Bratva funds—our funds—thinking no one would notice. He wasn't wrong to be afraid when I walked in. He just didn't realize I was the least of his problems.

I didn't pull the trigger, but I watched. Listened. Stood there while he begged, while I trussed him up and sent him off to my brothers to be punished. We wanted to make him sweat it out.

I played my part like I always do—stone-faced, silent.

Fucking complicit.

There's no way to explain that to Ember.

"You don't have to tell me everything, you know," she says after a moment, turning back to the fire. Her voice is casual, but I catch the trace of disappointment beneath it.

I push off the couch, closing the distance between us in a few strides. "If I told you everything, you'd run."

It's the most truthful I've been with her.

She studies me for a long moment, the firelight dancing in her green eyes. "Are you sure about that?"

I lean in, brushing my thumb over her jaw, and I feel her shiver under my touch. "You think you can handle the things I've done?" I murmur, my voice dropping. "The blood, the bodies, the lies?"

Her lips part, but she doesn't answer, and I don't push her. Instead, I settle back against the couch, my hand resting lightly on her thigh.

"I missed you too," I admit after a moment. The words feel unfamiliar, like they don't belong to me, but I mean them.

Her expression softens, the tension in her shoulders melting as she leans into me. Her head finds its place on my shoulder, and for a while, we just sit in silence, watching the fire dance in front of us.

Her hand drifts to my chest, the brush of her fingers tracing the jagged line of a scar across my ribs. She doesn't ask about it, doesn't speak at all, but her touch lingers. It's a quiet, deliberate thing—light as a feather but sharp enough to cut through me.

"You've got a lot of these," she murmurs. There's no pity or judgment in her tone. Just curiosity. A softness that both cuts and soothes me. "I want to trace them with my finger."

My hand catches hers, pinning it against my chest. My heart pounds under her palm.

Her lips part, surprise flickering in those sharp green eyes. "So much. They each have a story. A story that made you who you are."

"Yeah. Some earned. Some stolen." I let out a breath. "All of them mine."

Her breath hitches, but she doesn't pull away. She's braver than she looks, this beautiful, fiery woman who's dragged me into her orbit. "Do you ever tell those stories?" she asks, almost teasing.

Almost.

"No." I shake my head. "But I'll tell you this much—if anyone ever gave you a scar, I'd put them in the ground before the blood dried."

Her breath leaves her in a shudder, her cheeks blooming with a heat that matches the firelight. She tries to pull her hand free, maybe to hide how her pulse betrays her, but I don't let her.

"No one marks you," I growl, leaning closer until my lips brush her ear. "Not while I'm breathing."

She finally meets my gaze, a mix of defiance and something softer simmering in her expression. "What if I wanted to leave a mark on you?"

I smirk at her. "You already have, *kitten.*"

With a satisfied smile, she pads off to the kitchen. "I'm starving."

"Help yourself."

I hear her humming to herself, and it makes me smile.

A moment later she returns with a sandwich that looks like... a crime against humanity.

"What the hell is that?" I ask, eyeing the sandwich suspiciously.

"Peanut butter, pickles, and potato chips," she says, smirking.

"That's disgusting."

"Don't knock it until you try it," she says, taking a bite and chewing dramatically.

I narrow my eyes, then snatch the sandwich from her hand, taking a bite. I glare at her as I chew, waiting for the inevitable horror to hit, but—damn it—it's good. "Fine," I mutter. "It's... tolerable."

"Admit it," she says, grinning.

"Delicious," I admit grudgingly, shaking my head. "You're ridiculous."

She grins wider, her expression finally relaxing, and we settle by the fire, toasting marshmallows and falling into an easy silence.

"So mobsters chill, too? Huh."

"Call me a mobster again, little queen," I warn her. "I fucking hate that."

With a pout, she shakes her head at me. A crazy piece of hair flops in front of her eyes that she blows out impatiently. It's the cutest damn thing. "You can call me little queen, but I can't call you a pet name?"

A lazy grin spreads across my face. Goddamn, I love the way she makes me feel. "I didn't say that."

"Right," she says, her arms crossed over her chest. "I can't call you *mobster*, and I can't call you *Bratva boy*, so what else is there?"

"You could try daddy. Sir? My lord... hey!" Those little throw pillows on the couch are harder than they look. I palm one and toss it to the side before I reach for her. She almost gets out of my grasp, but I catch her just in time and pin her to the couch. "We don't hit people. We use gentle hands."

The way she snorts with laughter is so fucking cute. "*We?* I think you have a double standard."

I arrange her over my lap so she's facing me, her green eyes sparkling like emeralds under the dim cabin light, her legs anchored on either side of me. I stifle a groan. I trace the underside of her jaw. "Behave yourself before I have to put you in the naughty spot."

"Rodion," she says, her voice halfway between a warning and a giggle. The sound of it makes my chest tighten in the best way. "A time-out?" she repeats, her voice laced with disbelief.

"Mm-hmm." I brush my nose against hers, my smirk growing. "We'll sit down together, and I'll explain why your behavior wasn't acceptable. We can talk about your feelings. It's all about redirection these days, isn't it?"

She stares at me, biting her lip to keep from laughing. "Oh, this is rich. You, the poster child for violence as a first response, lecturing me about gentle parenting."

"Do you need me to reframe your choices?" I tease, tilting my head. "Offer you some age-appropriate alternatives?"

She arches a brow. "By all means, show me the light. I must've been mistaken because, for some reason, I thought consequences you'd mete out would involve ropes, a dark room, and some Russian curse words."

I tug a lock of her hair.

"You've been paying attention. But not swearing. Only praise, little queen. I'm a firm believer in positive reinforcement."

Her laughter is bright and genuine. "So did you learn your methods from your parents?"

I blow out a half laugh, half groan. "Uh, no. My older brother was my guardian after my parents died, and he's a loyal, devoted, but old-fashioned dick sometimes. Drill sergeant? Rules with an iron fist. Did I miss any clichés?" I grimace. "His motto was *pain builds character*."

A grimace flits across her features. "Your parents died, and your brother became guardian?"

I nod. "Yeah. I was still a kid, so..."

Her eyes on me, she smiles as her hand covers mine. "And even though he was hard on you, you love him?"

Ha. Like it's past tense.

Hope glints in her eyes as if she still wants to believe that siblings can love each other. That not everyone's toxic and hurtful. It'll be a sore point for her. But I'm not gonna lie.

"I love my family to my core. I'd do anything for them," I tell her, my voice a little hoarse. I swallow hard, unexpectedly choked up. I miss home. I miss my sisters. I miss my brothers ribbing me, bossing me around, and telling me stories of their ways. I miss my grandfather hobbling around on his cane, doling out Russian adages and wisdom. "I'd do anything for them."

"Anything?" Her brows knit together as if it's a concept she can't quite grasp.

"Anything," I repeat. "Including taking a woman I want to keep locked away from the eyes of everyone into the public eye. Where other men could look at her."

Not too far away, a wolf howls. I tug her in closer to me. This cabin's sturdy and secure, but we are in the middle of nowhere.

I wish we could stay here.

"I think I've read too many romance novels," she whispers, her eyes wide as she plants both hands flat on my chest.

"Yeah?"

Nodding, she continues. "For a minute, I thought that wolf might've been a rival shifter."

"A rival *what*?"

She's so pretty when she snorts with laughter. I lace my hand behind the back of her head and tug her to me so I can kiss her. This time, the kiss is gentle, almost tentative, as I tease her with the brush of my lips to hers. But when I taste her, I can't help myself. Our tongues touch the barest flicker. I bend her head back and touch my tongue to hers again, relishing the sound of her soft moan and the feel of her pliant body in my hands.

We pull away, panting. "Shifter," she whispers. "A possessive alpha who transforms into a wolf when someone threatens his woman."

"Ah." I nod as if I have a fucking clue what she's talking about. "Wouldn't anyone transform into a wolf when someone threatens his woman?"

The sadness in her eyes takes me by surprise. "No, Rodion. But I love that you asked that. *Love* it."

"You girls read the strangest things."

With a shrug, she stifles a yawn. I wore her out.

It feels like a badge of honor.

"Let's get you to bed. In the morning, we'll go back to your place and pack a bag before we catch our flight."

It will be a test for both of us. I haven't told her yet that my whole family has decided to come to New York. Turns out Polina wants to spend time with her family, and Rafail wants to meet the woman I'm bringing along. That led to Semyon wanting to scope the Romanov family stomping grounds, followed by Zoya saying she didn't want to stay home alone, and when Yana found out they were all going to New York, she booked a flight from Cape Town to tag along.

"I want to know more about you though," she says as she stifles another yawn.

I tilt my head, smirking as I lean in closer. "You're stalling. Don't make me sit here and make you go to sleep. I've got all night."

"You wouldn't dare."

"Oh, I would," I murmur, my voice dropping enough so that she shivers against me. "You want to test me? I'll even read you a bedtime story. Something uplifting, like *Crime and Punishment*."

"Oh god. The absolute worst way to punish a romance girlie. You're relentless."

"And *you* are overdue for some rest." My tone softens as she struggles to keep her eyelids open. I lift her, cradling her in my arms while I get to my feet and head to the bed. Wordlessly, I tuck her against one shoulder as I pull the blanket down and lay her on the bed.

This, this right here...

Taking care of her when she's tired, tucking the blanket around her, and watching the way she falls asleep... I didn't know I needed this.

She's asking questions. She deserves answers. Answers I'm not sure I know how to give while keeping her safe.

I wish I could wrap her in a bubble where no one could touch her. My gut says she had her innocence stolen once. I've watched her moon over her books, and while she might laugh it off as a pastime, I know better.

In her heart, she believes in the power of love. In her heart, she wants to be as loved and cherished as the women in her books.

And goddamn, I want to give it to her. All of it.

CHAPTER 17

EMBER

FANCY HOTELS and penthouses sound nice. But the smell of coffee and bacon in a log cabin before you open your eyes? It's the height of luxury.

I stretch before I open my eyes, aware that the hot water bottle beside me isn't there anymore. Dwelling on the memories of the night before makes me feel like I'm living in the pages of one of my books. Him kidnapping me, toe-curlingly good sex, followed by his adorably and surprisingly hot lecturing, before he tucked me into bed. I want to grab my phone and record a video, only... this one's just for me.

I open one groggy eye. Early morning light filters in through a small window near the door. The walls are made of polished logs, their warm, honeyed tones glowing softly in the dawn light. Thick wooden beams stretch across the ceiling. It's rugged and charming. Needs a little fluffy dog by the hearth who wants his ears scratched.

A stone fireplace dominates one wall, its hearth neatly stacked with wood. The faint scent of pine and ash and last night's fires lingers in the air. I sigh. There's a sturdy wooden dining table with mismatched chairs and a patchwork rug underfoot, adding a touch of color to the otherwise earthy palette. On the far wall, a narrow bookshelf made of wood holds a few leather-bound books and a glass oil-burning lamp. I don't see any of the titles on *my* bookshelf, but a few classic Austen and Brontë books make me grin.

I didn't know I'd describe a place like this luxurious, but here we are.

"Thought you couldn't cook?"

Rodion turns around, sexy as fuck wearing nothing but a pair of boxers. From here, I can see the scars I traced with my fingers the night before and the trademark ink of the Bratva. His muscles ripple as he moves. He's a fucking paragon of masculine perfection. I swallow and lick my lips.

"Uh, no," he says with a grimace. "It was the one lesson Rafail tried to teach me. I failed miserably."

"Rafail? He's your older brother, right?"

"Yeah." When he turns to me, he has a platter of food piled onto his plate. "This is precooked bacon, but the lady at the store promised me it was foolproof." He pokes at it with a fork. "Looks... good?"

I sit up in bed, suddenly starving. "Last night's sandwich is long forgotten, so unless it's burnt or raw, I'll eat it."

"Let me guess," he says, giving me a wary look. "You need pickles and peanut butter?"

"Do you think I'm pregnant?"

I'm unprepared for the way his gaze grows heated.

His eyes darken, the playful smirk slipping from his face as something raw and primal takes its place. "If you were..." His voice is low, rough around the edges, as though the thought alone has ignited something deep within him. "I could handle that."

Oh dear god.

My breath catches, and I blink up at him, taken aback by the sudden shift in his tone, the way his gaze burns into mine like he's claiming something that doesn't exist—yet.

"Rodion..." I start, unsure if I'm warning him or questioning him, but he steps closer, his towering presence pulling the air from the room.

His fingers brush against my jaw, tilting my chin upward so I can't look away. "It'd mean you're mine in a way no one could ever change." There's no teasing now, just a quiet, ferocious possessiveness that sends a shiver down my spine.

I should've known.

I wasn't prepared for this...

I've read about this, haven't I? Men like him. I joked last night about him being a wolf, but right now, I don't feel like that's far from the truth.

I shake my head, trying to snap myself out of the spell he's weaving. "That's... not how this works."

When he grins, it's dark and dangerous. "You sure about that, little queen? Because the idea of you carrying my child

—of you being tied to me in every way—feels like *exactly* how this should work."

"I was joking, Rodion." My gaze focuses on the tray. There's a pile of crisp bacon beside bagels and cream cheese and a cup of steaming coffee.

"I'm not."

"I know." I reach for the coffee. It unnerved me the first time he gave me one because he knew exactly how I took it.

But now? I love that.

We eat in amiable silence. I know we're heading back soon, but I don't want to leave this cabin. We just got here.

"Why the pout?" He bops me on the nose and raises a brow.

"I was just thinking I like it here. I think I got... used to my shitty apartment. It's home, and I tried to make it look nice, but being in a rustic cabin that looks like a modern-day rendition of *Little House on the Prairie*, and I realize I've been living in the slums."

The dark shadow that crosses his face and his grunt of agreement tell me all I need to know. He's never tried to hide how he felt about my apartment.

Also, and I will not admit this to him, not yet, but—it felt so fucking *perfect* sharing a bed with him. I never knew if I'd like sharing a bed with a man, but sharing a bed with Rodion? *Heaven.* He slept like a rock at my back, his heavy arm strewn across me. I was wrapped in a cocoon, blissful and content.

"Have you checked your account?" I log in while munching on a bite of bagel, crumbs scattering over the plate. Rodion's hovering over my shoulder, his presence impossible to ignore. He's not even touching me, but I can feel the heat radiating off him, the quiet intensity of his focus. It's unnerving how much I like it.

As my account loads, his arm brushes against mine, and I glance up to find him staring at the screen like it might explode. "You're practically breathing down my neck," I tease, trying to lighten the mood. I look at my screen. "Jesus."

"What?"

"Some troll…"

He doesn't laugh. Instead, his face hardens as he reads the comments.

"Relax," I say quickly, already sensing the storm brewing in him. "This is just part of the job. I deal with it all the time."

His jaw tightens, and I know he's about two seconds away from hunting this guy down. Before I can say anything else, another message appears—but it's from *his* account.

> **Careful what you say. You wouldn't want me to find out where you live.**

I freeze, my bagel halfway to my mouth as my followers erupt in the comments, flooding my feed with laughing emojis, heart eyes, and the internet's equivalent of chaotic squealing.

"Rodion!" I spin around in my chair, my voice half-scolding, half-horrified. "What did you just do?"

He shrugs, utterly unrepentant, his smirk sharp and danger-ous. "Handled it."

"Oh my god, you can't just threaten people online!"

"Why not? He deserved it," he says matter-of-factly, leaning down so we're face-to-face. "Besides, they love it."

He's not wrong. My followers are eating this up, and the comments are a chaotic mix of admiration and envy.

> Where do I get a man like this??

> Protective mafia vibes?? Yes, please.

> This is why I stay single. None of my exes could ever.

Before I can argue further, he straightens, his expression cooling. "We have to go."

"I like it here," I counter, reluctant to leave the safety of this little cabin bubble.

His gaze softens just a fraction. "Then we'll come back. But for now, we need to move. I want to check in on your place, and you've got that shoot later."

I texted him about that two days ago and can't believe I didn't remember it myself.

"Fine." I sigh, packing up the remains of breakfast. "Let's do this again though."

The drive back to my place feels weirdly... natural. Rodion's got some old Russian song playing low in the background, the kind of music that's surprisingly soft, even melodic. I glance over at him—one hand resting casually on the wheel, his other lying on my thigh.

I swallow hard to stifle a sigh. I can't help but imagine that this is my life, that I'm his, and this funny, sexy, protective man is... mine.

But I don't really know him.

And he doesn't know *me*.

Still, I like the casual way we just... fit. It feels easy. It feels natural. It feels... right.

I open my email, scrolling through a flood of work updates and invoices. It's quiet between us, but it's not awkward. For once, I don't feel the pressure to fill the silence. I let myself relax, sinking into the rhythm of the drive, his presence strangely grounding.

Then he speaks, breaking the stillness. "The gala is in three days."

I look up from my phone. "And?"

"And my family will be there. All of them."

Oh my god.

His family.

His whole *mafia* family.

My stomach lurches. "You didn't mention that part before."

He gives a casual shrug of his massive shoulder. "You didn't ask."

"Rodion..." I grip the edge of my phone, suddenly on edge. The thought of meeting his family—their sharp eyes, their inevitable judgments—it's overwhelming. But there's another thought creeping in, too, one I've been avoiding.

And if he's mafia, that means...

What *does* that mean?

Are they as ruthless and possessive as he is?

And if Shawn... wait. I haven't heard from Shawn. A sudden thought crosses my mind.

"Did you do something to Shawn?" I blurt, my heart pounding.

His head turns slightly, his expression unreadable. Not sure I like how good of a poker face he has. "Why?"

"Because he hasn't texted me. It's not like him to stay quiet this long."

Rodion's smirk is slow, deliberate. "Maybe he finally got the message."

"Rodion. *What message?*"

He doesn't answer, just turns onto my street, the tires crunching softly against the pavement. As we pull up to my apartment, I can't decide whether to be relieved or more freaked out.

"We'll talk about it later," he says smoothly, parking the car. "You've got bigger things to worry about. And no, Ember. I haven't touched Shawn." With a scowl I feel straight between my legs, he mutters, "Not because I didn't *want* to."

I glance over at him, my pulse thrumming in my ears. The way he's looking at me—like he owns every thought in my head—is both thrilling and terrifying. I'm so into him, and it's making me feel raw and exposed. Vulnerable in a way I'm not used to.

How can I hate *and* love it?

The door to my apartment feels wrong before I even touch it. The faintest shift in the air, like it's been disturbed. My stomach knots as I reach for the knob, but Rodion's hand closes over mine, firm and steady.

"You look nervous."

I lick my lips. "Something is... off."

"Wait," he says softly, his voice a mix of command and reassurance. He pushes the door open, stepping in first like he's daring whatever's inside to come for him. The sight of his broad shoulders—tense, ready for anything—shouldn't calm me, but it does.

The apartment looks normal at first glance, but as we step inside, the air feels heavier. My gaze lands on the corner of the coffee table, where my packages are piled neatly. Too neatly. My breath catches.

"Someone's been here," I whisper, my voice trembling. I walk to the bathroom, Rodion trailing me. Unlike the packages, here it's a mess, like someone's come in here and deliberately mussed things up.

I look away from the mess, bile burning the back of my throat. When I was a child, I always tried to keep things tidy and neat. It made me feel like I had a semblance of control. My mother would tease me, and even the teachers at school would write notes about my "borderline obsessive need for order and tidiness."

Shawn loved to mock me.

I stare at the rolls of toilet paper scattered on the floor, the towels disorganized, and my toiletries opened and tipped.

Rodion's jaw tightens. "Not someone," he says, scanning the room with predatory precision.

"What-what do I do?"

He turns to me, those dark eyes locking onto mine with an intensity that steals the air from my lungs. "He was probably looking for evidence that I live here," he says, his tone as calm as if he's discussing the weather. "Now that he knows I don't, he'll be back."

Shit.

A chill races down my spine. "When?"

"Tonight," he answers, no hesitation. "That's why we're leaving."

"Leaving?" My voice pitches higher. "Where—"

"New York." The word drops like a stone. His hand reaches for mine, grounding me in the storm brewing inside me. "I need you to trust me, *kotyonok.*"

My pulse races under his steady grip. Trust him? I search his face, looking for something—anything—to make this less terrifying. And there it is: the softness that shouldn't belong to a man like him. It lingers in the curve of his mouth, the faintest tenderness in his voice. It almost fools me.

But when he mentions Shawn, his entire expression shifts. That softness hardens into something dark, dangerous. Protective. And somehow... it makes me feel safer than I ever have in my life.

I know my answer.

I nod, my voice barely above a whisper. "Yeah. I trust you."

His thumb brushes over my knuckles, a fleeting touch that sends heat spiraling through me. "Good girl," he murmurs, and just like that, my knees go weak.

"New York," I say, more to myself than him. "I've never even left California."

Rodion's gaze cuts to me, softer now but no less intense. "Maybe it's time you see what the rest of the world has to offer."

He takes my hand again, holding it like he's afraid I'll slip away. And for the first time, I let myself lean into it, letting him anchor me in this new, terrifying, thrilling reality.

I can't shake the feeling that this is all just a fairy tale. Just a made-up dream of made-up people, and when I open my eyes and wake, I'll remember who I am and why I'm here.

I can't lie. A part of me can't help but imagine a future together. But that can't be.

I might fangirl over a masked man with tats and Bratva ties, but in real life... is this really what I want?

For now, I'm going to enjoy this.

For now, I'm going to... pretend this *is* real.

CHAPTER 18

IF THAT MOTHERFUCKER shows his face, he's a dead man walking. A fucking *dead man*.

I don't even know what the fuck he did to her when she was younger, but I don't need all the details. Any enemy of Ember's is an enemy of mine.

I make a quick call to Rafail. When he answers, I hear the baby's wail in the background and his wife Polina's voice, trying to hush the baby.

"Rodion." I can hear the underlying concern in his voice with one word. My brother's a hard-ass, and sometimes I wonder if he's fully human, but this is the man who gave up his entire life to raise our family.

He'd do anything for us.

"Everything alright?"

"Yeah, so far. Can you rearrange the flight details so we can fly out tonight?"

Without hesitation, he answers. "Of course. How soon?"

"The sooner the better."

"Give me a minute. You need to pack?"

"Yeah, we are doing that now."

"We," he repeats but doesn't pry. "Call me in thirty."

I hang up the phone to see Ember staring at me. "You can just... call for an airplane. Like I'd call for an Uber." I love when she bites her lip and twirls her hair, those bright green eyes watching me as if to see what will happen next.

I shrug. "Might not be a *plane.*" I feel I need to clarify so she doesn't get the wrong idea. "Might be a jet or helicopter or something."

The subtle shift of her brows heavenward means that didn't really help.

"So you have to get somewhere and *pow.* Here's a plane. Dude, do you know what we call that in the book world?"

"Did you just call me *dude?*" I wrinkle my nose at her, but she doesn't respond. She steps closer to me and places both of her hands on my shoulders, standing up on her tiptoes.

"Competency porn," she breathes out.

Not gonna lie; my voice is a little husky, and I kinda feel like a lovesick teen right now. "Did you say porn?"

Leaning in, she traces my lips with her index finger.

Well, fuck. *Who knew that was hot?*

I swallow, my hands framing her hips as our lips meet. The world falls away, just for a second, when we kiss. I wish I could deepen this, bend her over and kiss her until she's panting and begging for me until she's wet and needy, but I can't.

We have to go.

"Competency porn," I mutter, shaking my head. "I don't even know what the fuck that means, but if it makes you happy, I'll do it again. Now go. Pack your bags. And don't forget your camera. They'll be counting on it."

"Which *one*?" she moans, then under her breath, "Why do people always think I have *one* camera?"

"Ember," I warn. When she starts tossing things into a bag and clearing out the shelf in her bathroom, I give the place another look around. "You need help?"

"Nope!" she says with a look of triumph. "I'm packed. Let's go. Your place next?"

"I wish."

I've been trying to get her there since the day I met her. Back to a place where we can linger in a king-sized bed, shower in a place that doesn't look like the floor is going to cave in, and sleep where I know I've got top-notch security. She deserves better, and I aim to give it to her.

But today isn't the day. I don't have time.

"I'm fine. I'll have what I need in New York. I live there."

Our ride waits, idling at the curb. Rafail pulled through. I'll be driving this one though.

I reach for her bags. All she needs is a head shake and a grunt before she lets me take them.

As I load her bags into the SUV's trunk, I feel her gaze on me like a brand. I glance over my shoulder, and there she is, arms crossed, those sharp green eyes tracking my every move. She's doing that thing again—biting her lip like she's about to say something snarky, but she hasn't decided if it's worth the trouble.

"What?" I snap, slamming the trunk shut.

She raises an eyebrow, all mock innocence. "Nothing. Just marveling at how a guy like you goes from mafia muscle to luggage handler in under five minutes."

I stalk toward her, ignoring the smartass smile tugging at her lips. I don't stop until I'm towering over her, forcing her to tip her head back to meet my eyes. "You got a problem with that, *kitten*?" My voice drops low, rough like gravel, just the way I know makes her squirm. I can't wait to get her alone again.

Her smirk doesn't waver. "Not at all. Watching you haul my stuff around like a pack mule? It's kinda hot, actually."

She thinks she's cute. She's not wrong, but that doesn't mean I'll let her win. My hand shoots out, gripping her chin —not hard, just enough to make her breath hitch. "Keep running that mouth, and I'll show you hot."

Her pupils dilate, and her breath stutters, but then she snaps back, leaning into my touch with a wicked grin. "Promises, promises."

This woman. She's going to kill me.

Ember stares out the window, her fingers playing with the hem of her shirt, but I don't miss the way her thighs press together when my hand brushes against hers on the console.

I let the silence stretch. I know her. She won't stay quiet for long.

"So…" Her voice breaks the stillness, light and teasing. "Competency porn. Big fan of the genre?"

I smirk, keeping my eyes on the road. "You said the word porn, little queen. Didn't hear anything else after that."

She laughs, soft and throaty, and I swear it goes straight to my cock. "Of course you didn't."

Before I can fire back, she turns to me, her tone shifting. "Seriously, though. What's the deal with this gala? You're acting like it's some big mafia Oscars or something."

"It's not about the gala," I say, my voice cooling. "It's about who's going to be there. My family. My enemies. The people who think they own me."

Her eyes narrow, and I can tell she's turning that over in her head, dissecting every word. "And what happens when they find out about me?"

I glance at her, my jaw tightening. "You let me worry about that."

"That's not an answer," she snaps, her voice tight with frustration.

"It's the only one you're getting." My voice is steel now, sharper than I mean it to be. "I'm not going to let them hurt you."

She doesn't flinch, but I see her fingers tighten around the hem of her shirt. "You think you can just decide that? You can't control everything, Rodion."

"Watch me."

I whip the car to the side of the road, throwing it into park so fast the tires screech. The silence that follows is deafening. Her head snaps toward me, her eyes wide, but I'm already leaning over the console, caging her in with one hand braced on the door and the other gripping her thigh.

"Let me make something clear," I growl, my voice low and dangerous. "I don't give a fuck what it takes. I'll burn down the whole Bratva if it means keeping you safe. And as for you—" My fingers tighten just slightly on her thigh, drawing a gasp from her lips. "You're mine, Ember. You've been mine since the moment I saw you. So go ahead. Fight me. Push back. Tell me you don't need me. But don't think for one goddamn second I'll let you go."

Her breath comes fast now, her chest rising and falling as she stares at me like she's torn between slapping me and pulling me closer. "You're insane," she whispers, but there's no heat in it. Just something raw, something needy.

I lean in, my lips brushing against her ear. "You like it."

She shoves me back—not hard, but enough to show me she's still in this fight. Her smirk is back, razor-sharp. "Drive the damn car, Bratva boy."

I grip her hard to remind her she'll pay for that.

As we drive, she seems like she's holding something back, but it's a short trip, and I don't want to pry.

"Wait," Ember says, giving me a curious look. "This isn't the way to the airport."

"Who said we're going to an airport?"

"Ummm…"

"Not interested in commercial airports. We need privacy, speed, and discretion."

Ember blinks. I hint at the deer-in-the-headlights look she gets when I remind her that I'm not one of the book boyfriends but a real made man.

"…and maybe not the discerning eyes of TSA?"

"Exactly."

"So we're going…"

"To a small private airstrip nearby. It's a place that caters to private jets and helicopters."

"Oh, wow. Okay. And this is safe?" As soon as she asks the question, she snorts and shakes her head. "What the hell am I talking about? Of course it is. This is *Rodion*, after all."

My brother would laugh his ass off at that. I'm the most reckless one in our family, but when it comes to *her* safety? I'm not fucking around.

The SUV rumbles to a halt just inside the gates of the airstrip. The gravel under the tires crunches loud enough to echo in the quiet, open expanse. Dim lights buzz from overhead fixtures, casting long, skeletal shadows across the cracked asphalt. The air smells faintly of jet fuel and oil.

"Wow," Ember says softly, peering around. She takes it all in—the squat hangars with peeling paint, the hulking shadows of private jets sitting idle under pools of light, the Bratva muscle standing near the jet waiting for us. They're dressed casually—hoodies and jeans—but for the telltale bulge of firearms at their waists. One of them flicks a cigarette to the ground, crushing it beneath a boot as he nods at me.

"Safe enough for you?" I ask, cocking a brow as I pull her bags from the trunk.

She hesitates, glancing at the Bratva guards. "Let me guess. TSA's not invited to this party?"

"Not interested in their kind of scrutiny," I say, my voice firm. "This isn't a layover in Newark."

She presses her lips together like she's holding back a laugh. "And... no metal detectors, either?"

I grunt, shifting her bag over my shoulder. "That's your takeaway from all this?"

"Well, yeah." She waves a hand toward the guards and the jet. "It's all very *Mission Impossible.*"

I pause, watching her as she scans the scene. She doesn't flinch, doesn't balk. Just processes it like she's ticking items off some mental checklist. The way she takes this world in stride—like it's just another inconvenient plot twist in one of her romance novels—does something to me. I've seen men twice her size pale at the sight of my Bratva family. But her? She looks like she's filing it under pragmatic life decisions and moving on.

I take a step closer, lowering my voice. "You okay?"

She snorts, running a hand through her hair. "Am I okay? Rodion, we're about to get on a private jet because you have mafia guys hanging around like it's your personal valet service. This is bananas."

Her words say one thing, but her tone says another. Beneath her exasperation, there's something else. Something raw. Her shoulders relax as she looks at me like she's decided to let herself trust this. Trust *me*.

"You're safe with me," I say. It comes out rougher than I intended, but the truth of it leaves no room for softness. I nod toward the jet. "Now come on. The sooner we're in the air, the sooner we're out of reach."

The inside of the jet is utilitarian. The leather seats are dark, sturdy, and worn just enough to feel comfortable. The overhead lights glow dimly, and the hum of the engines is steady, almost reassuring. Ember takes the seat across from me, glancing out the small window as one of my men secures the luggage and closes the hatch.

She's quiet for a moment, her fingers fidgeting with the strap of her camera bag. Then she looks at me, her eyes sharp. "You keep saying that. 'You're safe with me.' But Rodion... we barely know each other."

Her words hit harder than I expected. Because she's right. We don't know each other in the ways most people would call normal. I don't know her favorite color or the name of her favorite grade school teacher. But I know her. In the ways that matter.

I lean forward, resting my elbows on my knees as I pin her with my gaze. "I know enough."

She raises a skeptical brow. "Oh, really? Like what?"

"I know how you take your coffee," I say, my voice low. "Which, let's be honest, is fucking crucial. I know you dream about a life bigger than the one you've settled for. I know you're stronger than anyone gives you credit for. And I know I've watched every single one of your videos on repeat because I can't fucking get enough of you. And in your videos, you're self-deprecating but funny and witty, and I suspect part of the reason you spend more time in your book fantasy world than real life is because you fear getting close to people."

Her lips part, but no words come out. For once, she's caught off guard. Good. I'm not done.

"I've seen the way you look at the camera like it's the only thing in the world that understands you. Like you've built this perfect little escape, but you're still waiting for someone to come in and shatter it. Someone who can handle the real you. Not the version you *think* people want."

Her breath catches, and for a moment, she looks so exposed that I almost regret saying it. Almost.

"Touché, sir," she finally says in that adorable mutter. "But you don't—"

"Don't know the real you?" I shake my head. "I know more about you than I probably should. And if that scares you, Ember, good. Because it scares the shit out of me too."

I lean back and smirk. "Now let's hear what you know about me." This ought to be good.

"Ahh, my turn." The emerald glow of her eyes melts me a

little. "You're hot as fuck, and it's definitely gone to your head."

I grunt at her but don't interrupt. I'll remember that one next time she's over my lap.

"Not that I blame you, with all those followers offering you their virginity and whatnot, but still." Her lips twitch. "You're confident. Strong. Able to take command. Fearless, even, the way I'd imagine a soldier would be. You're protective and intense. You come alive when you have someone to look over, a battle to win, a villain to fight. Which, if you think about it..." Her voice trails off, and she grows a little shy. "Is kind of ironic, yet charming."

I lean back in my seat and steeple my hands. Listening.

"Yet even though you're dangerous, you're somehow... familiar. Someone who's really more like my book boyfriends than they are, and on the one hand, I feel like I know you... but on the other, I feel like I've just scratched the surface." She leans in. "You come across as bold and fearless, but a part of you wants to prove yourself to... someone. Maybe your brothers. Maybe me." She shrugs. "Maybe yourself."

A part of me wishes I could pull the mask back down.

CHAPTER 19

EMBER

FLYING ALONE with Rodion feels like we've crossed some invisible line, hurtling forward faster than the jet's engines can take us. Something about being cocooned at 40,000 feet with him makes it feel... serious.

I don't want it to be serious.

Do I?

The great thing about book boyfriends is that you actually call the shots. You can escape into the fantasy and explore moral lines you might never have a chance to do in real life. But when the real-life hero is sitting right across from you... it's a lot harder to close the book.

Rodion lounges across from me, his sharp gaze watching me. I look down at myself and sigh.

"You have nothing to worry about, little queen," he says. "They'll love you."

"They?" My fingers play with the corner of my book, the paperback an anchor I don't dare look up from. "You mean your fancy Bratva crowd? Don't lie to me, Rodion. I don't fit in your world."

"You fit wherever I decide you do," he replies without missing a beat, a calm authority in his voice that makes my stomach clench.

Oh no he doesn't.

That sparks something in me—a mix of frustration and a heat I don't want to name. "Well, it's a good thing I decide where I belong," I shoot back, finally looking up. "And I don't need your permission."

Leaning forward, resting his elbows on his knees, his focus now is so intense it's almost suffocating. "Is that what you're worried about? That I'm going to control you? That you're some pawn to me?"

His voice drops lower, rougher. "I don't play with things I want to keep." Heat rushes to my face, and I'm grateful for the hum of the engines to drown out my shallow breath.

I decide to redirect. "What about you, Rodion? What's so important about this gala? Why drag me along?"

His jaw tenses. For a second, I think he won't answer. "This isn't just a party. It's a test," he says finally, his words clipped. "The kind of test where the wrong move could cost everything."

"Everything?" I press, my pulse quickening.

Surely not *everything...*

"My family. My place with them." His mouth tightens, and I glimpse something raw in his eyes. "You."

My heart beats faster. I know he's not saying it lightly, and yet, the weight of it...

I tilt my head, forcing a small, defiant smile. "That's dramatic, even for Mr. Bratvabloodline."

His eyes darken. "Say the word, Ember, and we turn this plane around. Right now. No gala. No danger. Just us." It's not the first time he's offered this, but...

I swallow hard. "That's not an option."

I can't imagine the trouble he'll get into, and what's waiting at home for me? I mull it all over, thinking, wondering...

"You're thinking too loud," he says, his voice low and teasing. Even the sound of his voice, all raspy and deep, sends a shiver down my spine.

"I wasn't aware my thoughts needed approval," I reply, my voice steady even though his gaze makes it hard to breathe. I'm teasing, though, because I know he is.

His rough hand reaches for mine and holds it. I stare at my small, pale fingers, the nails slightly tapered but unpainted, still in such sharp contrast against his darker, tanned, inked hand and blunt fingertips. It feels oddly symbolic, and I'm not sure what to do about it.

His smirk fades, replaced by something sharper. He leans forward, elbows on his knees, the full force of his attention pinning me in place. "You're right. You don't need my permission. But I don't need yours to keep you close." His words land like a punch, stealing my breath, and for a moment, neither of us moves.

When he speaks again, his voice is softer but no less intense. "You're mine, Ember. And they'll all see that."

Hmm. That's what he thinks.

Part of me wants this because I'm not immune, but a part of me still balks at his arrogant claims.

Also... *All. They'll all see that.*

All who?

My stomach flips. I tell myself it's nerves. It has to be. But there's something raw in his gaze that makes me feel stripped bare, and for once, I don't know what to say.

Instead, I look down at the book in my lap—my favorite kind of escape.

"Gonna read?" he asks, with that signature smirk. "Want me to read it to you?"

"Uh, no. I don't need you to point out the inaccuracies or poke fun at the dialogue or mock the sex scenes. I love it, and you can go watch YouTube or... analyze a spreadsheet or something."

Looking at the title, he shakes his head. "Oh god."

That does make me giggle.

When he gets up to go check in with the flight crew, I use the reprieve to pull out my phone. I open the app, the comforting, familiar routine settling my nerves. I am so overdue for a post, and this is the perfect opportunity.

"Plane reads," I murmur to myself, holding up *The Bratva's Own*—a title that hits me a bit too close to home—and hit record. The video is simple—just me showing the cover, my voice light and teasing. "Jetting off with my current obsession. Could you say no to this?" I glance at the camera and give a playful wink before ending the recording.

Satisfied, I tuck my phone back into my bag.

Rodion returns just as the pilot announces our descent, his presence immediately commanding the space. His hand brushes the small of my back as I stand, sending a rush of warmth through me. "Nervous?" he asks, his lips close to my ear.

I swallow hard, nodding despite myself.

"Millions listen to you because you've got something real to say. You dive headfirst into this fantasy crap because you show women they can own what they want in fiction *and* in real life." He brushes his lips over my cheek, his voice a low rasp. "Don't back down from that, beautiful. Own it." And for a moment, with his heat against me and his words grounding me, I almost believe him.

I take in every detail as we get into the back of a car that's supposed to take us to his family.

"Okay, alright," I say as if psyching myself up, as I rub my hands down the length of my jeans because the palms are damp. "I can do this. *We* can do this, right?" Just before I start a shoot or a video, there's a moment of nervous energy, like this time, I'm going to forget how to do this. This time, they'll all know I'm just a fraud—and when I push past it, I hit my groove. The nerves melt away, and I'm just... *me*.

I have to do the same now.

A soft kiss at my temple makes me draw in a ragged breath. "Yeah, little queen. We can."

"So what's the plan?" His fingers lace with mine as we drive through the city. "When's the gala?"

"Tomorrow." Leaning in, he nuzzles my neck. "So I have you all to myself tonight. We get to sleep in. In the morning, we meet my family."

My stomach drops out from under me.

Already?

The car ride is smooth, the kind of luxurious glide that makes me hyperaware of everything. The leather under my fingers, the faint scent of his cologne, the way his hand rests possessively on my thigh. I can't stop fidgeting, my palms damp despite the chilly air-conditioning.

"Relax," Rodion says, his lips brushing against my ear like it's the most natural thing in the world. "Breathe. You're with me."

"With you," I echo, forcing a tight smile. "That's what I'm worried about," I quip.

His laugh is low and rich, wrapping around me. "You're going to make it through tomorrow night just fine. My family doesn't bite—but I might."

I shoot him a glare. "Not helping."

We pull up to a towering hotel, all sleek glass and stone, and my nerves are back to full throttle.

It feels all a bit surreal—armed guards and uniformed assistants, every detail dripping with luxury and discretion. As we step into the private elevator, I let out a shaky breath. The space is pristine, with mirrored walls reflecting Rodion's sharp gaze and my wide, uneasy eyes. I stare at the buttons, watching his hand move to select the floor, but instead of pressing it, he hesitates.

Uh-oh.

I know that look by now. I know the way his eyes grow heated and dangerous, and maybe it's my romance-cultivated imagination, but I swear this is when he transforms from human into beast.

"Rodion." I put my hand out in a futile effort to stop whatever he's going to do. "What are you—"

Before I can finish, he slams the emergency stop button. The elevator jolts to a halt between the floors. The sudden stillness is deafening, save the rapid beating of my heart.

"What the hell?" I snap, turning to face him, but he's already moving, stepping into my space, swallowing the distance between us.

"You're on edge. Scared," he says simply, his tone infuriatingly calm and controlled. "I don't like it. And I want to remind you who you belong to before we take another step anywhere."

"You don't like it?" My voice rises, my fists clenching by my sides. "Of all the nerve! Well, excuse me if meeting your family of actual criminals in person has me a little wound up."

Leaning in, his hand curls at the back of my neck. I stifle a moan at the instant flood of heat that rushes through me, grounding me in an instant.

How does he *do* that?

"They're not going to touch you, little queen." His thumb brushes the sensitive skin at the base of my skull, and *damn him—it works.* I stop trembling.

Was I the one who moved closer, or was it him?

I'm against the wall of his chest, and a very small part of me still wants to push away, but the mirrored wall is behind me, leaving me nowhere to go. "This isn't fair," I whisper. "You can't just...*trap* me to calm me down."

"Says who? Why not?" His voice is velvet-wrapped steel, the dangerous purr of a predator, but I want... *more.* "And who says my plan is to trap you to calm you down? Maybe I have other plans."

I open my mouth to argue when he lifts me up, his hands under my ass as he perches me on the elevator railing. The sudden intimacy of it all makes my skin prickle with heat and my breath catch. "Rodion..."

This time when my voice trembles, it isn't from fear.

Leaning in so close, I can feel his breath against my jaw and smell the raw, masculine, heady scent of his cologne, he whispers, "Go ahead, little queen. Tell me to stop."

How does he read my mind like that?

Of course I can't. I don't want to.

His lips graze my neck, his teeth scraping just enough to send sparks shooting through me. "You've got two choices, Ember. First, you can fight me—because I know you want to, even though I'll win. Or second, you let me show how I deal with nerves."

Uhhhhhm.

Let me...show you...

But I'm not the girl who rolls over and splays her belly. Nuh-uh. I *want* to be overpowered. I *want* to push back.

I want him to handle me.

My hands are already against his chest, pushing, testing, even though he's as immovable as the damn wall on the rooftop where we first met.

"Ahh," he says with a smirk and that familiar greedy gleam in his eyes. "You want a fight."

When his hands tighten against my hips, pulling me flush against him, the pressure is maddening. The hot, sturdy feel of him between my legs sends my need into overdrive.

"You're playing a dangerous game," he says in a gravelly whisper.

"You started it," I bite back, lifting my chin in defiance.

His mouth at my ear, he nips at my earlobe. "And I'm going to finish it," he promises as he slides me off the railing. "Turn around and put your hands on the railing. If you move them, you'll force me to remind you what happens to naughty little queens who disobey their kings."

Gah.

What is he going to *do*?

I'm hyperaware of the sounds he makes as he deftly unzips the bag with my camera. What is he—oh god.

His movements are unhurried, measured, and maddening. He knows I'm watching, already on edge, trapped between floors, conscious of every subtle shift of his body, every quiet click of the camera's clasp.

With deliberate precision, he unfastens the leather strap around the camera and folds the ends in his palm so it makes a supple loop.

Is he—

"Jeans off, Ember," he commands, his voice like gravel.

I don't move. I can't.

He steps closer, his height and breadth overwhelming me. His knuckles brush my hip as he grips the waistband of my jeans, unbuttoning them with a single, deft motion. The sound of the zipper lowering echoes in the small space.

"Don't make me repeat myself."

I'm trembling as I push them down my thighs. Cool air licks at my bare skin, and I hear him hitch in a breath as I step out of them. My pulse is deafening in my ears.

The leather strap brushes over the curve of my thigh as he drags it slowly upward, teasing. A shiver runs through me.

"You think it's cute to challenge me?" His words are a low growl in my ear, sending a jolt straight through me.

"I—"

"Why don't we see if this will help."

Then, without warning, his palm presses on the small of my back. The strap cracks against my ass, and I cry out, my voice breaking between pain and a rush of molten heat. He snaps it across my ass again. I come up on my toes and gasp, even as the sting melds to warm, sultry arousal.

"No more talking back, little queen." The strap comes down again, harder this time. I'm gasping for breath. "No more second guessing or waffling. I told you what to expect, and I told you to trust me. No more running that pretty mouth of yours when you already know who's in control."

The strap lands again, crossing the line of heat already throbbing. I whimper, and it feels so much more like surrender than protest. My fingers dig into the bar in front of me, bracing against his command. I nod, even while I know I'm welcoming another lash of the strap.

The leather cracks down harder, and my knees buckle, my fingers clutching the bar like a lifeline. My breath is shallow, each sting searing through me, blurring the lines between pain and pleasure.

"Yes," I manage to croak. "Yes."

"Good girl." His free hand smoothes over the heated line of my skin. "You like this, don't you? The way I handle you. The way you can finally stop trying to carry everything yourself."

He brings it back and snaps it again, another line of pain lighting up the first. "Hands on that bar, Ember. Just like that, baby."

Again, he spanks me with the strap before he unfurls it, slides it between my legs, and then lifts it like a reverse saddle. He drags the leather upward, teasing and deliberate, until it presses against the slick ache he's created. I'm so wet, so aroused, I wantonly shimmy my hips across the leather.

"Such a bad girl," he says, shaking his head as he leans in behind me and whispers in my ear. "You want to come again, don't you, baby?"

He slides the strap back and forth, slow and torturous, and the friction sends a jolt through me. My hips jerk, and I'm aching for relief.

"Look at you," he says approvingly. "So eager. So willing to take what I give you."

My body trembles as I arch into his touch.

"Beg me, little queen. Say it. I want to hear you beg."

"Please—let me come, please." My voice is barely audible as I'm fighting the heady rush of arousal and need, taking all my effort to hold myself up.

The strap tightens between my thighs. "Not yet. You'll come when I say you can."

And then it's gone. Cool air and emptiness in its wake.

His mouth to my ear, he tortures me. "That's the prettiest fucking pussy I've ever seen. The sexiest spanked ass I've ever laid eyes on. When you meet everyone, I want the vision of this at the forefront of your memory."

"Rodion—"

If he doesn't let me come—

"Patience, little queen. I want to get you to the penthouse first. We'll talk there."

With his warm mouth on my shoulder, he plants a scathing kiss on my collarbone before putting the strap back in place.

"We're almost there," he says with a wicked grin.

"*Noooo*," I whine.

I topple against him, but he rights me and holds me.

"I promise you. The wait will be worth it." I whimper when he drags my jeans up my sore ass and rights me.

"I can't believe you're—"

But my words die on my lips as the elevator door opens.

My stomach flips at the sight that waits for us.

CHAPTER 20

RODION

Son of a bitch.

Well, if it isn't the Kopolov family, here en force, ready to greet me and my little queen.

They could've warned a guy. And why do they all look so *pissed*?

Ember's grip on my hand tightens as we step off the elevator. The tension in the air is suffocating.

"I didn't expect such a welcome party," I say smoothly, aware of Ember's nervous breathing and shaking beside me. I know the sight before her is probably terrifying—Rafail, his dark, assessing eyes narrowed on the two of us, his lips curled in a not-quite-there smile. Semyon, his gaze cold and calculating behind thin glasses, as aloof and threatening as always. My cousin Matvei, large and looming with his weapon *drawn*, beside them. All are dressed in business casual as if they're ready to step out to grab dinner with consultants.

"Put it away, Matvei," I say in a low voice. "Jesus."

After a moment's hesitation, he slips the gun in a holster, but his stance doesn't change.

"So this is the girl you brought," Rafail says.

Well, thanks for the warm family greeting.

"This is Ember. And yes, she's with me. Why the welcome party?"

We step off the elevator. Jesus, I hope no one heard her moans in the elevator shaft.

Rafail's tone is icy. "You sure this is a good idea, Rodion?"

My fingers tighten on Ember's hand, my voice as sharp as a razor. "Excuse me?"

"This is the one you asked me to expedite home."

Rage threads through my limbs as I shake my head. I don't appreciate the note of derision or how he's talking about Ember like she's fucking cargo. "Obviously, yes. Someone want to tell me what the fuck is going on? Where are the girls?"

Rafail jerks his head to the corner of the room. "Kitchen. Before you see them, we have to have a little talk. What the hell are you two playing with, Rodion?"

I haven't heard this tone of voice since I was a fucking child.

"What are you talking about?"

Oh, shit.

Maybe they found my social media account. If they found my account, I'm fucking screwed. But then... why are they looking at Ember as if she's the enemy?

Rafail shifts, tucking his hands in his pockets, but it doesn't make him look more casual, just more calculating. He and Semyon share a knowing look.

What the fuck?

"I didn't know you allowed her to post videos online about us," Rafail says.

What?

"What are you talking about?"

Semyon pulls out a tablet and taps a few buttons. Are they really going to give her shit about having a book account about mafia men? Those are fiction. They should know—

Oh no.

I stare at the video, cold awareness curling in my gut.

Jesus.

"When did you take that video, Ember?" I ask, my grip on her tightening. I'm careful not to hurt her, even though I want to *shake her.*

It's her on the plane, holding a book up. On *our* plane.

"Where was I?"

It's a viral post, with thousands of messages and millions of views coming in as we speak. Damning. Incriminating.

"I don't know what happened," she says, shaking her head.

Even though her eyes are wide with fear, her voice is tinged with the ferocity I love about her.

Get it, girl.

"Yes, I have an account, but it has nothing to do with *you*. It's about romance books. I post about fiction, not *you* guys. I don't even know who *you* are."

"Look at this," Rafail says, obviously seething as he points to a corner of the screen.

Ember's hand covers her mouth. I don't say anything at first, as I'm trying to stay calm.

"I asked you a question, Ember. *When?*"

"On the plane, you got up to talk to the flight crew, and I took the opportunity to post a quick video."

"Maybe you shouldn't post quick videos," Rafail snaps. I hate the way he chides her as if it's his fucking place. My hands ball at my sides. "Maybe you should take the time to edit them before you fucking post."

I take a step toward him. How fucking dare he. "Maybe *you* should shut the—" I clamp my mouth shut at the searing glare he sends me, just as Semyon snaps, "*Rodion.*"

I can't lose my shit, not here, not now, not with my brother the pakhan.

Ember's eyes flash at my brothers, and her nostrils flare. "I didn't even know the Bratva was fucking real until like two weeks ago, so excuse me for not knowing I couldn't take a video on a plane I was *invited on.*" She turns to me, her eyes bright with unshed tears. "You know me. You know I would never do anything to intentionally hurt you or your family."

Rafail jabs a finger at the video.

Right in the corner of the screen are all the details—a crest in the background with our family name. The caption suggests Bratva themes, and the whole thing *maybe* could've been shrugged off as fictional, if not for the comment section.

"Holy fuck," I whisper, shaking my head. *No.*

Someone looked it all up and posted all our information for the whole damn world to see. It's the top comment.

"Delete it," I snap, but she's already on it, her hands shaking as she unlocks her phone and pulls it up.

"It's gone," she whispers, not voicing what all of us are thinking: deleting the post doesn't remove the screenshots or views. The leak is out there, and there's no taking it back.

"I didn't know. I had no idea. I thought I was just taking a video for my account. It's part of my income, you know? I need to keep posting, and I haven't posted in days. I had no idea you guys would have information on the plane that would identify you. I didn't mean—"

"To mock our family?" Rafail snaps. "To make us the laughing stock of—"

"*Rafail.*"

I step between Ember and him. I never wanted to have to choose between my family and Ember, and I don't want to have to now.

"Stop. She didn't mean it. It was a harmless accident. This is what she does, and she didn't mean anything by it."

"It's *not* harmless." His nostrils flare. "This has gone wider than you know. We have to talk to you alone, Rodion." His voice sets my nerves on edge.

What the hell happened?

"Fine, but no one touches her," I warn, steel in my voice. "If one fucking hair on her head is harmed, you'll answer to me."

Rafail's brows rise. Semyon whistles under his breath, and Matvei silently makes the sign of the cross.

Rafail narrows his eyes on me. "Your sisters are in the kitchen. Bring Ember there while we talk."

I definitely have no choice, but she won't like being separated. Hell, I think it's bullshit myself, but I know better than to push back now.

So I take her by the hand and lead her to the kitchen. I'm still shaking. Still waiting for the fallout from overstepping my place with Rafail. He'll fucking kill me for that.

"I'm sorry," Ember says in a whisper. Her eyes are blurred with tears.

"Just do what they say for now. Let me deal." I kiss her cheek. "You didn't mean it. I know you didn't. I know you have reservations about everything, and I know you were just trying to post a video. But I do have to talk to them privately, and I'll make it better. Hang out with my sisters." I roll my eyes. "They're better company anyway."

The little kitchenette is attached to the living area but secluded, so we can't see or hear my sisters until we walk through the door. Sweet little Zoya, petite with dark hair and warm brown eyes, and my sister Yana, taller and slenderer than Zoya, stand up against a counter.

"Hey," Yana says warmly, extending her long, slender fingers out to grasp Ember's hand. "I'm Yana. This is Zoya. And you are..."

"This is Ember. Take care of her, girls. I have to go talk to Rafail."

Zoya grimaces. "Good luck. I'm sorry, he's in a *mood*, Rodi." She wrings her hands, always nervous around my thundercloud of a brother.

Yana, however, is less easily intimidated. "Come on, Ember. Let's get you something to eat. They'll work things out."

"I love your account," Zoya says with a grin. "I can't believe it's *you* here. I feel like I'm meeting a celebrity. Your book recs are life."

"Zoya!" I'm shocked by her admission. I still think of little Zoya as a child, the youngest sister. And I've read those damn books...

"What, Rodi?" She waves her hand dismissively at me. "Relax, will you? Did you forget I'm an adult now?"

"Barely," I mutter. My brothers will be getting impatient. "I need to get out there. Take *care* of her."

I go back to my brothers. They're waiting in the sitting area.

The vodka's out, of course.

At least I know Ember's safe in the kitchen.

I walk straight to the vodka, thankful my brothers brought the good stuff. "Anyone want a drink?" I'm deflecting but don't fucking care. I walk over and pour myself a few fingers.

"I don't want a drink, Rodion," Semyon says with a sigh. "I want answers. We all do."

But to my surprise, Rafail stands and walks over to me. He's as tall as I am, but it took me a while to catch up. I know when I've pushed too far, and god knows I've done it before. He's always been like a father to me, but maybe now, in some way, he's more a father than a brother.

When he reaches for me, I stifle a flinch, prepared for anything after what happened out there, but instead, he pulls me into a hug.

Something in my chest loosens.

I tamp it back down again.

"Good to see you, brother, even if I want to wring your damn neck."

Well, that's about as tender as Raf gets.

"Good to see you too."

We step back from each other, and I sip the vodka before I take a seat next to him. "Alright. I'm going to tell you everything. Just relax, okay?"

Rafail leans against a small wooden desk and shakes his head, crossing his arms over his chest. "No. Talk."

This is not going to go over well.

I take another sip. God, I missed this shit. It tastes like home.

I blow out a breath. "I was doing the job you told me to do. And then... I saw the video Matvei sent of the mafia thirst traps, and I thought... I thought maybe I'd have a little fun."

"What the fuck did you do?" Semyon asks in a growl, shaking his head.

Time to tackle this head-on and brace for the fallout. Ember can't shoulder the responsibility alone.

"I started an account," I admit. "But I didn't let *anyone* know who I was. I was masked the whole time since that's what everyone likes right now anyway."

"Not everyone," Semyon mutters. "Do go on. I can't wait for the rest of this."

Rafail growls but doesn't say a word.

I swallow hard. "No one had any idea it was me."

"Which fucking account?" Semyon asks, his voice dangerous. "Show me."

God. Shit. I am in so much trouble. Still, I pull up the account and show them.

"Motherfucker," Rafail mutters under his breath. "What the hell were you *thinking*? Were you that hard up for attention?" He looks like he wants to throttle me, and honestly, right now, I wouldn't blame him.

"Wow," Semyon mutters, peering at my phone. "750,000 followers already? And you barely started? That's impressive, brother."

"What the fuck are you talking about?" Rafail looks like he

wants to single-handedly beat the shit out of both of us. Wouldn't be the first time.

"It takes a lot to get this many—"

"I don't give a fuck how popular he is!" Rafail thunders. "The more popular he is, the more fucking vulnerable we all are! This is the stupidest shit I've ever seen." He turns to me. "Go on. Get to Ember. Let me guess. She's one of your stupid followers."

I don't even realize I'm on my feet going after him until Semyon and Matvei both pull me back.

"Sit *down*, brother," Semyon warns. I look away. Rafail is the oldest, but Semyon's older than I am, too, and no slouch. I have to get my shit together.

I glare at Rafail. "We need to have this conversation. I need to make it fucking right. But you need to show that woman respect just like you would Polina."

Rafail's brows rise. "You want to compare Ember to Polina?"

I'm seething and doing everything I can not to say something I can't take back. "You have no fucking idea who she is to me."

I hate that they know her name, but it was inevitable. I can't have her in my life and have her be anonymous. My family and I are one. It's the law of the Bratva, steadfast and dependable, and even I won't challenge something as unmoving as family loyalty. Hell, it's carved into me.

I hate that she's in another room, apart from me, but I'm relieved she's with Zoya and Yana.

Rafail simmers but finally nods. "Go on but watch your fucking mouth. I'm giving you a lot of grace, Rodion, only because you did every damn job I gave you with perfection and only because I know you'll be the one digging yourself out of this. Make it fast. My patience is wearing thin."

You don't say.

"Okay, so... I kind of got a crush on her." Understatement of the year, but I'm not clarifying. I'm deeply, madly, head-over-heels in love with the woman.

"Like fuck you did," Semyon says, shaking his head. I go on and pretend he doesn't exist.

"We, uh... so we started messaging each other." I look away. I hate sharing this with them. It feels special and sacred, and I don't want to desecrate what's ours. I have no choice.

"I tried to stay away, I was going to delete my account, but I couldn't. It's the first time since I fucked shit up that I felt... like something was going right. I thought the videos were ridiculous, and then...I saw Ember. And everything changed." My voice trails off and I shake my head. I release a shuddering breath. "So we started... flirt-texting. And then I met her, and I... I can't help it. I maybe stalked her. She's got this fucking stepbrother, man, and I—"

"Rodion." Rafail's gaze hasn't softened a lick. "Even for you, this is fucking dumb as shit. But now we need to fix this with your little date."

"She's not a little fucking date," I snap, my voice rising. I clench my fists and glare at him.

You do *not* talk to Rafail Kopolov like that. Never in my life have I raised my voice to him. Never. Not even when I was a kid. I always respected him, feared him—but I can't stand for it now, not when Ember's on the line.

"Rodion," Semyon groans.

Rafail is on his feet as he shrugs out of his suit coat. *Fuck.*

"You want to repeat that?" When Rafail goes quiet, shit's about to go down.

He might be my brother, but he's also fucking *pakhan* of the Kopolov family. I've pushed too hard.

I stare him in the eye. I don't care what they do to me. I'm a member of this family, and I won't let them fuck with Ember.

"She's not a fucking date, Rafail. This isn't a teenage crush." I have to tell them the truth. I have to bare my neck and admit to them what I haven't even admitted to myself yet. "I love her. She's my one." My voice breaks. "I'd do anything for her."

Rafail studies me. Silent. For once, his gaze actually softens.

"He doesn't understand," Semyon says quietly. I look from one to the other.

Matvei only shakes his head. "We haven't shown him everything yet."

I swallow, ice pricking my spine as Rafail opens his phone. "See this?" he says in a voice I know all too well, the same voice he used when I was in the principal's office about to be expelled, or when I took his car and totaled it, or when I fell off the roof of the garage and broke my leg. The calm before the storm.

"The location of our enemies. This is the man you killed last week, yeah? You made an example of him. Well, there's fallout, Rodion. They didn't know who was behind it. Now that they've traced Ember's account to LA, with the Kopolov name on that plane, they *know* you were there."

Fuck.

I thought I was so careful. I knew I was playing with fire.

If they brought me in here to get rid of her, if they fucking hurt one hair on her head—

"What are you planning to do to her?"

I'm on my feet, but Semyon steps in front of me, his voice low and cold.

"Sit the fuck down, Rodion."

He pulls up a tablet and shows me footage of Ember drinking tea with my sisters. "She's fine."

I sit back down, but I don't relax.

"If you guys hurt her—"

"We're not going to fucking hurt her," Rafail says. "Not if you do what we say. What have I told you every goddamn night you were in California? What did I tell you I needed you to get?"

I stare.

"A wife."

A wife?

"Yeah, I said you need a wife," Rafail repeats. "After the shit Semyon put up with." He shakes his head. Arranged marriage to men like us is more complicated than it seems. Our reputations precede us.

Rafail goes on. "So these are your choices. You have two. Get rid of her, or wife her up."

I stare. "She's not one of us, Rafail. You can't just—"

"Not *yet*, she isn't."

Women in her world don't just leap into marriage to save their lives.

Do they?

"You know I wouldn't hurt her." I shake my head.

My god. She's gonna lose her shit.

"I do know. But you know what our family requires." Rafail's voice drops lower. "I would hate to order a hit on a woman you're attached to. Or maybe even love."

The coldness in his gaze makes me look away.

Jesus.

He hasn't given me two options. He's given me *one.*

Marry her? She's not ready for something like that, no fucking way. Of course she isn't.

"How long do I have to figure this out?"

Rafail stands. "I'll give you an hour. Should be long enough for you to figure out what you need to do."

"This is temporary, Rafail."

"We don't do temporary, Rodion. You know that."

He jerks his head at Semyon and Matvei, who get to their feet and follow him, and calls out, "Yana! Zoya! We're leaving."

The girls come quickly, Ember trailing behind them.

What the fuck am I going to do?

Rafail turns to me before he leaves. "I believe you. I'm going to forgive you overstepping tonight, with one condition: make it better."

Yana reaches out and squeezes Ember's hand before she gives her a little wink. On the way out she gives me a hug too. "Danila will be here tomorrow. He's missed you guys," she says with a smile. Her husband's been away, and she came here without him, but it seems the Romanov gala will be a reunion of sorts.

I hug her back in a sort of stupor and watch as Zoya waves goodbye to Ember. "I'll bring that book tomorrow! And you have my number if you need anything."

Well. Ember's already won over my sisters. I guess that's something.

Ember stands alone, wide-eyed and pale, as the door clicks shut behind them. She turns to me, and it breaks my heart when her face crumples.

No, no, no. I'll do anything to stop that. I reach for her, but she steps away, shaking her head.

"I'm sorry, Rodion. I didn't mean to—"

"I know." I collapse into a nearby chair and lean forward, resting elbows to knees.

How the fuck am I going to tell her this? She barely trusts me, and maintaining her agency is of the utmost importance to her. I can't just... strip that away.

I have to.

She'll never forgive me.

Khristos.

"What did... they say? Your sisters wouldn't tell me anything. They were sweet, but they said you'd talk to me."

I nod, unwilling to put this off for another minute. "Come here, Ember."

She swallows, her eyes on me warily, but she does as she's told. When she reaches me, she slides onto my lap and sits with her back upright as if afraid to get too close.

Fuck that.

I reach for the back of her neck and drag her mouth to mine. Our lips brush, and our tongues touch before she moans and sighs into me. I kiss her until I feel strong again, ready to do what's next.

"They didn't say much to me, Rodion," she repeats, obviously nervous as fuck.

I nod. "I know. That's because they said it all to me."

The tension hangs between us like an impending thunderstorm, heavy and damp.

She traces a finger along my jaw. "You look like you've seen a ghost."

"Yeah."

I need to get this out of the way. Lay it all out.

Be ready to chase her if she tries to run.

"They gave me an ultimatum, and I know which one I'm going to pick."

Licking her lips, her gaze meets mine. In the distance, a dog barks and a clock ticks on the mantle.

"And... what's that?" she asks in a whisper. "Rodion..."

"Your post drew out our enemies. They were able to identify my location and yours. It's not good."

"Oh shit."

"Yeah."

"You knew I was Bratva, but I don't think you understood the consequences, what that meant—" Shaking my head, I go on. "But I'm not going to blame you. I was the one who pursued you. I was the one who convinced you to spend time with me." I look away from her. "We only have two choices, and I won't hurt you, Ember."

Her wide green eyes register mild surprise but nothing more.

"And the other choice?"

"Marriage. Immediately. You and me."

She acts like I've just prodded her with a hot brand. She leaps off my lap as if burned. "I can't marry you, Rodion. Are you serious right now? *Marriage?*"

I grab her hand and yank her back down. "Dead serious.

You can, and you will because I won't allow the alternative. But listen—" I gentle my voice. I can't snap at her.

She shakes her head. "*No.* I won't marry you. I can't. Look at the trouble I caused today—"

I take her by the shoulders and shake her. Her hair bobs around her face as she shakes, trying to get away from me, but I hold her tight. "There *are* no other choices, Ember. I won't hurt you. I won't lose you because of this bullshit."

I let her go as if she's on fire. I hate the way she's staring at me like that.

I brush a hand through my hair. "It's temporary. We marry, show face at the Romanov gala, and this blows over. We look at it as temporary. And then, after things settle down... we go our separate ways."

CHAPTER 21

"Well, that escalated quickly." The calm tone of my voice doesn't match the energy of the rapid beating of my heart or the way my brain short circuits at the word *marriage.*

Rodion snorts. This is probably going to be our downfall, not gonna lie. Never taking things seriously enough. Honestly? That's why we're in this situation to begin with.

I swallow hard and try to talk, but I don't know what to say or how to proceed.

Why does it make me fearful to hear the word "marriage" but want to cry when he follows that up with "temporary"?

I never thought I wanted to be... *married.*

Most especially to an actual man of the Bratva.

"Is that what you want?" I ask, my voice hoarse. "To get

married on a temporary basis like we're two drunk, horny bastards at an Elvis chapel in Vegas?"

"Of course not." His voice is husky. I can't tell if he's angry or emotional or what. "You're the most beautiful woman I've ever seen. And I don't care that we haven't known each other for long. I feel alive when I'm with you. And for the first time in my whole life, I... feel like I can actually imagine a future with someone. But I can't force you to love me."

Could anyone? And does love have anything to do with this?

Because I don't trust myself. I don't trust the way my heart beats faster, imagining a life with Rodion, while at the same time, my brain is trying desperately to find a way out of this situation.

What he doesn't know is... I'm halfway there. I have reservations, yes, but I love being around him. Marrying into that family though? I saw those ruthless men. One of them was *holding a gun.*

I know what Rodion is capable of, and the thought of—of spending the rest of my life with a man like Rodion makes me melt like ice on a frying pan.

"You said it's only temporary? Until this blows over?"

My throat tightens, the reality of the situation crashing in on me.

"Yeah." But he doesn't meet my eyes when he says it, and I can feel the tension in his body.

Rodion doesn't want temporary.

And I'm starting to fear that...neither do I.

"Do I have a choice?"

When his gaze snaps back to mine, my heart stutters. I see the raw, ruthless man who's willing to burn the entire world down if it means keeping me safe.

His eyes darken with something I can't quite name.

"No."

I look away from him. I was the one who fell for a man I knew to be dangerous, a full-fledged man of the Bratva. I let fantasy color my judgment, and now...

There's no turning back.

"I know I'm not a good man, Ember," he says quietly, but there's no softness or regret in his tone. Nothing but sheer, brutal honesty.

And isn't that one of the things I love best about him? "I've ended lives and ruined others, more than you'll ever know. I'm Bratva. I will always be Bratva. And that doesn't change because I love you."

I blink. My breath catches. I try to drag air into my lungs. The word hangs between us like a fallen star, brilliant and unexpected.

Love.

"I didn't ask for this," I whisper, even as a part of me leans into him, leans into *us*, and I wonder...

Did I?

"I didn't either." He cups the side of my neck in his large, rough palm, his thumb brushing the spot where my pulse races as if reassuring himself that I'm still here. "But here we are. And I'm not letting you go."

His words are a vow, said with finality and surety. I know what he's offering me isn't hearts and flowers, but something deeper, weightier, undeniably bloodstained and dangerous... and bigger than both of us.

"I don't know how to do this," I whisper, my words choked.

He leans in, pressing his forehead to mine. "Maybe we learn together."

I wrap my hand around his shoulder. Bracing myself. "Are you *sure* we have no other choice? None?"

"No." One word that falls like a gavel.

There is no other choice.

I close my eyes, but he lifts my chin up, forcing me to look at him. "You want the truth?"

I swallow. "Always."

His gaze hardens, something lethal flickering in the depths of his eyes. "If another man ever tried to touch you, I'd break his hands. And if he tried to take you from me, I'd tie him to a chair, making him watch me ruin you—slow and raw, before I cut out his eyes and left him to bleed out, knowing the last thing he ever saw was me owning you."

Oh dear god.

There's no hesitation. No apology.

"I'd bury his body and sleep like a fucking baby, Ember."

His soft touch, a thumb brushing over my bottom lip, belies the utter violence of his words. "You understand me, little queen? Do you know what you give me? I don't share *my wife*."

It's so very different hearing those words in real life, hearing the sincerity and devotion and knowing he means every word of his declaration.

His promise.

There is no choice, but he's telling me what I'm getting into.

"One more thing."

I don't know if I can take another. I swallow and nod.

"You have to delete your account," he says in a rush of heated words. "*Now*."

My heart sinks. I close my eyes, fighting the rush of tears. I poured so much into that account. My identity as a romance lover is part of who I am. For the first time in my entire life, swooning over a shared love of all things romance makes me feel like I'm part of something bigger, a community of people who haven't yet given up on dreaming and who still believe that everyone deserves to be loved passionately. That everyone deserves a happy ending.

When I open my eyes, he's still staring at me.

Can I give up this part of who I am for what could be the real thing?

"I know," I whisper. "I figured as much." But when I pull up my account and see my friends, the notifications, the videos waiting to be watched, my heart aches. I feel like I'm losing an actual part of myself.

But I got in too deep. I took things too far. And now, I'm facing the consequences.

With trembling hands, I click the big red button and confirm the next step. I blink. A hot, fat tear rolls down my cheek.

"It's done," I whisper. My head falls to his shoulder. "And yours?"

He exhales. "It's already gone. I should've known better. It was too risky." My heart swells when he kisses the top of my head. "But I know it was harder for you than me, little queen."

And then I'm crying. A part of me feels like it's silly for me to react like this, but it isn't just the account or the followers or even romance. I've severed a part of who I am and what I love, something I forged with my own two hands. I faced imposter syndrome and took risks. But I worked so hard, hours upon hours crafting the perfect videos and photos, reading thousands of books, distilling feelings, hopes, and dreams...

I'm still pressed against his chest, his arms wrapped around me. I drop my head to his shoulder and cry. It's not just the account, it's everything.

Shawn coming back into town and knowing he'll be there when I go back home.

Meeting Rodion's family and knowing what they think about me.

My choices going up in flames and being forced to make a life-changing decision.

Losing so much of what I've fought for, built…

His hand slides slowly up and down my back. Steady. Grounding.

And despite everything, I melt a little. The thoughts and fears begin to quiet. I didn't know it could be like this.

"You didn't lose it all," he whispers into my hair, his voice low and rough. "You built it once, and you can build it again."

I sniffle as he continues. "And you kept what mattered most."

I look up to him. For the first time since we got here, his eyes are dancing with that familiar heat-laced humor that drew me to him to begin with. Rodion will never take life too seriously, and it's the hottest damn thing I never expected to need.

"Oh?" I ask, my own voice lilting with humor. "What's that?"

He snorts. "Me, obviously."

I open my mouth to protest when his mouth crushes mine. He tastes like victory and danger, and I'm fucking here for it. He swallows my moan as his hands grip my hips hard enough to bruise. I straddle him, gasping against his mouth, but he doesn't let me go.

I don't want him to. "Don't hold back," he growls, dragging his lips like a brand down the side of my neck before he bites hard enough to make me jolt. "We're alone now. Let yourself go." He traps my hands in one of his much bigger ones and whispers in my ear. "*Let go*, little queen. Give yourself to your king. Tell me you're mine. I want to hear you say it."

I look up into his eyes. I want him to claim me. I want him *in me.*

"I'm yours," I whisper.

I watch as something snaps in him. *I feel it.*

With effortless ease, his muscles bunching, he lifts me and carries me to the huge bed in the corner of the room. He drops me, his movements hurried, almost feral, as he reaches for my clothes and tears them off me. Fabric rips and pulls. In a hurried frenzy, I rush to help him. I've never wanted a man inside me so bad in my life.

His shirt hits the floor before I can blink, and I take a moment to touch his beautiful, perfect body. *None* of those videos did him justice. They didn't capture the raw power and strength or the way he holds himself back so he doesn't completely annihilate me. My mouth dries at the sight of him before me—all muscles, scars, and lethal, heartbreaking beauty.

"You're staring." That smirk makes my ovaries cry. But there's a darkness in his gaze that half dares me to look away.

"Maybe I like what I see."

He's on me in seconds, grasping my wrists and pinning them down before he drags his teeth down the column of my neck. His tongue lashes out, and I arch into him with a moan I can't stifle. "You're mine," he whispers against my ear. "Every heartbeat. Every breath. *Mine,* my sweet, beautiful little queen. Am I clear?"

"Crystal," I say with a moan.

I lean into him, my legs tangled with his as he shoves his knee between my thighs, parting them. Heat coils in my stomach, pressure builds a desperate ache between my thighs. I lift my hips, wordlessly begging for him to take me.

And then he slows as if savoring me. The hurried kisses grow softer. More passionate. He takes his time, his rough palm running the length of my body as if memorizing me, as he brushes his lips to mine. His hands explore me as if it's the first time we've ever touched. His cock swells, pressed up against me, and I whimper.

"Don't moan like that," he grates. "I won't be able to hold myself back, Ember. I'll fucking break you."

I arch into him and release a low, desperate moan, deliberately pressing into the hard length straining against his jeans, my hips rolling. "Maybe I want you to."

Rodion's grip on my hips tightens, his fingers digging in hard enough to bruise. His mouth brushes the shell of my ear, his breath ragged.

"Ty khocheš', shtoby ya tebya rastyanul na etikh prostynyakh i zastroil tebia krikami, da?"

I don't have a clue what he's saying, but it makes me shiver. The words sound hot and sinful, and I love it.

I have *way* underestimated how hot his Russian is. *Way underestimated.* I'm going to make him record his voice so I can play it on repeat while I—

His hand is on my neck. Pressing.

I told him to break me. I wanted this.

Do I?

I drag in a shuddering breath. I can still breathe.

Yes.

Heat floods my core at the feel of his heavy hand on my neck, the possessive look of his straining muscles, with the knowledge he *could* break me but won't.

"What did you say?" I ask in a whisper, relishing the slow, wicked smirk that's all Rodion. "The Russian."

"I asked if you want me to stretch you out on those sheets and fill the room with the sound of your screaming."

I swallow hard, my pulse thrumming beneath his palm. I nod.

"It's easy in Russian," he rasps. Say, "*Da, Rodion.*"

I lick my lips, barely able to form the words. "*Da, Rodion.*"

His responding groan is music to my ears. "*Khoroshaya devochka.*" He kisses my cheek. "Good girl. Show me what a good girl you are."

His hand tightens in my hair, my scalp aching deliciously, until my neck arches under his touch, baring my neck to him. His breath is hot and ragged against my skin, and I love the way his teeth scrape along the curve of my jaw.

His lips trail down my neck, but he doesn't kiss—he bites, sharp enough to make me scream.

"That's what I want to hear, little queen." He kisses where he bit before he bends his mouth to my breasts. They're full and aching for him, so when he tugs a hardened nipple between his teeth, I let myself go and scream out loud. My need for him becomes wet heat between my legs, aching for him.

He suckles my breast and flicks the other, then nips and grazes his teeth along the sensitive skin. "You're trembling. Is it fear, little queen? Or something else?"

"Uh. Both? Can I say both?"

He grins. "You can say anything you want."

I can't hide the way my hips shift beneath him, chasing friction. He chuckles darkly, his free hand slipping under my ass and squeezing the sore place he spanked with the leather camera strap before sliding between my legs, his fingers grazing over the heat pooling between my thighs.

"That's my girl," he whispers. "*Vot eto moya devochka.*"

I moan as he strokes me, slow and deliberately teasing, just enough to drive me *mad*. When he pulls his hand back, he leaves me writhing and desperate. Aching.

"Soaked," he says with mock disapproval. "You think I'll let this slide? You think I won't punish you for being such a bad, wicked little slut?"

I tilt my head back in silent surrender. "What are you gonna do?" I barely recognize my own voice. "Punish me? Ohhh. I'm so *scared.*"

I should be. I very much *should* be. I'm well aware of the fact that the spanking he gave me on that elevator was nowhere near what he was capable of, and if he even begins to think of orgasm denial...

"You really want to play that game?" he asks, shaking his head. "I thought you wanted to be my good girl?"

I give him a silent pout and turn away.

"Look at you, so fucking beautiful."

He pushes away, and I whimper at the loss of his heat. "Rodion!"

I stare as his hands nimbly unfasten his belt. Dear god, he's a thirst trap in human form as he tugs the belt free and loops it. He just spanked me. He's not going to—

In seconds, he rearranges me on the bed so I'm facing away from him, my wrists in his hand. "You said you like competency, didn't you? What was it you said, competency porn?"

"Well, I didn't—I mean—*Rodion*," I protest, as he loops the belt around my wrists and tugs, securing them.

"Let's see how competent I am at making you come."

Oh my fucking god. Why does that fill me with dread and delicious expectation at the same time?

"You can't—you—well, I—"

"Quiet, little queen. One more word, and I'll gag you. You want to surrender to me? *Do it*."

I open my mouth to protest when I feel him beneath me. What is he—oh *god*.

Rodion lies on the bed beneath me and arranges my thighs on either side of his face. "Sit on my face," he growls, his breath hot against my thighs. I have enough room to move my hands up and down, even though I can't get away.

Grabbing my thighs, he tugs me down. I'm shaking at the feel of his mouth between my legs. My eyes flutter closed. I can still feel the throb where he spanked me, his hand at my throat, the brand of his mouth on me, as his tongue lazily laps my clit.

I gasp. "Rodion!"

His palm slams against my ass. I hiss in a breath.

"Take it," he orders, his voice muffled between my thighs. "No talking without permission. And if you come without permission, I'll show you exactly what I can do with that belt, beautiful."

I clamp my lips together and shudder at the feel of his lips closing around my swollen clit. My back arches, and my body tightens. I'm so damn close already. But he... he said... I can't think anymore.

My hips arch as I desperately try to remember. I can't talk except to ask him to come. If I come without permission, I'm toast. And that might sound hot, but I definitely think it's one of those things I'm not *quite* ready for.

"That's my girl," he whispers just before he plunges his fingers into my core. "Good girl. Are you ready to come, gorgeous?"

I nod wordlessly. "Please," I whisper. "May I?"

"Come, baby. Come on my tongue." His voice is a low growl, vibrating against me as his mouth works me mercilessly. His hands clamp down on my thighs, holding me open, denying me any escape. I arch, straining against the belt. The leather bites into my flesh, grounding me.

"Give it to me, baby. I want to taste you. Come," he orders with a harsh slap to my thigh.

That's all it takes. I shatter beneath him, a raw scream ripping from my throat as pleasure floods my limbs, violent and overwhelming ecstasy.

He groans beneath me like a man starved, lapping up the aftershocks as I'm helpless.

His tongue slows, teasing me through every pulse until my breath is ragged and uneven.

"Fuck, look at you," he whispers, dragging his mouth up my body as he gently pulls me away from him, open-mouthed kisses along the curve of my stomach and underside of my breasts. "So fucking beautiful when you break for me."

I'm still gasping when he frees my wrists, but before I can catch my breath, his hand slides to the back of my neck, fingers tangled in my hair. He tilts my head back and forces me to meet his gaze.

"I'm not done with you yet."

I stifle a little squeal.

"I'll make you come until you forget your own name."

I'm boneless and pliable as he arranges me beneath him, on my knees, my hands planted in front of me. I feel his hardened length at my ass. "Rodion," I manage to protest when I feel him moving, and the next thing I know, warm lube drips down my ass. I gasp as his thick fingers press into my ass. A second orgasm takes me by surprise and eclipses the first. "Oh god. Oh my *god*." I moan, coming on his hand just before the head of his cock presses to my entrance.

I arch into him, so eager for his heat to fill me. To be connected even more than we've ever been. I'm still coming as he pushes into me, stretching me inch by inch until I'm gasping, my fingers digging into the mussed sheets. I didn't know I could be this full, this stretched, this *turned on* even after I've come.

"You take all of me so fucking well, baby. Such a good girl." His voice is strained as if he's holding himself back.

He doesn't move for a moment, just holds me there, with him buried to the hilt, my pussy tight and stretched, his cock pulsing inside me. I feel every inch of him, every pulse, every beat of his heart.

This man is going to be my husband. *My husband.* He promised to violently end anyone who threatened to take us apart. Being with him will mean surrendering in ways I never imagined. Yet right now? I want nothing more than *him.* Him in all his power and brutality, danger and darkness, *all of him.*

"Take me." I breathe. "I want you to take me."

With a low growl, he fists my hair, tugs my head back, and slams into me. I cry out, nails digging into the bed once more, but it only makes him drive into me harder, deeper, building a rhythm that's ratcheting me up to another climax. He curses in Russian, the words rough and desperate.

"*Krichi dlya menya, Ember.* Scream for me, baby."

His hands grip my hips as he thrusts again and again, and I do exactly what he says. I scream as he makes me come again.

And again.

And again.

When he pulls out of me, still hard as fuck, I moan. "Rodion, what are you—"

And then he's dragging me to the edge of the bed and falling on his knees before me as if to worship. "I can't, Rodion, I—"

A punishing spank silences me. "You can and you will. Open your legs for me."

He pries my legs apart, and his tongue dives between them again. My back arches. My *god,* I'm so wet, so slick, so tender I bite back tears as he licks my clit again. I'm impossibly aroused as need builds again, this time faster. I can't think beyond the need to climax again when he laps my swollen clit and orders in a harsh growl, *"Come."*

I shatter into another climax, this one more intense than the last. I can't breathe. I can't think. Stars blind my vision as I gasp for enough breath to scream. I'm still coming, still wrapped in ecstasy and all loss of control when he's on me again, and he's filling me again.

My legs wrap around his torso. He holds me beneath him, his gaze searing as he thrusts. I'm pliant and softened beneath him as he wraps his hand around my throat.

"Tell me you're mine," he whispers.

It feels like surrender and victory when I whisper, "I'm yours." His hands on me tighten, and I dig my fingers into his back hard enough to leave marks, pulling him closer as his forehead touches mine, and he grinds out a stream of Russian. His head drops to my neck, and he growls, softer than before, *"Mine."*

I come again, softer this time, sweeter, meeting his thrusts and ecstasy with mine.

He nuzzles my neck. It tickles, and I squirm and smile. "I'm proud of you, baby," he whispers. "Shhh."

I can't move. I'm immobile. I can't think. I'm half-asleep, blissed out, as he arranges me on the bed. A warm cloth comes between my legs a moment later, followed by a soft towel and silky sheets.

A pillow under my cheek.

The weight of a blanket over my shoulders.

Rodion curled up beside me.

Sleep.

CHAPTER 22

RODION

IT'S DARK OUT. *The lights outside our estate have flickered on, armed guards at the gates as always, as I wait in Rafail's office. I can't remember what I did this time or how I got here, but I know the routine by now—lecture. Disappointment.*

Punishment.

When the door to his office opens, I feel the weight of his disappointment before I see him. "Rodion, are you ever going to fucking learn?"

This time, Rafail isn't alone. He's brought... everyone. My grandfather leaning on his cane, his wizened face lined with disapproval. Semyon, frowning and not meeting my eyes. My cousin Matvei. They pour into the office and don't meet my eyes.

I open my mouth to protest but find I can't talk. My lips are sealed together. Mounting frustration builds in me, and I'm on my feet before Rafail snatches me back down with a growl and promise of a worse punishment if I don't sit.

I try to tell them she needed me. I try to tell them I didn't mean to. I try to tell them I won't let them down. But I can't open my mouth, the words won't come...

I wake from my dream with a start, blinking in the early morning quiet. I pat the bed next to me and find it empty.

The dream fades, but the sting of it remains.

"Ember?" I call out her name but don't hear a response. I sit up in bed, my heart slamming against my rib cage, and tell myself to calm. Just because she's—

Water runs in the bathroom. The door's slightly ajar. I turn my head to see—Ember's standing at the bathroom sink, her hair in a messy bun on top of her head, brushing her teeth with vigor.

I let out a breath.

She's wearing my tee.

It reminds me of a video she did, one of her viral ones, where she sighed and said she lost her mind over a scene where the heroine wears her boyfriend's too-big tee. Mine is *way* too big on her. I stare at her. When she lifts her arms to put the toothbrush back, the hem of the tee rises to show the curve of her bare ass.

I know this might not be what she ever imagined for herself, but I'm going to make every damn day feel like a scene only her favorite writer could ever dream up.

I swallow hard.

It was just a dream. Just a fucking dream.

I watch in silence as she splashes water on her face. She's humming to herself. The sound is haunting and makes my heart ache.

My memory drifts to the times I let my family down, some of them not too recent.

If I *hadn't*, I never would've been in California. I might have never met Ember. Still, the sting of being the goddamn black sheep of the family lingers, and I know I'm doing it all over again.

I told Ember this was temporary, knowing full well a temporary marriage to Bratva's an impossibility.

"Hey," I call out louder this time. I want to touch her again and drown out the memories of the past and the fear of the future. Turning to me, she gives me a little wave.

"Morning. Hey, aren't you Russians super superstitious?" When she cocks her head to the side like that, she looks so innocent.

"Yeah, why?"

"Shouldn't we, like, not see each other on our wedding day?"

"Too late for that now." I push out of bed and head to her.

"But what if our future is doomed now?" That sweet little pucker between her brows...

Our future. Let's stay here a minute.

"Then I guess we'd better make use of the time we have together before doom sets in." I bend and kiss her bare shoulder, where the tee's fallen down. Her eyes flutter closed as I kiss her neck next, my hands anchored on the warm softness of her hips.

"What time is it?"

"Eight thirty-two."

Eight.

Eight?

"*Fuck!*"

I let her go like she's branded me and turn to head to my phone. "Rafail said to be ready by nine at the latest. Sending a car to take us to the Romanov estate."

Oh god.

"Rodion!" Her eyes widen in panic as she tosses the brush down and looks around the room wildly. "What do I wear? You didn't tell me!"

Stifling a groan, she runs into the room and rummages through her things.

"Doesn't matter. They'll have everything there." I'm checking my phone to make sure I didn't fuck something else up, reading through the messages from my sisters. They've got shit sorted with Rafail's wifePolina and her mother, the Romanov matriarch.

My phone is ringing, Ember's flying around the room trying to get her shit together, and I'm cursing myself for not getting my ass out of bed earlier. I don't want to start our day like this.

She'll fucking lose her mind when she realizes our wedding isn't temporary, and it feels like all of this is an omen.

"What?" I snap into the phone. Rafail, of course.

I hear him blow out a breath on the line and mentally curse myself for not keeping my shit together. I expect him to tell me to get us outside because they're waiting for us, but he doesn't.

"We've got bad news, brother."

Ember looks at me, and I look back at her as I listen. I stand up straighter. If anyone's going to hurt her, if anyone's planning on—

"Yeah?"

Rafail doesn't speak right away, and that's what sets me off. He's not the type to hesitate. Not unless it's something big— something that could derail everything.

"Rodion." His voice drops, low and sharp. "Her fucking brother's here."

What?

My entire body locks up. Across the room, Ember freezes like she knows, as if she can feel the news straight through the phone.

"What do you mean, *here*?" I grit out. The fucking audacity of this goddamn prick.

"I mean, he's at the gate. Says he's her family, and he's demanding to take her back."

How fucking delusional can one person be?

Ember's staring now, wide-eyed and pale, her lips parted to speak. "What is it, Rodion?"

Rafail keeps going, his voice clipped. "He knows about the wedding. About her. Too much, Rodion. He's not just some jealous asshole from the past. He's been digging, and he's not alone. Looks like he's made some friends in all the wrong places."

"Like fucking who?"

"Feds."

Of all the fucking—

The words get stuck in my throat, as Rafail's meaning sinks in. Shawn isn't just sniffing around to make trouble, he's weaponized his obsession with her, *using* her as leverage. A small pebble in the ocean, causing a ripple that reaches miles.

Jesus.

Rafail's voice cuts through the haze of fury. "Looks like he's been feeding them information. Could be nothing, could be scraps, but you know how the Feds work. They'll turn a crumb into a fucking feast if it gets them close to us. He's probably selling it like he's a fucking golden boy, a good citizen. And now they're circling."

I grit my teeth.

"Why the hell do they care?"

"They could use her. Think about it. Get your head out of your ass and use that brain."

I pinch my lips together as he continues.

Should've fucking ended Shawn before we left Cali.

"She doesn't have to talk. They could use her to track your movements, trace your calls, watch her every step."

"Then we get him out of here," I growl, pacing toward the window like I might spot him through the damn gates of the hotel.

"Already tried," Rafail says. "He's not leaving. Not without her. And if we make a scene… well, Romanov hospitality only stretches so far. I promised Polina."

I'm going to fucking kill the son of a bitch.

But how, when I can't do it in the open when my hands are tied?

And would Ember ever forgive me?

I can practically hear the underlying warning. This isn't our family's territory. The Romanovs have their own rules, and our alliance with them is tenuous, at best. If Shawn pushes his connections with the Feds, instead of a wedding day, I'll be led out in handcuffs.

Ember's already at my side, eyes burning with questions.

"Give me ten minutes," I tell Raf, ending the call.

"What is it?" Ember stands in front of me. I hate the way her lower lip trembles.

"You won't fucking believe this." I shake my head when recognition dawns on her.

"There's only one person from my past who could fuck this up. It's him, isn't it? *God.* This is what I tried to tell you—that he isn't harmless. You can't just treat him the way you'd treat a normal predator. He-he'll stop at nothing, Rodion, nothing. Oh god."

She closes her eyes, and two fat tears roll down her cheeks.

I won't let this happen.

I reach for her.

She pushes me away.

"You don't understand. Shawn doesn't stop. He doesn't... doesn't *break.*"

I pull her to me, this time not taking no for an answer. She breaks into a sob. "He could never let me have anything good or normal or healthy."

I can't help but smirk at her. The situation is fraught; she's a mess, my brother's pissed, and I have no idea how I'm going to get out of this situation, but I can't always take shit so seriously.

"So you take it all back? Marrying me is good and normal and healthy." I nod as if proud. "Honored, babe."

"*Rodion.*"

I sober and pull her to me. I kiss her forehead fiercely and pull her into a hug. "I'm teasing, baby. I've got this. You said he doesn't break?" I hold her out in front of me and tip my finger under her chin, meeting her gaze. "Doesn't back down? *Neither do I.*"

CHAPTER 23

I'D GIVE anything to go back to the safety of one of my books right now. Back to where there are always happily ever afters, and the bad guys never win... *unless* they're the bad guy you fall in love with.

Like me.

Because right now, I'm in the back of an armored car next to my soon-to-be husband, forced into a marriage he tells me is temporary when I know better, fleeing from the vindictive son of a bitch I've spent years trying to escape.

In the books? This is an easy one. My Bratva hottie saunters in, impervious to the laws and consequences. He defeats the bad guy and claims me as his own; we suspend disbelief, and there's no legal fallout. Maybe I have his babies, and somehow, our two extremely different lives meld into a happily ever after.

But this is nothing like that. Right now, my nerves are so raw I'm nauseous. Rodion's anything but romantic as he curses in Russian and gives me short, cryptic answers, as he's glued to his phone.

Right now, we're hurtling toward our *wedding day*.

I want to keep my mind in the present, to ground myself in the reality of what's tangible and real.

I'm safe.

We're getting married.

We will make this work.

He loves me.

Loves me? I feel like I'm saying one of those affirmations they tell you to say as if saying *I'm beautiful, I'm rich, I'm perfect,* will somehow make it so. But there's a disconnect between the words and reality.

Loves me?

How do you really, truly know someone does?

"Here we are." Rodion doesn't look at me, his jaw clenched as he stares out the window. I want to reach for him. I want to bring him back to me. I want to see that passion in his eyes I saw last night. I'd give anything for that smirk right now.

But instead, I see nothing but the cold, impassive face of the Bratva. My future husband.

"Here we are," I echo. I sigh and look away.

The Romanov estate stretches out into the sunset as if it's carved straight from the earth—unyielding and imposing, as old as sin. With the brief conversation I had with Yana and Zoya last night, I gathered the Romanovs practically own everything in The Cove here in New York, nestled between Coney Island and Manhattan.

The car comes to a stop, but I don't move.

He said Shawn was here. Where exactly is he? How safe are we?

"Let's go."

"Rodion—"

When his eyes meet mine, something in me softens. I feel vulnerable and afraid, and no one, *no one* has ever made me feel as safe as Rodion has. My words come out in a shaky whisper despite my bravest attempts to speak up. "Where is he?"

Rodion reaches for both of my hands, his gaze burning into mine. "Rafail said he's gone for now. Told him he'd be back, and there would be hell to pay." He shakes his head. "As if he thinks he can take on the Romanov and Kopolov family combined."

But there's a flicker in his eyes. This isn't as simple as it seems.

I try to mask my feelings, try to pretend that I'm not a nervous wreck knowing Shawn's flown all the way here to end whatever there is between me and Rodion. And right then, for one fraction of a second... I'm relieved we're getting married. Even if it isn't my choice. Even if it's temporary.

I can feel the tension beneath Rodion's calm exterior, his pulse rapid.

I can feel my own.

Rodion wraps his fingers around the back of my neck and brings my mouth to his. The kiss is tender and chaste, a reminder that he's going to do everything in his power to protect me. To keep us safe.

I have to hold onto that.

"You're strong, Ember Steele. Even your name is fire. Unyielding." He shakes his head, holding my gaze with his. "And no one, not even me, is going to take that from you." He leans in and whispers in my ear, his breath hot on my neck. "*Especially* me."

I have to believe him.

I have no other choice.

While the rest of this situation feels fraught and uncertain, there's one thing I know for sure: the Romanovs don't do *modest*. Do any of them?

For one fleeting second, I don't feel like Cinderella in a borrowed gown, waiting for the clock to strike midnight before I turn back into a pauper. No. I hold my chin high, and for a fleeting second, I don't care about Shawn. I don't care about temporary or forced or whatever restrictions we want to put on my marriage to Rodion. For one fleeting second, *I belong here.*

Maybe I *am* a queen. His little queen, yes, but... a queen.

The world outside the window looks something like a dream. The gorgeous estate is sprawling and beautiful despite the marble, steel, and sharp edges of a New York winter. Ice crystals decorate the bare branches of the weeping willows that line the walk to the house.

Silhouettes of spire columns stand dark against the morning light backdrop.

Even from here, I can see sparkling chandeliers glinting from massive windows and staff inside milling about with efficiency and decorum. The magnificent display of ice sculptures takes my breath away, silver garland glinting on the wrought iron fences and rail that line the home.

And then there are the people.

I don't know most of them, though I recognize Yana and Zoya, as well as Rodion's brothers Semyon and Rafail. I've always struggled to remember names, so I didn't make myself memorize more than those few.

For now.

Yana stands beside a man I don't know, with dark skin and snappy black eyes. He has a wide, handsome, friendly face. She holds his arm with elegance. Her husband.

Zoya fiddles nervously with the red velvet edge of her sleeve. She offers me a small, hesitant smile and a little wave.

"She's sweet," I whisper to Rodion.

"Somebody has to be," he mutters back.

Behind Zoya, Rafail stands like a shadow, broad and imposing. His expression is thunderous as if the permanent scowl he wears is carved into his features. Semyon lingers just a step behind, his eyes flicking between me and Rodion as if cataloging our every move.

He probably is.

And then there are the guards.

Armed men stand at every corner and entrance, their black suits pressed and sharp, not even bothering to hide their guns.

Well, then. I guess this is how we roll now.

They're not subtle. Neither is the Bratva wealth that exudes from the entire setting as well as every person here—the stretch of imported cars, the perfectly curated lawn, even frozen in mid-winter.

Rodion steps out first and adjusts his tie. My god, why is that so sexy? My romance-cultured brain short-circuits at the sight of him dressed in a tux I had barely processed before now. We were so rushed, and I was so nervous. He fills out the suit with perfection, his tall, lithe, powerful form barely contained. The tiniest hint of a tat peeks out from under his collar, his eyes somehow both serious and dancing.

My heart swells. I love that about him. I love that so much.

He holds a hand out to me silently, palm up. It feels oddly symbolic. I wish I could capture it in a picture. For now, I'll have to commit it to memory.

His hand is rough as I place mine in his. The warmth of his touch is the only thing grounding me as I step into the cold air.

Every eye is on us. I know somewhere out there, Shawn takes in every detail.

I hope he notes my *future husband* in detail.

Rodion's grip tightens as he leans down to whisper in my ear, "Smile, little queen. Everyone's watching."

I lift my chin, my heart pounding against my rib cage, and let him lead me forward.

"Ember. I'm Ekaterina Romanova. Welcome." A woman with a swath of silver hair tucked into a bun smiles at me, her eyes stern yet welcoming. Ah. A woman with a spine of steel but with heart. I like that. I suppose it's a combo that would serve a woman of the Bratva well.

She extends a hand, and I take it gratefully. Next, she turns to Rodion. "And welcome, Rodion. I've heard you two have quite the circumstances surrounding this whole ordeal." Stepping back, she leans into my ear. "I love romance too, Ember. It's so... *escapist*, isn't it?" With that, she turns and gestures for us to follow her.

"Fortunately, we were in full preparation for tonight's gala, so a simple wedding ceremony was easy to pull off."

She goes on about flowers and food, a simple guest list and plans, while I follow Rodion, his family trailing behind us.

I can feel the tension beneath Rodion's calm exterior, his pulse rapid.

"It's freezing out here. They didn't all have to come out," I say in a small voice to Rodion as he opens the door.

"They came out in case they're needed."

Ah. So beneath those elegant, sleek clothes, they're all armed to the teeth.

Yana winks at me, and little Zoya squeezes my hand as Ekaterina leads us into an elegant living room. I barely notice the details.

I'm about to be married.

"Aren't there... legal things we need to do?" I ask Rodion.

"Taken care of."

I give him a half smile, and he snorts under his breath. "Competency porn?" he whispers.

"Mhm."

At the sight of the officiant, however, I freeze.

This is real.

I'm going to be married. *In real life.*

Into the Bratva.

Rodion's wealthy and charming and dangerous as hell, and I have... mixed feelings.

Shawn is breathing down our necks like the predator he is, but the Kopolov family presses in on all sides, reminding us of who they are and what we promise.

This is real.

But as the officiant drones on, I hardly hear them.

Is this really how it ends?

I glance at Rodion, uncertainty swelling in my chest. I feel like I'm waiting for a sign that, at any moment, he'll give me the signal to run or drop another bombshell on me.

But there's nowhere to run.

And this is all too real.

We take our vows in a rush of whispers. This is nothing like the formal weddings I've read about in the books, but fast and pragmatic.

When he slides the ring onto my finger... it feels heavier than it should.

Done.

This isn't the wedding of my dreams.

And when I look at Rodion, I wonder.

Is it his?

I stare at the ring on my finger, my breathing shallow. I feel like I should say something, but I don't know what, as the room erupts into cheers and someone starts pouring vodka. I take the shot glass thrust into my hand, even though I haven't eaten breakfast and morning vodka sounds like a terrible idea. I'm afraid if I decline, I'll break some type of unwritten rule.

Rodion's eyes meet mine, anchoring me in place. When he brushes his fingers to my jaw, he leaves a trail of heat across my skin. Leaning in, he kisses me. And I remember why we're here.

I remember his promise last night. I remember the way he said he loved me, the way he held me. The way he told me he would never let anyone hurt me, not ever again.

I remember how he promised to protect me and devote himself to me.

We may be new to this but hope blossoms in my heart.

Rodion is trying. So will I.

"Done," he mutters, his hand resting at the small of my back as he steers me away from the officiant.

"We have coffee and breakfast for all in the dining room," Ekaterina says with a smile. "Let's celebrate."

After Rodion and I sit down, Yana approaches with her husband. "Welcome to the family," she says with a wide grin. "Try not to cause too much trouble. I've heard about those books."

I let out a laugh, the tension in my chest easing a little. "Don't believe everything you hear."

"Oh, I don't," she replies with a wink. "I've...seen the covers."

Zoya is next. She steps forward with an almost apologetic smile. The poor girl is so timid. "If you need anything at all, please let me know," she says with a smile and a swift hug. "It can be overwhelming at first. I know Polina had her work cut out for her though..." Her voice trails off. "She had other challenges too."

Overwhelming is one way to put it.

Semyon is the one who makes a shiver trail down my spine. His eyes are ice, his tone even colder. The mood shifts like a cold wind. He stands apart from the rest, his movements deliberate and measured, as if he's sizing me up.

"Welcome," he says without a trace of a smile. The words are polite. The tone isn't. He lifts a drink to his lips.

I muster a tight smile. "Thank you."

Rodion's stiffened posture beside me feels like a quiet warning, but before the tension can thicken, a booming voice breaks through.

"Ah, so this is the woman that think she knows all about us!" Matvei strides over, his grin wide and devilish. "Rodion, you didn't warn her about the initiation, did you?"

"What initiation?" I ask, narrowing my eyes suspiciously.

Matvei's grin widens. "The one where you have to prove you can survive in a room full of men who think your mafia book heroes are a joke."

"Matvei," Rodion says in warning, but his eyes are dancing.

"Oh, don't forget the part where they're all billionaires," someone else chimes in. "Damn it, I missed the sign up."

"Tell me," Matvei says, "in these books do the men walk around in suits all day? Even when fighting off entire armies with their bare hands?"

"Bare hands and six packs," Zoya chimes in, giggling.

I can't help but laugh even as my cheeks flame. "I don't *write* them, I just read them, okay?"

"But you're the expert!" Matvei says, sitting down across from me with an exaggerated lean forward. He unfastens the top button of his shirt and gives me a wink. "So tell me how accurate they are. I *am* single..."

"Better start working on that six-pack. I mean, more accurately...*nine* pack, right?" Yana asks with a snort.

I glance around at them, realizing that for all their dangerous edges and reputations, there's one thing the books get right: the sense of family loyalty you can't ignore.

I look over to see Rafail standing next to a man the rest seem to be deferring to. He looks about Rafail's age, with a tall, muscular build and tanned, golden skin. I watch him chatting with Rafail, their voices rising and falling, even when they maintain decorum.

"Mikhail Romanov," Rodion whispers in my ear. "This is his home. His sister Polina is married to my brother."

Oooh, right. I forgot about that. This is why they had to come and prove themselves, something about making a good show of things.

It doesn't feel like a ceremony. I don't feel... *married.*

But Rodion? His hand closes over mine, solid and sure, as he talks to the Romanov family.

I don't know any of them and won't be able to remember their names. I'm lucky I remember *mine* at this point. But there's a tall, dark, and classically handsome one talking about biometric tracking and drones with Mikhail's wife, a spitfire of a woman with glasses and a mane of curly hair, alongside a few lethal, menacing-looking Bratva types, as well as one who's so big he has to turn sideways to walk in the room.

The estate glows with candles, the atmosphere softened with streams of classical music. It's nearing lunchtime when

Ekaterina says it's time to begin preparations for the gala. In the meantime, Rafail wants us to get pictures taken.

It feels so surreal. I long to escape into one of the expansive rooms in this mansion, just me and a book, preferably with a pair of noise-canceling headphones. The sound, sights, and intense atmosphere are almost oppressive. I don't want to be on anymore. I don't want to pretend to fit in with people I have nothing in common with.

"Smile," Rodion murmurs, his voice a low vibration in my ear. "You're mine now, Mrs. Kopolova. It's time to play the part."

I feel the weight of those words. The expectation.

But I smile until my face feels sore. I savor the weight of his hand on my lower back and the way he says *my wife*.

And when it all feels like too much, I remind myself that it's only temporary, that this won't be my life forever... even as the thought of separation from Rodion makes my heart ache.

I can't have him and pass on Bratva life though. The two are irrevocably entwined.

"Ember? I just wanted to wish you congratulations."

I turn to see a tall, willowy blonde with pale blue eyes and a ready smile extending her hand out to me.

"I'm Polina Kopolova, formerly Romanova. My mother's arranged for you and Rodion to have a room on the third floor so you can regroup and get a little rest before tonight." She snorts. "It's the room marked with white balloons. She's so cute."

I shake her hand. "Ah, thank you. Wait, so *you're* the one who joined these two families together?"

"Oh, well…" she begins hesitantly. "I… am still in the process of *trying*."

"And doing an excellent job," Yana says. "Old habits die hard and all that. You know how pigheaded our brothers are." She rolls her eyes.

"Yup. Listen, Mom needs me in the kitchen. We'll catch up later? We have so much to do," Polina says. "Mom gets a bit frantic before the gala."

"They do it every year," Zoya explains. "It's *epic*."

"We have to," Polina continues as she turns to head to the kitchen. "It's our way of keeping local people pleased with us and keeping money in the community coffers." She gives me a slight grimace. "Believe me, it helps."

She flits to the kitchen as Rodion joins Rafail and Semyon. I sit heavily in a chair. The dress I'm wearing feels so heavy, too stunning, too extravagant for someone like me, like a costume for a role I haven't rehearsed.

Rodion's in a heated conversation with Rafail, even as his gaze constantly assesses the situation. I watch him eye every exit, every window, and every person who walks in the room.

"When will people start arriving for the gala?" I ask Zoya. Yana's gone off with her husband, and I'm left alone with the shy youngest sister.

She bites one of her nails thoughtfully. "Hmm. Shortly after they're supposed to, is my guess."

"Oh?"

"Mmm," she says with a nod. "These are not the types who show up early for events." She rolls her eyes. "Everyone has to make *an entrance*." She sips a glass of champagne. "It isn't here, though, but offsite in a gallery or something?"

"Did you ask Rafail for permission for that, Zoya?" Rodion quirks a brow at her.

Zoya's cheeks flush adorably pink. "They poured it for me."

My heart thumps at the way he quirks a brow at her. Rodion as big brother is so damn cute.

He gives her a stern look. "Do you think Rafail would take that as an excuse?"

Zoya sighs. "*Rodi.*"

"He wouldn't mind a little champagne, would he? It's our wedding," I tell him, my hand on his chest. Seems ironic a man who deals in everyday illegal activity would balk at his sister having a little bubbly.

"You really don't know Rafail," Rodion says with a grimace, scratching at his jaw. "Make it your last, Zoya."

She nods. Poor kid. It must be insufferable to be under the watchful eye of all those bossy brothers.

Before I can wade in and defend her, his phone buzzes. He glances down, his body tensing.

"Something wrong?" I try to peek at the screen. I swear to god, if Shawn—

"Nothing I can't handle," he replies, slipping his phone in his pocket.

"If it's Shawn…"

"Ember. I said I'll handle it. Trust me." I place my champagne down and press my hand to his chest. I can feel the rapid beating of his heart beneath my palm just before his hand closes over mine, trapping it against his heartbeat.

I draw in a deep breath, and I… release it.

Whoosh.

Can I trust him?

He kisses my cheek.

"I need to step out a minute."

I nod. "Polina said they have a room upstairs for us to rest in if we want to."

Of course, red-blooded alpha male that he is, he wiggles his eyebrows at me. "I would love to *rest.*" He somehow puts air quotes around the word *rest.*

"*Rodi.*" I stifle a giggle, repeating Zoya's nickname for him just because I love the way his eyes narrow in on me.

"Call me that again, little queen." He clucks his tongue at me. "Go, Ember. Rest. I'll be up in a few minutes."

But it's hard to rest knowing Shawn is out there, that he's never going to walk away from me, knowing I shunned him and knowing that I just *married into the Bratva.*

What does that even mean?

I consider taking the dress off, but in the end, keep it on because… well, if I'm honest, I want *Rodion* to take it off. So sue me if I still have book boyfriend fantasies I want to live out.

I lie in the bed, propped up on a variety of pillows, and pull out my phone. My heart rate races when I see I got another message from Shawn.

I put the phone down.

I pick it up again.

I stare at it as if it's a lethal snake about to bite me.

I finally click the message to read it, despite everything in me screaming at me not to.

Shawn: you looked beautiful today. White always suited you. You look beautiful now. Careful not to wrinkle the dress, Ember

I sit up in bed, my heart racing. Footsteps sound outside the door. I try to remember everything about self-defense, but I haven't practiced, and my mind is a blank of nerves and fear.

Oh god.

Oh god.

I look wildly around the room, but it's just a simple guest room, well-appointed but simple. Pillows, blankets, and— my eyes come to rest on a bottle of champagne on the dresser.

I could break it. If I have to, I can use it as a weapon, and I could—

The door handle jingles. Someone pounds at the door. I scream.

CHAPTER 24

EMBER

"It's me! Ember. Open the door!"

Oh god. It's Rodion. Of course it is as if Shawn would get past the wall of armed guards downstairs.

I choke back a sob as I open the door to find Rodion frantic and half-mad, his eyes blazing as he pushes past me into the room, a gun in hand.

"What are you—Rodion, you can't—"

"Where is he? You screamed. Your heart rate went through the fucking roof. What happened?"

I show him the texts. "He's lying, baby. It's a lie, I promise. He can't be watching you."

My voice is trembling. "But what if he is?"

Rodion's gaze grows heated. "I hope he shows his fucking face."

I should stop him. I should tell him no, that I can't do this, not now, not when I'm tense and afraid and I—

I *should.*

But the second he spins me toward the window, pressing me up against the glass like he can't stand the space between us, I forget how to breathe.

His hands fist the layers of fabric of my wedding gown, dragging it up slowly—too slowly. I know exactly why he's doing this.

I'd tie him to a chair, making him watch me ruin you—slow and raw, before I cut out his eyes and left him to bleed out, knowing the last thing he ever saw was me owning you.

Cool air kisses the back of my thighs as he lifts the dress higher. I press my palms flat against the glass to steady myself. It's frigid, like a sheet of ice, the edges painted with ice crystals, when something colder and harder presses up against my thigh.

"Here's your wedding gift, little queen. A weapon from your king."

My heart swells. I can't think of a better gift than him taking me without apology and handing me agency, all at once.

I might love this man. I think I do.

I can see us in the reflection of the cold glass—him, behind me, dark and possessive, his eyes burning with something untamed and wild. I barely recognize myself, my lips parted.

"You're shaking, baby," he whispers, his voice rough against my ear as he grips my thighs hard.

"Rodion..." My breath stutters. It sounds like a plea. I don't know what I'm asking for.

His teeth graze my shoulder, scraping over my skin before he bites down hard enough to make me squirm.

God.

My forehead drops against the glass with a quiet thud as heat rushes between my legs.

"Don't hide," Rodion growls, his hand fluttering over my stomach as he yanks me back so our bodies collide. I love the feel of him at my back. His voice drops lower. "I want him to see exactly how good you look when you're mine."

I can still see myself making a video, holding my favorite dark romance book, waving it in front of the camera while I gushed.

And then he fucks her, right in the open, so the enemy can watch everything.

But right now... I open my mouth as a shudder rolls through me.

I don't pull away.

I can't.

Because some twisted, broken part of me... *wants it too.*

I'd bury his body and sleep like a fucking baby, Ember.

Rodion knows exactly what he's doing.

"Rodion," I whisper, squeezing my eyes shut as his mouth drifts lower.

"Open your eyes, Ember." His voice is rough, demanding.

I hesitate a second too long. His teeth sink into my shoulder to punish me. "Eyes on the glass, Ember."

A desperate sound escapes me as I force myself to obey him. I want to push back, to challenge him, but I'm melting, and I want this escape so badly.

"Good girl," he whispers, dragging his tongue along the mark he just made.

"You wanted this, didn't you?"

I can't answer.

Because... yes.

I did. I do. I want it still.

A part of me needs to push back, needs to fight him. A part of me needs to fight for control and have a little bit... just a little, taken from me.

But the moment his teeth sink into my earlobe, his breath hot against my skin, with the knowledge that if I disobeyed him right now, it would not go over well, and I would prob-ably *love* whatever he did in response... the outside world floods in, cluttering my thoughts.

Loud. Unforgiving.

The cold glass is a shock against my skin. His teeth drag along my shoulder as if to remind me exactly what he's capable of, that he's holding himself back... and exactly *who is in control*.

I shudder against the glass, my breath fogging the surface in front of me. His grip tightens on my hips, a reminder I'll feel tomorrow. The wedding gown is bunched around my waist, but he doesn't care.

Neither do I.

"You're shaking again, little queen," he whispers. "You like this, don't you?"

I nod wordlessly.

I bite my lip hard, trying to hold myself upright when my legs feel like jelly.

His hand trails down my stomach, then lower, teasing just under the hem of lace. I squirm, but he presses me harder.

"Don't fight it, baby." His words spread heat across my chest.

"Already so wet," he murmurs, satisfied. "That's my girl."

My god, I love when he says that.

I can hardly breathe. My eyes flutter closed when emotion sweeps over me, but he claps a hand hard across my ass. "Eyes open, Ember. Wide open."

He pulls my thighs apart, his hand sliding between them, and I hear the telltale whir of a zipper being undone.

I swallow and lick my lips, arching my back because I want him so fucking bad.

I cry out at the first perfect thrust, every nerve in my body alight.

"Louder," he rasps, his grip on my hips brutal and intense as he pulls me back against him with every hard thrust.

I can't stop the sound that escapes my lips, a mixture of moans and gasps. I don't care who hears or sees; *I need him.*

"You see this?" he growls, his voice low and animalistic, making my need ratchet higher. *"You're mine.* Fucking *mine.* No one will ever touch you again. No one will take what's mine."

His words cut through me, raw and possessive. The tension builds, my need to climax taking over.

"Rodion," I breathe out.

I claw at the glass, nails scraping along the flat, cold surface, my body trembling as he drives into me.

"Come, little queen. Come for your king."

Climax tears through me, flooding my body with euphoria. I cry and moan as he growls in my ear, his hot seed spilling into me, hips grinding into mine. I can hardly breathe, my chest heaving. If he didn't hold me up right now, I'd fall to the floor, boneless.

I meet his gaze in the reflection.

The cold glass wakes me from a fog.

I just let him fuck me against a window where anyone could see, knowing full well *that was his intent.*

"Stop." My voice is so low I'm not sure he hears me at first, so I say it again, louder this time. "*Stop.*"

"What's wrong?" He pulls away from me and peers out the glass. "Did you see him?" His voice is laced with concern as he rights my dress and zips himself up. I swallow hard, untangling myself from him, but the miles of fabric make it clumsy and awkward.

"I can't—this is too much." I shake my head, stepping back from the window. I can't stop shaking.

I can't stop the flood of memories that assault me. It seems the harder I push them away, the harder they attack.

I'm brushing tears from my eyes and shaking my head.

Maybe book boyfriends are safer.

Maybe being alone is safer.

"Ember." Rodion watches me carefully, his hands hanging loose by his sides.

I can't look at him. Not now. *I can't.*

Because the thoughts claw at my mind with vicious pain.

What if Shawn really is watching?

What if I've made a terrible mistake?

What if there is no escape?

I swipe my phone off the nightstand, ignoring Rodion's look of concern. The messages stare back at me, but there's another now.

White always suited you

But I preferred you in red.

Rodion steps closer. "What does it say?"

I shake my head. "It doesn't matter."

"The hell it doesn't."

I turn away. "You can't just fix things by... by *claiming* me, Rodion."

A part of me fears I'm pushing him away because I don't know what to do with all these pent-up fears, and he's the closest target.

Another part tells me I have to test him; I have to make sure this is real before it all goes up in smoke and vapor.

"That's not what this is, Ember."

"I'm not just a prize you can parade around." I back toward the door. The words hang in the air between us when I remember what he said before.

"Wait. When you first came in here. You said something about my heart rate?" He looks away and clenches his jaw. "Rodion. How do you know that?"

With a frown, he reaches for his phone and shows me. "Biometrics, of course."

"You check *my biometrics*?" It seems like a violation.

"Of course. How else was I supposed to know you were okay when I wasn't there?" He says it as if it's the most natural thing in the world.

Seriously?

I stare, abashed. "What else have you been checking you conveniently decided not to tell me about?"

Rodion smirks, slipping his phone into his jacket pocket. His eyes hold that infuriatingly hot glint, the one that makes it impossible to tell if he's being playful or deadly serious.

The one that made me fall in love.

"You want the full list now, or should I spread the answers out?" he asks, tapping his chin. Reaching for me, his hand grazes my hip, thumb brushing over the silk of my dress in a way that makes shivers tingle my spine.

"I'm not joking, Rodion." I'm trying to stay serious, but he makes it hard. My voice is husky, affected.

Leaning in, he kisses my cheek. "Little queen, neither am I."

Something dangerous simmers beneath the surface. "Let's see," he begins. "I know you sleep on your left side when you're anxious. I know you clench your fists in your sleep when you've had a bad dream." His voice drops lower, his mouth at my ear. "I know you stop breathing, just for a second, when I touch you here." His hand skims down, pressing lightly against the curve of my waist.

I stop breathing, just for a second.

Heat creeps up my neck. I swallow hard.

"You've been watching me that closely?"

He doesn't answer right away, but his eyes are focused on my lips. I lick them because I love the way it makes him groan.

"You're mine, Ember. My wife now. Watching you is the least I've done." His eyes grow darker. "And I don't plan on stopping."

I know I should say something sharp and witty, but the words seem to catch because a part of me... *likes* this.

A lot.

That's the dangerous part, I think.

His hand lingers at my waist as if to remind me how easily he could pull me closer… but doesn't.

I should remind him I need some space, that I'm still mad, that I'm not some prize to be watched or guarded.

"I know you like it," he whispers.

Get out of my thoughts.

I turn away, but he reaches for my chin and drags my gaze back to his.

I can't deny it. I won't.

Because he's right.

Somehow, when my eyes meet his… all the anger and fear and worry melt like snow under the blazing sun.

I want to let go.

I want to relish in the freedom of surrender.

How can I give him that and still maintain… *me?*

How do I not totally lose myself to him… to us?

My phone buzzes with a text. Rodion takes it straight out of my hand, and we read it together.

"I'll fucking kill him," he says in a rush of words.

> **Shawn**
> He can never protect you
>
> You can run but I'll always find you

You fucked me over and you'll fucking pay
for this, you liar

My throat tightens because I know two things...

First, Shawn has signed his death warrant.

Second... this isn't temporary, and it never was.

CHAPTER 25

EMBER

"Rodion. Come here." Rafail stands in a doorway by three other men.

Rodion blows out a breath, kisses my cheek, and whispers in my ear. "Stay right here."

They all want him, everyone wants to talk, to network, to congratulate him.

He leaves the terrace outside and heads in. I welcome the garden air. The faint hum of voices inside fades, muffled by the tall hedges that line the estate.

A few minutes later, Rodion is locked away with his brothers and those official-looking men. I know he's here on business and that his brothers are trying to make the most of their time here. So I spent the next hour with Polina and Zoya, but I miss being alone, on my own.

I live alone because I like the solitude. It feels suffocating in here. It was nice, comforting even, to chat with the girls, but eventually, it felt like the air around me was pressing in on me.

Now, the quiet and cold make me breathe a bit easier. I tilt my head back, closing my eyes. Above me, bright stars are deeply embedded in the night sky, flickering above the haze of the city. I give myself space to breathe.

The sound behind me comes so softly, at first, I almost miss it. The faint crunch of footsteps on gravel. But before I can turn, a hand slips over my eyes.

A blindfold.

"Rodion."

This isn't the time or place. If he thinks he's going to—

A hand catches mine, wordlessly pulling my hands behind my back. Rope—maybe silk? Tightens around my wrists.

"Shh," a voice whispers behind me.

This doesn't... feel like Rodion. I can't tell if it sounds like him, but...

I sniff hard, trying to see if I recognize his scent, but it's impossible in the frigid air. Rodion smells like cedar and gunpowder, sharp and dangerous, and so utterly masculine it makes me ache. This... this is different.

Unfamiliar.

And even though Rodion can be rough, he never hurts me.

The grip on my wrists isn't just restrictive—there's an underlying roughness that feels *wrong*.

Rodion would never hurt me.

It feels like this person might.

"Rodion?" I whisper again, my pulse spiking, praying that he'll give away some clue that it's just him, and he's just enacting one of my fantasies again. Maybe he has a secret room or a shed he'll bring me to, maybe—

A hand over my mouth is my only response.

CHAPTER 26

RODION

I SIP MY DRINK. Cold air bites through the open balcony. I should be inside. Playing the part. Shaking hands. Smiling like I belong here.

I married Ember and lied to her. I told her this was temporary, that we'd get my brothers off my back. I appeased the Bratva gods, knowing if I showed up married, my entire family would be cast in a better light.

I knew that.

And yet... and yet...

I can still feel her. I can still hear her.

Somewhere along the line, I fucked up.

This is too much.

I came on too strong, maybe.

Was it the stalking?

The forced marriage?

Or maybe fucking her against the window...

I smirk and shake my head.

I told myself I would do things right, but the more I stand out here I realize... I'm lying to myself.

I take another sip and polish it off.

It does nothing to steady my nerves.

I need more.

Ember thinks I don't know what she's doing, that I can't see the way she's unraveling beneath the weight of this.

I won't have her looking over her shoulder the rest of her life for *him*. Shawn.

His name is a curse I want to rip out of our lives.

She deserves a life free from worry.

I don't have many regrets, but at the very top of the list is that I didn't kill him the second I found out from her exactly what he did.

I look inside. She's standing near Zoya, her head tilted slightly. Even from here, I can see the way her hands tremble around the flute of champagne she hasn't touched.

Trying to hold herself together.

But when the person next to Zoya turns to me, I see it isn't Ember after all.

Where the hell is she?

Go to her.

I walk to her as if she cast a spell on me, and I'm helpless to fight against her incantation.

Fuck. Maybe she did. My little queen, the sorceress.

I push off the railing and head to her, back into the crowd. The faces around us blur—the Romanovs, Bratva leaders, our rivals, and our friends. Polished socialites wrapped in designer clothing, all pretending that an art auction charity event will somehow buy their way into the good graces of all. None of that matters.

I can't find her.

"Rodion?" A heavy hand falls on my shoulder. Rafail.

Fuck.

"I was just telling Mikhail about what you found in California. One more minute. Can you tell him the rest?"

His grip tightens slightly as if to warn me. Mikhail Romanov stares at me, his gaze unyielding. "I heard you had some blowback. Tell me what happened. I have friends in California."

I look for Ember but don't see her.

"I will," I say with a nod. "I need to talk with Ember first."

"Rodion—"

I shrug out of Rafail's grip and head for Ember.

"I'll be right back."

But I can't find her. Anywhere.

The Romanov estate is an enigma, rooms upon rooms, and

everywhere I go, I find more people, more uniformed staff, clinking glasses, and small talk. Everyone... but her.

I barely stifle the need to scream her name, to raze this fucking party to the ground to find her.

I should've stayed right next to her.

Logically, I know I shouldn't fear the worst. The Romanovs have a legion of guards and protective measures, but tonight... tonight, there are so many people.

Where is she?

I weave through the crowd, my pulse hammering. The air in here feels suffocating, and my patience is at an all-time low. *Where the fuck are you, Ember?*

That's when I see it, the faint shimmer of white turning around a corner at the far end of a corridor.

Her dress.

I move fast, my steps silent against the marble, but when I turn the corner? Nothing.

Just another empty hall.

"Ember?" No response.

I find Polina and Zoya chatting in a library. "Hey," I say, trying to keep myself calm when I run my fingers through my hair. "Have you two seen Ember? I can't find her anywhere."

"She was outside?" Polina says. "I told her we had open access to the garden..."

My heart races. It doesn't matter if she went outside because the Romanovs have this place locked down tighter than the Kremlin.

But still... still...

I head to the garden when I hear a scream.

I turn the corner, my pulse racing and gun in hand, when I see—I come to a halt.

It isn't Ember but a woman I've never met before, her cheeks flushed. "You shouldn't sneak up on me like that!" she chides a young man who's laughing his ass off.

I turn away before they see me.

Not Ember.

I tear through the frigid gardens, looking for a clue. She couldn't just disappear...

And then I know. *I know.*

I won't let Ember go. I told her what I thought would appease her, knowing that my brothers wouldn't accept anything less. I told her what I thought would keep her here, knowing that if she's with me, I'm the one who will protect her, no matter the cost.

I know I love her. I love her feisty, indomitable spirit and quirkiness. I love that she raves about the books that bring her joy while she clings to her independence. I love her fire and defiance, the way she burns brightly even when the world wants to snuff her out.

I love the way she challenges me with a single glance.

There's a stubbornness in her that grates on me—and I love every fucking second.

I love her creativity and vision, her bravery.

She might blush and pretend she doesn't like what I have to offer, but I see the spark that craves not just flirting with danger but embracing it.

I need to find her. As I turn over room after room, fear begins to grow.

I'm so caught up in my quest to find her, I've completely forgotten the trackers she hates. I hide in a doorway, pull up my phone, and quickly check. A red flash warns me on the screen: *Alert: elevated heart rate, oxygen levels dropping.*

Fuck.

She's panicking.

I slide the screen over to the tracker and see the blinking dot that shows me where she is. I hoped I would find it somewhere right here in the house, but my worst suspicions are confirmed—the blinking dot moves erratically. Sharp turns, wrong paths. Ember isn't running.

She's being taken.

My chest constricts as I zoom in and track the rapid shift of her location. West gate.

I sprint through the estate, slipping through the side entrance just in time to catch the rumble of tires on gravel and the squealing tires of a black SUV.

Shawn.

I don't need to see his face to know. *That bastard.*

I pull my gun from my waistband and race toward the line of cars waiting for valet parking, their keys conveniently still in the engines. I slide into the driver's seat of the one at the very end, a sleek black Mercedes.

My phone vibrates. A message from Ember's tracking app.

Signal lost.

My gripe tightens on the leather steering wheel. I try to soothe the rapid beating of my heart with another deep breath. I have to stay focused and alert. Too many times, I've lost my temper and fucked up. This time... this time will be different.

Shawn should've killed me when he had the chance.

CHAPTER 27

EMBER

I KNOW IT NOW, with every cell of my body, this isn't Rodion. He plays games, dangerous ones, but they're just that—*games.* He teases and torments me and leans into making those fantasies come to life.

But he doesn't hurt me. He loves to tease me, to play around a bit with the element of fear. But this? This is next level.

This is not a game.

I have to keep my head on straight. I have to stay the course. I can't lose my shit, not now.

Someone shifts in the front seat. Then his voice, the same one that's plagued me for years.

"You don't have to be afraid, Ember."

Shawn.

My worst fears are confirmed.

His tone is soft, almost coaxing. "I know what you really want, Ember. It's alright that you're playing hard to get. I know you really want me; you just haven't admitted it even to yourself yet."

My heart thuds painfully. He's delusional, a fucking psychopath, and *I hate him.*

"You say you only like these mafia men and dangerous situations in your books," he continues. The car turns sharply. "But I know the truth. You crave danger. You're not afraid of it, not at all." He chuckles. "You kinky little girl."

I squeeze my eyes shut as bile burns the back of my throat.

"I know you better than he does. He's not like us." His voice drops to a dangerous register. I want to scream at him, but I'm gagged and incapable. "He's playing at being protective. Pretending he didn't use you to build status when that's exactly what he did."

What?

"I see you, Ember. The real you. And you know I love you, even if you've disappointed me."

Tears burn my blindfold. I fight a sob that threatens to break free as I twist my hands and try to find a weak spot.

Does Rodion know I'm gone?

Is he tracking me?

Shawn's words press on me like the cold, steel edge of a blade to my neck. "You can fight me, but I know the truth. I'm the one who deserves you. Not him."

My breathing hitches.

No.

My body might tremble, but my heart steadies.

I think back to Rodion's smirk, the way he'd lift my chin when I got riled up. He let me fight him. He let me push back, gave me agency and free will. He knows how much that matters to me.

Maybe that's why I love him. *I love him.*

Here, in the back of Shawn's car, I see so clearly now it makes my heart ache.

I trust him.

Maybe my book boyfriends offer safety in danger, a place where I can explore but stay in control. The fantasy was never about submission but about trust.

I'm not going to lose him.

I *want* him to protect me. I want that fierce, sometimes irrational, unapologetic dedication to keeping me safe. *Owning me.*

I want all of it.

Shawn won't win. I'll be sure of it. He won't.

An engine roars behind us, growing louder.

Oh god, oh please, please be Rodion.

I can still see the lethal flicker of his eyes as he promises brutal retribution to anyone who tries to hurt me.

I'd tie him to a chair and make him watch me ruin you, slow and raw, before I cut out his eyes...

Rodion doesn't bluff. He gives me all of who he is, the brutal and the beautiful, every ounce of morally gray that I crave in my books right here, in all his Bratva glory, tats and weapons, and the fierce, undying protection of a man who loves me.

You don't want a gentleman, little queen.

I don't now, and I never did.

"He's too late," Shawn growls in the driver seat. "He can't have you."

I twist my wrists harder, feeling my skin burn under the ropes.

Come on. Come on…

The car swerves violently as Shawn tries to lose whoever's trailing us. I stifle a whimper, completely unable to stop myself from crashing headfirst into the door. Pain radiates along my skull with these stupid restraints holding me tight.

Gunfire explodes behind us. Shawn screams and curses, the car tilting dangerously to the right.

Shawn seems to be fighting for control, but whoever it is, is gaining on us. Something bumps the back of the car.

Has he caught us?

I can imagine exactly what he's going through right now because I know him. Rodion wants to catch us and punish Shawn, but he doesn't want to hurt me.

The way Shawn is driving, he might get his wish sooner than later. I'm straining against my wrists when I feel something hit my palm. Is it—I trace it with my fingers and realize it's the tail end of the restraints he sloppily tied.

I work at the knot and feel a shift of movement. *I can do this.*

Rodion slipped a knife into a sheath on my thigh. If I can get to it—

I have to keep my head in the game, have to stay on task here. He won't notice if I undo my restraints. I shift the fabric of my dress, cursing the layers, when I feel the cold, hard metal of the knife at my thigh.

I swallow hard. Yes. *Yes.*

Who the fuck am I?

Maybe I *am* cut out for mafia life.

I'm the wife of a hero.

Slowly, carefully, I move the knife out. It scrapes against my thigh as I pull it out and palm it. Shawn's swerving and cursing. He hits something hard, and I stifle a scream when I prick my own damn leg with the blade.

He never would suspect I had my own weapon.

With trembling fingers, I slide the knife into my palm and shave at the restraints. I can feel it yielding even as I can't see. Finally, my wrists swing free. I grab the blindfold at the back of my head and yank it off.

Shawn's face is a mask of fury as another gunshot rings out. I contemplate stabbing him, actually tearing into someone's flesh with a weapon, and the thought makes me want to vomit. But I have to get away. Does it make sense to hurt him while he's driving though? My thoughts go crazy, and I can't reel them in, no matter how hard I try.

Shawn curses, swerving dangerously close to a guardrail. The SUV scrapes alongside it, sparks flying. Another shot rings out. I hear a pop, and the side of the car immediately swerves. Another gunshot followed by another *pop*.

He's here, and he's shooting out the tires.

The SUV screeches to a stop because he can't drive it another foot. It slams against the guardrail with a sickening crush.

My ears ring.

Silence.

I sit still, not sure where I can go next, what to do—

Heavy footsteps.

Measured. Unhurried.

He's here, and he's going to enact brutal justice. I tremble and breathe a little more easily even as my belly clenches.

The driver's side door wrenches open as Shawn tries to flatten himself against the other side of the car. Rodion reaches in and, with his massive, tatted hand, grabs Shawn by the neck. But he doesn't move him, doesn't drag him out like I suspect. Instead, he turns to me, eyes blazing into mine.

"Are you hurt, baby?"

I do a quick mental tally and shake my head. "No," I whisper.

Shawn tries to take advantage of the opportunity and wriggle out of Rodion's grip, but that is not going to happen.

"Get out." Rodion's voice is cold. Lethal.

I'd bury his body and sleep like a fucking baby.

Shawn shifts, reaching for something—a gun, maybe a knife. But Rodion doesn't hesitate. Two hands on Shawn's shirt, and he drags him out of the SUV like he's a rag doll. The sound of bone cracking echoes like thunder.

Shawn's body crumples against the pavement.

I look wildly about me. We're on a vacant road at night, illuminated by bright overhead lights. No one's here. Behind the guardrail is a row of tall pines, a natural barrier.

I can hardly breathe as I see Rodion's sure, deadly aim. I can't hear him from here but can gather a mix of Russian and Shawn's pleas for mercy before Rodion takes one of Shawn's hands in his and breaks it. I cringe but can't look away. Shawn screams, writhing, as Rodion pins him to the ground beneath his foot and reaches for his second hand. He yanks it back with brutal efficiency, and Shawn's cries of terror and pain echo in the night.

Rodion looks to me. I stare at him through cracked glass. Dark. Dangerous. Blazing with a ferocity that calls to the deepest, darkest parts of my soul.

I reach for the handle of the door and try to open it, but the metal's crumpled, and the door won't budge. Rodion sees me struggling, takes a look at Shawn, then heads over to me, his gun poised at Shawn. Shawn wriggles away, and in one quick movement, Rodion points his gun at him and pulls the trigger. His kneecap explodes.

I watch. I can't look away. Shawn screams, a mess of broken bones and blood, but Rodion just pulls the trigger again. His second kneecap explodes.

As he nears me, he calls over his shoulder, "You'd better not fucking die. I am *not* done with you yet."

Rodion reaches me, grabs the door, and yanks it hard, but it doesn't budge. Behind him, Shawn cries like a baby, trying to move his broken body on the ground, blood dripping from his open wounds, but he doesn't get far.

I climb over the console, fall into the passenger seat, and Rodion pries the door open. I fall into his arms.

"I should kill him now," he mutters. "But not yet. I want him to suffer, Ember." His eyes flick back to mine, and he does that thing that I love. His finger under my chin, he holds my gaze. It's never felt more poignant. I shiver, looking at raw brutality and undying devotion wrapped into one. "Tell me you want this, Ember. Say the word, and this ends."

My breath catches. I swallow hard, my eyes locked onto his.

"Yes, please." My voice shakes. "He won't stop. It will be another woman next. He's insane, Rodion. A predator. I can't let him go on."

Rodion's smirk is razor-sharp. Terrifying.

Rodion, in real life, makes every book boyfriend I've ever met pale in comparison.

Leaning in, his lips brush over my ear.

"He'll watch first," he murmurs, his hand already tugging at my hips. "*Then* he dies."

My pulse races, and the blood roars in my veins, adrenaline thrumming. I didn't know until I was here—until I truly *felt* this—that I've never felt more owned in my life.

His mouth claims mine, bruised and unforgiving. The knife I still hold slips from my hand as his fingers tangle in my hair, tilting my head back to deepen the kiss. I melt into him, my body arching as heat surges through me.

"Need one minute." He breathes into my ear. "That son of a bitch is trying to get away. I want him to watch. Come with me, Ember."

My skin crawls as my pulse ratchets higher. I nod and walk with him, the cold night air biting at my skin. Shawn screams and begs as Rodion yanks him around and ties him with the same restraints he used on me.

"I don't want to hear your fucking voice," Rodion says before he gags him and slaps Shawn's cheek. "There ya go, asshole."

God, I love him so fucking much. I don't know what that says about me, but I don't care.

I want him.

I want him to burn the memory of every painful touch I've ever felt from my mind. I want him to sear himself into my memory, to break down every wall I've constructed and show me what it means to be well and truly loved. I want him. I want *us*.

I want it all.

Rodion stalks over to me, and just like that first time I saw him, he's dripping with lethal Bratva energy. My body sings. My heart soars. When he reaches me, his mouth burns mine with a ferocity that takes my breath away. He grips my ass, and I shift the miles of fabric to hitch my leg up. I love the feel of his hot, strong hand on my thigh.

He lifts me in his arms and carries me to the clearing sheltered beneath the pines. His hot skin on mine warms me despite the cold. Moonlight filters through the trees.

Rodion's grip tightens around my waist. When his mouth meets mine, everything else falls away. His kiss is feral and bruising, the kind that leaves marks.

I feel the rough scrape of his stubble against my skin as his hands grip my ass, pulling me closer.

I lift my leg, sliding the fabric of my dress up, giving him full access to the bare skin of my thigh. He wastes no time, fingers searing into me, teasing until I don't feel the cold anymore, and I feel the brush of his rough knuckles against the heat between my legs.

I break the kiss, gasping against his lips.

"Rodion."

His growl vibrates against my throat as he lifts me effortlessly, cradling me in his arms as if I weigh nothing.

The rough bark of a pine scrapes against my back as he pins me there, his body pressing into mine, his breath hot against my neck. His hands roam, dragging down the straps of my dress until the cool night air hardens my nipples.

He steps back, eyes burning into me as he drinks me in.

"I'll burn everything before us from your memory," he rasps, reaching for his belt buckle in one fluid motion. He tugs it from his pants in one pull. "Do you understand me?"

I nod, breathless and aching.

His mouth trails down my collarbone, teeth grazing, biting, sucking until I'm dizzy with need and panting for him. His fingers push aside the fabric pooling at my hips, where I'm already wet and waiting.

"You're so fucking ready for me," he whispers, voice thick with approval. His thumb circles my clit slowly, torturing me.

"Rodion." I moan.

He gives me a wicked grin full of promises.

"Beg for me, little queen."

I can't stop the moan that slips free as his fingers slide inside me, curling just right. His other hand cups the back of my neck, pulling me into another fierce kiss.

I come apart for him, trembling, gasping his name, but he doesn't stop. I feel the hot, hard press of his cock against my legs.

"Tell me you want this." His voice is rough, barely hanging onto control.

"I want this, Rodion. I want *you*. All of you."

Pulling back, his eyes meet mine with surprise. He knows as well as I do what that means. Every bit of him, the hardened criminal and wise guy, protector and husband. *All* of him.

He drives into me in one hard thrust. I arch into him, legs

wrapping around his waist as he fills me. I love the way he stretches me to the edge of pleasure and pain.

Rodion doesn't hold back—he pounds into me, wild and relentless, each thrust pushing me harder against the tree. I'm begging and pleading, wild with need, as we hold each other so tightly we'll leave marks.

"You're mine, Ember. *My wife.* No one else touches you."

I cling to him, shattered and whole.

"Yours."

He drives deeper, his hand fisting my hair to tilt my head back so he can kiss the tender skin at my neck.

"I love you," I whisper. The world and everyone in it has ceased to exist. All that matters is *us*.

Pleasure explodes in my veins, hot and relentless, as he comes inside me. I gasp for air, gripping him, everything around narrowed to just the two of us.

"I love you," I repeat as his hot seed spills into me, and I pant through the aftershocks of bliss. "I love you."

Rodion growls against my skin, his lips tracing down my neck as if committing me to memory. I hold onto him, the heat of his body against mine a shield. The cool night air barely touches us.

His thumb brushes along my cheek, tender in a way only I ever see.

"Say it again," he whispers, his voice raw.

I cup his face, stubble scraping my hand. "I love you."

Rodion closes his eyes for a brief second, exhaling like the words loosen something inside him.

"You're mine now, Ember. No running."

I smile at him. "I wasn't planning on it."

His lips quirk in the boyish smirk I've come to crave before he looks behind him.

He tightens his arms around me, shielding me from the sight. But I can't turn away.

This is me. This is *us*.

"You know what I have to do."

I swallow hard and whisper, "Yeah, I do. Bury his body and sleep like a fucking baby."

He kisses me, hard and passionate, a silent declaration of solidarity.

Rodion presses a kiss to my forehead before slipping his jacket over my shoulders. "Shh, baby. This is almost over."

He steps back toward Shawn, who groans to himself.

"I told you once," Rodion says in a low growl. Deadly. "You'd regret laying hands on her, didn't I? I told you to leave her alone. I told you I never wanted to see you near her again. Didn't I?"

Shawn begs, his eyes wide with terror, but Rodion doesn't care.

Neither do I.

Rodion's gun presses to Shawn's temple before he looks my way. I meet his gaze, steady and sure. This isn't just vengeance. It's cleansing. It's retribution. It's ensuring no one—not me, not another innocent girl—ever gets hurt by this monster again.

Rodion pulls the trigger.

The shot echoes through the night.

I don't scream. I don't look away. I need to see that he won't hurt me or anyone else ever again. I watch Shawn's body fall to the ground with a thud, his blood saturating the earth around him.

When Rodion finally stands, it's with the slow deliberation of a man who's made peace with his choices.

I love him for that.

I pull his jacket tighter around myself. It's warm, and it smells like him. It feels like a symbol of Rodion as my shield.

He makes phone calls before he returns to me and gathers me in his arms.

"Are you ready to go back to the gala?"

I stare at him in surprise but think it over. I swallow hard.

"Let me change into something a bit more comfortable?"

He smirks in the darkness.

CHAPTER 28

RODION

I DIDN'T SET out to test her. But I know if we return to the gala, she'll be permanently immersed in my world—brutal, unforgiving, but loyal.

I'm checking her for signs of shock, but she's only quiet, clinging to me.

"Stop," she finally says. "You have no idea. The memory of what he did haunted me so much worse than what we just did. That was awful, yeah, but I'm...god, I'm relieved. But I need a stiff drink, stat."

The gala is in full swing when we return. Laughter spills from the open doors, mingling with strains of violin music.

I get her a stiff drink. Actually, two.

It should feel surreal—stepping back into the world of glittering celebration. It doesn't for me.

I feel nothing but relief. Maybe that's fucked up.

"You alright?" I ask Ember. She's cleaned herself up and changed, with fresh makeup and her hair down her shoulders, loose and wavy.

"Yes," she says with that majestic energy fitting of the queen she is. She stands next to me, her chin held high, her fiery red hair cascading over the silk of her dress.

She doesn't shrink back or hide.

Maybe she's as fucked up as I am.

God, I fucking love her.

I watch the way their eyes track her, both men and women alike, as if they're drawn to her beauty, her magnetic energy, and can't quite put it into words. A part of me wants to growl at all of them to look away.

Because she's mine.

But when Ember turns toward me and buries her head on my chest, I wrap my arms protectively around her. It was a lot tonight, but she's handling it so well.

"You sure?" I whisper in her ear.

"Yeah," she repeats. "I feel like I should be a lot more upset about what happened, but I..." Her voice gets a little choked, and she doesn't complete her sentence. "I needed closure. I needed to know there's no going back, that it can't possibly happen again."

"You don't have to explain. I understand." I tip my finger under her chin and bring her gaze to mine. I stare into her bright green eyes, and my heart swells because I know—I'm staring into my forever. "But I want you to trust me to handle the details. The rest of this. Can you do that?"

Holding my gaze, she nods. "Yeah."

Ekaterina swirls her champagne, oblivious to what we just did or what we're talking about, but I know that even if she did know details, she wouldn't judge. After all, it was her son's cleanup crew I borrowed.

"I've heard you're a photographer, Ember?" she asks with a welcome smile. "We hired someone, but they didn't show." She rolls her eyes. "Sometimes our reputation gets in the way of such things."

"I am," Ember says. She stands up tall. "Do you want me to take pictures?"

"Just while we hand over the big check," she says with a wink.

Ember slides into artist mode, her eyes trained on various people. I watch her take snapshot after snapshot until finally, she lowers the camera and turns to me, her cheeks either flushed from the heat of the room or from the weight of my eyes on her.

"Done yet?" I'm getting impatient to have her alone. My thumb grazes the small of her back.

Rafail and Semyon join us, their hands in their pockets. Rafail gives me a curt nod. "All taken care of."

Semyon nods. "Anything you need from us now?"

I shake my head. "A promise that nothing happens tonight that will tear me and my wife from much-deserved rest."

Rafail nods. "Granted."

I turn to Ember. It feels like we've had three nights rolled up into one, and I'm at the end of an exhausting marathon.

"Let's get some rest. No more eyes on anyone else, baby."

Her breath catches before her hand slides along the front of my jacket, tugging me closer. I grin at her.

She gives me the barest hint of a kiss, but it's enough to make my blood hum.

Let them see. Let them all know exactly who she belongs to.

I pull back, brushing a strand of hair from her face and tucking it behind an ear. "Let's get out of here."

"Don't we have to, like... wait until people are going home?"

I shake my head. "Nope."

We head to the room. Ember's fingers are threaded through mine as if to ground herself to me. Leaning into me on the landing, she presses her cheek to my shoulder. "We survived the night."

"Yeah," I say on a breath. "All of it. It feels like we've lived a full lifetime in twenty-four hours."

"But we did it together."

"I knew we would."

Back in the room, I lock the door and throw every dead bolt into place.

I don't say anything. I tug the zipper on the back of her new dress down, watching the silky material peel away. It pools at her feet, leaving her bare.

Wordlessly, she reaches for me next and unfastens every button on my dress shirt before pulling it off. Leaning in, she kisses the swell of my bicep. "So hot," she whispers with a wink. "So fucking hot."

"Oh yeah?" I flex just to show off, and she predictably whimpers. She leans over and kisses my cheek next.

"Shower?" she asks, her eyes flicking up to mine.

"That sounds good. And food?"

"Mm. I'm starving. Can we order delivery or something?"

"Anything for my queen." I pull out my phone and open an app. "Anything in particular?"

"Pizza," she breathes out. "New York style, with pepperoni, and if they have any cheesecake... supposed to be pretty good around here."

I grin at her and order a large pepperoni pizza and a few slices of New York-style cheesecake. I text Yana and ask her to bring it up when it arrives, since she's the one most likely to mind her own business.

I turn the shower on and toss our dirty clothes to the side. Steam billows up around us. I open the shower curtain and gesture for her to step inside. I welcome the hot water as it curls around our bodies.

On a normal day, this would be like foreplay. Tonight? Sex is the furthest thing from my mind, and I want to make sure that she feels safe and taken care of.

It seems she wants the same for me. The way she touches me tenderly, smoothing a washcloth over the suds until the water runs clear.

The shower is small, not really built for two, but we make it work.

"I don't realize how unnaturally huge you are until you're squashed under a showerhead," she says, her lips twitching.

I pinch her wet ass with my palm, and she squeals. "I'll give you unnaturally huge," I mutter before I grip her other cheek and knead. I bend and kiss her.

Water streams over us, the rhythmic sound of it soothing like rain on glass. She leans on my chest, her forehead pressed to my collarbone. My hand rests lightly on the back of her neck, fingers tangled in the wet strands of her hair.

I spin her around and tilt her head back. Her eyes close when I massage shampoo into her hair, suds it up, then rinse it slowly. Conditioner next, then another rinse.

I imagine we're washing everything away. The memory of her assault. The lies between us. Anything that will tear us apart ever again.

Neither of us speaks. We don't need to.

My chest rises and falls beneath her touch when she turns to face me, soap bubbling under her palm. I haven't let anyone take care of me like this in... god, I can't remember. My parents died when I was so young, and Rafail had his work cut out for him with a houseful of kids. We learned independence early.

I reach for her hand and kiss her palm.

"Thank you, little queen." Her soft smile warms me through. When she draws closer to me, I stifle a groan. My cock stiffens between us, but this isn't the time.

"Happy to see me?" she says with a smirk, her brow raised. "Or…"

I bend and kiss her shoulder when she yawns widely. "Always. But you're exhausted."

"Yeah." Her voice is a breathy whisper.

"You have to stay awake until the pizza gets here, and then you can sleep for days for all I care." She needs to eat.

"I can handle that," she says on another yawn.

I turn her around to rinse her off.

It feels like we've walked through something we can't really name—an unspoken battle neither of us wants to admit we were fighting.

It's more than Shawn. More than her fears and mine. Neither of us does vulnerable easily—and yet here we are. We stand under the stream of water, bare in more ways than one.

I shift, reaching past her to adjust the water temperature. I move carefully, almost reverently, as if I could shatter this moment between us. But there's nothing fragile about the way she turns to me and holds on, her arms about my waist.

Steam coils around us. My scars stand out against the warmth of my skin. Wordlessly, she traces one of them, brushing over it as if committing it to memory.

My hand covers hers, stilling the movement. My thumb grazes over her knuckles in slow circles.

Her fingers slide down my arm, stopping just above my wrist. Slowly, she traces the thick gold band on my finger.

Her voice is quiet. "What if I don't want temporary, Rodion?"

I bend my head, kissing her temple. "What if I don't either?"

She draws in a sharp breath as if she wants to believe me, wants to believe herself, but can't quite trust it all yet.

I brush the wet hair from her face. "Listen, Ember. I'm not going anywhere. Tonight was about survival. Survival is only the first step."

She swallows hard, her fingers tightening around my wrist. We stand, wrapped in the heat and silence, letting the pounding water drown out the rest of the world until our skin is wrinkled and her stomach growls audibly.

I reach behind her and shut the water off just as a knock sounds at the door. "Food's here!" Yana shouts.

She smirks. "Guess you really are staying, then. One way to keep you here."

I smile at her. "Are you really afraid I'm going to leave, little queen?"

She holds my gaze for a long moment, searchingly, before she finally shakes her head with a sigh. "No. I don't think you will."

"Woman, you couldn't chase me away if you tried."

I wrap her in a towel, then wrap another around my waist. Wordlessly, she sits up in bed, and I get the food outside the door. We open the box on the bed.

"Rafail would kill me for this," I say, lifting a slice and handing it to her.

She swallows and licks her lips. "Rafail can fuck off. I can't think of a better way to honeymoon than pizza and cheesecake. You?"

I take a bite of the pizza and groan. "I would've said sex, but right now, this pizza tastes better than sex."

Ember laughs softly, tucking her legs beneath her. The towel falls off her shoulder and pools in her lap. The warmth in her eyes lingers longer than usual. "You know," she says with a twinkle in her eye. "If I were still making videos, I'd be running to make a video about this scene right here."

I shake my head at her. "Why?"

She shrugs. "We can talk all day about a hot, tatted guy taking care of us. But being comfortable enough to share a pizza, half-naked, in bed... could be the hunger talking, but this is the stuff of dreams."

We eat in silence. In the distance, we can still hear the muted sounds of people talking and music playing, but it seems we're almost a world apart here.

She tilts her head up just enough to meet my eyes. "I meant what I said, you know. About not wanting temporary."

"You say that now..." I want to believe her; of course I do. But I want her to say the same thing after she's accepted what this really means. I'm not built for soft edges and quiet endings. I don't like the thought of my world swallowing her whole.

But when I look down, she's already watching me, eyes steady and unwavering. Like she sees the storm inside me and isn't afraid of getting caught in it.

"I mean it," she says softly, her fingers tightening around mine. "I know what I'm asking for."

She drops her crust in the box, grabs another slice of pizza, and takes a huge bite.

I take her crust and bite it.

"Things sometimes go to shit, Ember. We don't always have happy endings. Sometimes—"

She stops me with her hand on my arm. "Rodion. I get it. I know." Shaking her head, she smiles at me. "I've read all the books, remember?"

"Oh, right." I grin at her. "You're an expert."

She giggles. "I don't know if I want to kiss you or write fanfic about you."

"Oh, really?"

She sighs and says in a lilting, teasing voice, "The way he's morally gray in all the right ways..."

I snort.

"The way I need you to *ruin me*, sir."

I shake my head.

"Do you have a tragic backstory, a deep emotional wound, and a loyalty kink with a heavy side of competency porn?" She sighs dramatically and brings her hand to her brow. "I'm *dead*."

I finally get it. "Oh my god. You're pretending to be a fangirl."

"Yes and no," she says with a shrug. "I'm not really pretending. Listen, Rodion. I know you're worried about me losing it when things go sideways, but I... I know what you're like when things go *right*."

That hits deeper than I thought it would. I tilt her chin up with two fingers, holding her gaze. She licks her lips adorably. "And anything else we can figure out."

She smiles back at me. "That's what happily ever afters are made for."

CHAPTER 29

EMBER

Moscow. Is. *Beautiful.*

Turns out, no one could tie Rodion to anything and my video caused momentary suspicion but no more.

We still decided to leave town for a bit.

I thought I would want to go back to my apartment, but I find that the memories of Shawn are too hard to shake. I knew it was time for me to leave, and now I have good reason to.

I always wanted to travel the world. And after seeing homes like the Romanov mansion? I have no interest in going back to that apartment. I'm also not leaving Rodion's side, and he needs a bed and shower big enough to accommodate him.

And what better way to practice my photography?

I sit on the balcony of the home Rodion grew up in, my

camera perched in my lap, and wonder... is home really a place? Or is it who you're with?

Maybe home is the weight of Rodion's jacket on my shoulders, the faint scent of him reassuring. Maybe it's the quiet hum of voices drifting from inside the house, voices I'm slowly learning to know and trust.

Maybe home is a place you return to, a place where you're accepted and cared for, no matter your past. Maybe it's a sense of belonging that's unshakable. Because here, with Rodion, he's *home.* And when I'm with him... this is my home too.

I lift my camera, framing the snow-dusted trees that line their property. Their home is right outside of Moscow but has the perfect view of the iconic city. A light fog curls around the bare branches, chilling yet beautiful, as if softening the sharpness of winter.

Rodion steps onto the balcony behind me, leaning against the railing. "Of all the things you could steal from me, I never thought it would be that old jacket."

I shrug. "What's yours is mine."

I love the sound of his low, dark chuckle. "As long as you're mine, that's all I care about."

I smile. I know. He has more clothes in his closet than I've owned in my lifetime, a testament to the wealth he grew up with, but he doesn't care about any of them.

His hair is still damp from a shower, curling slightly at the temples. It gives him an almost boyish charm. He watches me quietly, something he does a lot these days.

We've been in Russia now for a full month. I'm absolutely terrible at speaking Russian, but fortunately, his family has infinite patience.

I take photo after photo, moving around the balcony for different angles. He watches me in silence.

"You keep looking at me like that, and I'll have to charge you for portraits." I lower the camera just long enough to meet his gaze.

He smirks. "I'd pay."

I grin at him. It feels so good, so freeing to just smile and let it all go. To enjoy the moment without worrying about tomorrow. To know that I have all I need, right here.

When I shiver, he reaches for my hand and frowns when he finds my fingers cold. "That's enough of this. Inside with you. You're turning into an icicle."

"I want to take one more—"

"Ember." His tone is implacable. It still makes my heart do a little somersault in my chest.

"Mmm?"

"Do what your king tells you, little queen," he whispers in my ear. "Behave yourself."

I know he's right, but it's fun to push back a little.

We head downstairs, the sound of laughter coming from the living room. I glance through the glass doors, catching a glimpse of Zoya and Polina sprawled across the plush sofa, their heads bent together as they watch something on a phone.

Yana's gone back with her husband, but the rest of them are here still. Zoya lives here with Polina and Rafail, and though Semyon and Rodion both have a place of their own, it seems we spend more time here than anywhere else. Not that I'm complaining. This place is *epic*.

Semyon lounges in the corner, his arms crossed, but there's an uncharacteristic twitch to his lips. Rafail sits near the fireplace, a glass of whiskey in hand, watching them all with the quiet authority of someone who doesn't need to say much to command a room.

It all feels... normal. Strangely domestic for a Bratva family. I expected them to be colder, more aloof.

Rodion's arm slides around my waist. "They like you, you know."

I lean into his warmth. "And I like them," I say softly, watching as Rafail ruffles Zoya's hair, and she swats his hand away. "Your family."

"They're not always this... easy," he says.

"I don't need easy, Rodion. I need real."

A sharp knock at the glass startles us. We pull away like two teens caught making out behind the school. Zoya stands on the other side of the doors, grinning at us. She motions for us to come inside, mouthing something I can't quite make out.

Rodion presses a quick kiss to my forehead. "Let's go. You want to see real?"

I let him pull me inside. I love it here, but I do feel a little shy around all of them.

Zoya barely waits for us to step inside before she plops down on the couch, swinging her legs over Polina's lap. "You're late," she says teasingly. "We saved you a seat, but you were too busy making out."

Polina snickers and playfully smacks Zoya's leg. "Behave, little sister. I told you they'd come in eventually."

Rodion huffs, guiding me to a vacant loveseat. "You're lucky we put up with you two."

Rafail's gaze flickers toward us. "Part of the deal. Family, you know."

Family.

I do know.

I clear my throat and decide to dive right into what's been plaguing me. "Has there been any... you know... talk or blowback or whatever because of Shawn?"

"Yes," Rafail says soberly, meeting my gaze. "Several women have come forward to the press in California, stating that he sexually harassed them at work, and one says she's a former girlfriend he assaulted. The general consensus is that they're glad he's missing but not surprised."

"There's even talk online from a few women saying they hoped the women he hurt finally banded together to bring, what did they say... *poetic justice.*"

My heart aches. It isn't the answer I expected. Rodion's hand squeezes my knee.

Now that Shawn is gone, it feels like I can start rebuilding in a way I couldn't before, when I was always looking over my shoulder, always waiting for the next shoe to drop.

"This has all made me think, Ember." Rodion's gaze snaps to Rafail as if he doesn't know what to expect. I wait myself.

"Yes?"

"Maybe you should start doing your book reviews again."

I feel my jaw drop open. "What?"

The room stills for half a second.

I don't know if the rest of them know how much this matters to me. I was willing to table it all for the sake of his family, but it feels as if I lost a part of me in the process.

"You... want me to pick up reviews again?"

Rafail leans forward, resting his elbows on his knees. "You can thank Zoya for this. She pointed out that no one will ever actually believe that you married into a Bratva family. Even if the media or commenters catch on, it will seem like it's part of the fun of it all."

Polina grins. "It's true. You look way too innocent."

"Thanks?" I laugh, tucking my hair behind my ear. My cheeks feel hot. Rodion's arm falls heavily over my shoulders.

"She's right," Zoya chimes in. "Think about it. No one thinks of us as... well, normal. But you? You break that stereotype." Her eyes shine with something I can't quite place. Pride? "Plus," she continues, shaking her head. "I haven't had a good book rec in *ages*, and I'm dying for another."

I laugh. "I can give you plenty one on one."

Zoya's eyes shine bright. "It's not the *same*, Ember. Plus, I'm not the only one who wants to hear from you."

She's right. I look down at my hands, suddenly bashful. I still get messages and emails from my friends, and the truth is... I miss it. I think I'd see the book world in a whole new light now.

Like my photography, my love of all things romance is a part of who I am, an extension of my hopes and dreams. I live through the pages of my books in a way that's hard to explain. I love romance because it's a constant reminder that even normal people deserve to be loved, that it's healthy to want to dream, and that everyone deserves a happy ending.

"Maybe this is Rafail's version of a local gala," Rodion whispers in my ear. "Charming the locals and all that."

I turn toward Rafail. "I don't know if my unhinged book reviews will... butter up the locals."

He shrugs. "We'll see."

For a moment, I don't respond. They've offered an olive branch. It's not just the suggestion but the knowledge that I belong here. This family that I expected to keep me at arm's length is drawing me in. It's the underlying acceptance beneath it.

Rodion presses a kiss to my temple. The book world had one thing right: it is the very sweetest thing to be kissed that way. I stifle the need to ask him to do it again.

"See?" he whispers in my ear. "Told you they like you."

I nudge him playfully. "Careful, I might start believing I belong here."

"Woman," Rodion growls in my ear. I shiver and lean in closer.

"God, get a room," Semyon says, but his eyes twinkle at us.

I don't know what I expected from them, but it wasn't this.

I settle deeper into Rodion's side, appreciating the warmth of him beside me. It's hard to imagine that only a few months ago, I only dreamed of a Bratva boyfriend, and now... here I am. His family—*our* family—keeps talking, laughing, filling the space with a comfort I didn't know I craved. Because even though they live by a code of ethics I never knew, the undying loyalty that weaves them all together makes me feel part of something so much bigger.

Polina looks over at me. As I've come to get to know her better, I've been drawn to her resilience and down-to-earth nature. "So? What's your first review going to be, Ember?"

"Ooh, I don't know. But definitely something *Bratva*, no?"

Zoya gasps, sitting up straighter. "You must have at least ten books waiting for you by now!"

"Minimum," I say with a laugh.

Rodion's hand tightens at my waist. "Careful, little queen. You'll start giving them ideas."

"Sorry, not sorry," I mutter, which gets me a vicious tickle. "Hey!"

But the question lingers in the back of my mind long after the laughter dies down. *Can* I go back to the way things were before? It seems like the old Ember is a different person. She's not gone... but changed.

I used to sit in my apartment alone, making sure the spider cracks in the walls and the peeling paint didn't make it into the videos. I hid behind a string of fairy lights, glowing about the latest book boyfriend... and now that I have a book boyfriend of my very own, the fairy tale doesn't hold the same appeal.

Or does it?

Just because this is my life now doesn't mean I can't still live a thousand other lives in the pages of my books. Isn't that what it's all about? Not just finding the most perfect book boyfriend but... finding friends. Being understood. Feeling heard.

Finding *love* of all different kinds. Romantic, yes, but so much more—I look around the room at sweet Zoya and Polina, Semyon and Rafail.

Zoya throws a pillow at Semyon when he teases her again, and Rafail calmly palms the pillow and gives them both a warning look. Polina tugs on his shirt sleeve and whispers something in his ear that makes him soften a bit.

I take in a slow breath and release it.

This *is* my life now.

"Maybe I'll start with that latest book they're all talking about? The one about the girl who felt like she didn't belong anywhere... but found her home in the most unexpected place."

Polina grins. "Sounds like a bestseller to me."

CHAPTER 30

I SIT CROSS-LEGGED on the floor of my apartment, camera propped up on a stack of books, a coffee mug that's gone cold beside me. The room is more than half-empty—boxes stacked in the corner, half-packed, ready to go. But my reading nook is still in place, the familiar stack of books in my hand as comforting as a weighted blanket, twinkling under the glow of the white light. Fairy lights will forever hold magic for me.

Rodion hangs up the phone with his brothers. I told him once he was competent, and he's shown me that in spades in the past few days. When his enemies out here couldn't prove anything he'd done, following an investigation on the sudden disappearance of Shawn Steele, I watched my husband...*my husband*...handle every detail. He methodically extinguished every fire with a precision that was unnerving as it was impressive. No panic, temper, or hesitation. Every step he took was deliberate, every detail accounted for as though he'd mapped it all out before the events unfolded.

I'd knew he had a dangerous mind but watching him handle every facet of a high-stakes situation, I saw how terrifyingly capable he can be.

That *thrills* me.

The little red recording light blinks at me, and for a second... I hesitate. It's been so long since I faced this screen, this world, that I've almost forgotten who I am in the book space. But then I remember Zoya, her eyes alight when she talks about all things romance... and I face the screen.

I decided it would be fun to come back in a live feed. Why not?

I lean in, my heart beating faster, grinning like I've kept the biggest secret in the world. "I'm *baaaack.* And oh, how I've missed you all!"

The words echo in the room, playful and familiar, and it feels so damn right. I sigh contentedly.

"I know. I disappeared for a little while. You probably thought I got kidnapped by one of those morally gray mafia boyfriends we're all swooning over." I pause dramatically, ignoring the way Rodion chokes on the beer he's drinking. I'll have to edit his choking sounds out. I pause, tucking my hair behind my ear. "And I'll tell you... you'd be not that far off."

The chat lights up. I can hear notifications pinging, but I ignore them for now. I lean back, folding my arms.

"So... what have I missed? Besides every single mafia romance released in the past *month*?"

A shadow moves at the edge of the frame, just out of focus. I pretend to be surprised like we didn't plan this whole thing.

I fight a smirk. "I *was* going to do this whole video alone, but it seems someone decided to lurk."

Rodion leans against the doorframe, his arms crossed over his bare chest. He watches me with that dark, unreadable expression that always makes my heart race. I don't know if I'll ever get used to the look of him shirtless, sweatpants hung low on his hips, a black mask covering the lower half of his face.

Zing.

I turn the camera slowly toward him. "See? On brand, girls."

He cocks his head, eyes narrowing on me. "What is that supposed to mean, little queen?"

At the "little queen," the comment section goes wild.

I grin. "Exactly what you think it means, sir," I tease, shifting my focus to him. "Look at you. You *are* the mafia trope come to life."

He steps forward, tugging the mask down just enough to smirk at me. "Careful, little queen. You're skirting the edge. Keep saying things like that, and I might have to play the part."

I toss the back of my hand to my brow. "No. No. Please don't."

The chat *explodes* as he prowls closer to me and fists my hair.

Yum.

Didn't know I had a voyeuristic streak, but here we are.

Maybe I'll need another theme for my account...

"Can you take your mask off?" I say in a low voice, biting my lip.

He drags it off, facing only me, so they can't see his face on-screen. He drops it on the stack of books beside me. I grin and face the camera. "I would say I created a monster, girls, but believe me when I tell you... he was firmly established in that role before we first met."

Rodion leans down and brushes his lips to mine. "Camera off now, little queen."

I lean in with a little cackle of glee and shut it off.

"I am never going to hear the end of this, you know," I say with a laugh, even as my heart beats faster and arousal pools between my legs. Who knew that bringing my two lives together, my fantasies and hopes and dreams, right here in the open with my real-life book boyfriend, would be so utterly addictively *hot*?

His gaze lingers, dark and heavy, the corner of his mouth tugging into that smirk that always makes my pulse skip a beat. The soft hum of the city outside buzzes in the background, but here, it feels like we exist in our own world.

"You enjoyed that too much," I murmur, leaning against the pile of books behind me.

He follows, one knee pressing between my legs, as he braces his hands on either side of me.

Oh yes. *Love.*

I love that so much.

"I'm not the only one," he says, eyes flicking to where I nervously tug my bottom lip between my teeth.

I smile, not bothering to deny it.

His hand skims down my side, then back up again, before he hooks a finger in the string of fairy lights.

"Rodion," I say warningly. "Don't you—"

"Careful, little queen. You're not about to tell me what I can and cannot do, are you?" His eyes glint dangerously at me. I bite my lip. "That's what I thought," he finishes, tugging the fairy lights into a straight strand.

He bends and snags the hem of my dress with his teeth, dragging it up so he can divest me of my clothes. The little dress I wear falls into a heap at the foot of my bed, followed in short time by my bra and panties.

Oh my god.

I watch, mesmerized, as he loops the string of lights around my wrists, down under my breasts, over the swell of my belly, between my legs, and finishes at my ankles. I'm trussed up like a Christmas tree. I couldn't get away now if I tried.

The first real kiss is slow, deliberate. His mouth claims mine with a kind of unhurried patience that makes my body sing with need. The books behind me shift slightly as I arch into him, the fairy lights casting soft shadows across the room. I kiss the edge of his jawline when he bends closer to me, my wrists too secured for me to touch him.

"Is this safe?" I ask, jerking my chin at the fairy lights. "These books aren't exactly pillows, Rodion—"

"Quiet, Ember. It's my turn now."

He arranges the pillows and blankets so I'm cocooned on either side, the books arranged all about me, ensuring I'll never look at them the same way again.

I gasp when he takes two of the thickest ones and slides them under my ass.

"Shh." He bends his mouth and licks the side of my thigh. He suckles, teeth scraping the tender skin. My hips rise, needing the wet heat of his mouth just *there*.

"I told you," he whispers in my ear. "I'd let you make those videos under the condition that I'm your only real-life book boyfriend."

"Hmm, I don't know about—*oooh*."

He silences me with a firm swipe of his tongue right where I need him most. Oh my god, it feels like heaven and hell wrapped all together.

Yes, please.

He teases me with the tip of his tongue before he licks lazily, anchoring himself on my hips with a groan of pleasure. Somehow, hearing how much this excites him makes *me* even hotter for him.

My mouth is dry, and I'm stifling a pant when he suckles again, the perfect pressure of his tongue making my hips jerk with need. Again and again, I'm drowning in pleasure when he reaches for my nipples and tweaks them. Pleasure cascades down my spine like molten lava, and I shiver in glee.

"Please," I whisper. "Yes, *please*."

His low, dark chuckle between my legs makes me whimper. Again, he licks me before he slides one hand down between my legs and thrusts two thick fingers inside me. Pleasure bursts inside me, and I whimper out a moan.

"*Rodion*," I whisper. "Oh my god, please, yes, yes, right there."

"Beg for me," he grates against my thighs, his breath hot on my skin.

"Please. Please let me come. I want to—oh god, yes— please!"

"Come for me, little queen," he whispers. "Come on my tongue."

My back arches, and the books beneath me shift, but Rodion doesn't stop.

His fingers dig into my hips, anchoring me to the bed as I shatter, gasping his name in a moan. My thighs tremble around him, every nerve on fire as waves of ecstasy crash over me.

I'm still shaking when he finally lifts his head, his mouth trailing lazy kisses along the inside of my thigh. His eyes meet mine, dark with satisfaction. I didn't know I really wanted to be owned by someone like him... and now I do.

"There she is," he says, pressing a kiss to my pulse at my wrist. "That's my girl."

His dark, whispered approval makes me want to sing. I live for this.

I can't find the words just yet. I'm boneless and breathless as he gathers me in his arms and untangles the lights around my legs. His hot, thick cock presses into my belly.

"I love you," I breathe out, still blissed out beneath him, as he presses my thighs apart with his knee and glides his cock to my entrance. My hips jerk when he moves through my slick heat, and I hold my breath when he nudges my entrance.

"I love you," he whispers in my ear just before he thrusts into me. I love the feeling of being so full, so completely his.

I gasp as he sinks deeper, stretching me with perfect, deliberate strokes. His hands press into my hips, grounding me. The heat between us is so strong, so pervasive, as the world shrinks to just the two of us. I cling to him, to his raw power, as he thrusts again. He stills, buried to the hilt. My pussy clenches around him, eager for more.

He kisses my cheek, working a perfect rhythm in and out, filling and teasing, until I'm a blubbering mess, arching into him between strokes. I shudder, a wave of pleasure overtaking me, pleasure building again as I tighten around him. Desperate for more.

"Rodion—" His name falls from my lips, a half prayer and half plea.

I grip his hair, dragging him closer to me. He thrusts harder, his breath hot against me. "*Mine.*"

"Yours," I gasp, echoing the sentiment. My legs tighten around him, pulling him closer, deeper, until the two of us cease to exist as we meld into one.

The coil inside me tightens, winding until I'm panting and begging incoherently.

"Come, baby," he demands, his own voice hoarse. "Come when I do."

I break apart beneath him as he drives deep, chasing his own release. He spills into me with a shudder and a groan as pleasure crashes through me. I'm half-blinded, drowning in ecstasy.

He collapses gently beside me, his weight comforting as he traces lazy kisses on my shoulder. The fairy lights flicker like a silent reminder of the magic between us.

Finally, after a while, he lifts his head. "How'd I do?"

I slap his massive shoulder and snort.

"Not bad, Bratva boy. Might need another round to do a comparison test."

He groans and flops beside me. "Of all the times to test me, woman..."

We curl up in bed. The half-packed boxes can wait.

He reaches for my phone and hands it to me. "Go ahead. See what they said. Maybe tell them you were otherwise occupied, wink wink."

I take my phone and kiss him. "Stop being so perfect already."

"Oh yeah? I can take your phone away and make you worship me as your king. Would that destroy the fantasy illusion?"

I grumble. "Yes, actually, it would."

I love the way he chuckles when I slap his arm playfully with a book. I click on the notifications and nearly squeal.

This is so fun.

> Girl noooo. You've been keeping him from us the whole time? Where do I sign upppp 

> The way he took off that mask and whispered in your ear? I need holy water, rn 

> Not me rewatching the video on repeat to catch every detail of his shadow lurking in the background…

> OMG. Welcome BACK, "little queen!" 🤪

> The way he looks at you like he will LEGIT burn the world down for you. 🫠 🩶 🔥

> Forget the book recs. I just need to know when the second part of this video drops, pretty pretty pls 👀 🍿

I grin at him. "I knew they'd love you."

We read through the comments and reply. I swear his head grows three sizes.

"Stay humble, Bratva boy."

"Call me that one more time, and I'll reopen my account *just* to post that video of you over my lap."

I can't help but giggle at that.

He kisses my cheek. "Baby, they love *you*. You're the one who keeps the fantasy alive. Who keeps the hope alive." He shakes his head. "And I love that for you."

I sigh and look around my apartment before I shut the phone off. I rest my head against his chest, feeling the steady thrum of his heart beneath my cheek. "I guess I'm just nervous. It feels like closing a door."

Rodion tilts my chin up, his thumb tracing my jaw. "Then leave it open. Just don't let it keep you from walking through the next one."

He's right.

There's nothing tying me here anymore. Shawn is gone, and for the first time in a long time, I'm not looking over my shoulder. This apartment—the one I once considered my safe haven—now feels like something I've outgrown.

"Alright, let's finish packing. I still owe Zoya about ten book recs before we leave."

"Not sure how I feel about that."

"Not sure it's your business." I narrowly dodge his outstretched palm.

The apartment grows quieter as we work, the shelves slowly emptying. But even as the space becomes less *mine*, I feel it —the excitement thrumming just beneath the surface.

Moving to Russia isn't the end.

It's the start of something new.

EPILOGUE

RODION

THE FAINT GLOW of a winter dawn filters through the window, but I'm mesmerized by the sleeping form of my wife.

My wife.

Those two words hold a world of meaning they never did before. Her fiery red hair spills on the pillow—a satin pillowcase she tested for her new online store, saying something about it leaving hair softer and untangled. I don't much care about that part, but it twisted nicely into makeshift bonds last night. Heh.

She's quiet now, her breathing steady, but the tension in her brow still lingers a little. Not every day is a happy ending, and not every night sweet dreams. She has nightmares sometimes. I don't ask her what they are. They could be memories of her past or even more recently, the blood-stained ground the day of the gala.

I only pull her closer and whisper against her ear that she's safe. That I'm here. That I'll protect her. I stroke her hair until she's softly sleeping against my chest.

I never go back to sleep, though. I can't. Vigilance was burned into me by my brother, and that won't change, especially now that I have someone to be vigilant *for*.

Sometimes, I wish I could dig up Shawn's fucking corpse just to kill him all over again. But I can't go to the past to rectify the present. Instead, I'll focus on the here and now. I promise to slay whatever demons threaten to rob her peace.

Happily.

I give my everything to my wife, and that won't ever change.

"You're thinking too loud," Ember whispers, her eyes still closed, echoing my own teasing line to her.

She stirs, her gorgeous emerald eyes blinking up at me. For a moment, she looks dazed, and so vulnerable she's almost childlike. When she sees me, her lips curve into a soft smile that brings an ache to my chest.

"Morning," she whispers, her voice thick with sleep.

"Morning, *Zveda Maya*." He brushes his lips over mine. "You alright? Bad dream?"

She shakes her head. "Not anymore."

Her fingers lace through mine.

She lays against me as her phone buzzes on the bedside table.

"Did you forget to silence those notifications again?"

"Mhm. *Someone* distracted the hell out of me."

I shake my head. "I'll have to have a talk with Zoya. You don't have to be her personal book assistant."

Laughing, Ember pushes my chest. "As if."

"Seriously, baby. You've become a star in your own right." Her account has absolutely exploded, earning more than she ever imagined. Her follower count has skyrocketed. Here in my home outside of Moscow, she doesn't just have a little nook enchanted with fairy lights to hide the cracked ceilings and fading wallpaper. Oh hell no. My little queen has her own library.

Built it myself and I'm damn proud of it. The grin on her face was worth it.

"Oh, please," Ember says on a yawn. "My account is doing well because of *you,* not me."

I stifle a snort. "Yeah, no. My occasional cameo has nothing to do with it. It's *you,* babe. They want to see you. You let your authenticity shine, and that's what they're here for. You tell them to keep dreaming and all that."

Her eyes narrow playfully. "You mean all those reviews about dark, brooding alpha males? Who could I possibly be drawing inspiration from?" She snorts. "Not my husband, who hardly shows his face on my feed."

"Right. You just let the books keep doing their talking, babe." I shove the covers off and give her ass an affectionate slap. "Let's go. Gym time. You said your New Year's Resolution was to get back to the gym so you could wrestle me. No more slacking."

She throws her pillow at my head. "It's not my fault you keep railing me every time I get dressed in my gym clothes."

I shrug. "No regrets."

As she tugs her leggings on, she sighs.

"What?"

"I miss the attention I used to get at the gym."

She is baiting me, and she's going to fucking regret that.

"Behave yourself, woman."

Smirking, she ties her shoe laces. "It's harder to get attention at a home gym."

"You really need more attention?" I push myself off the dresser and stalk over to her, but she squeals and runs toward the kitchen, likely to grab the protein shakes she prepped in the fridge last night.

I shake my head and chase after her, but when I find her, she's rummaging through the cabinets. "I can't find the peanut butter."

"Peanut butter?"

"Yes," she says with a sigh. "I am *dying* for a peanut butter and pickle sandwich."

I stare at her. She hasn't asked for one of those since we went to the cabin. It feels like a long time ago now. Here in Russia, Zoya cooks for all of us at the family home, and Ember happily partakes, as we all do.

"Are you serious right now?"

"I just... it sounds so *good* right now, and I'm a little nauseous..."

We both turn to face each other at the same time.

"Ember." I hardly trust my voice.

"I—I'm not ready, Rodion. I—I can't, not now, not yet. We used protection!"

I am trying to be sympathetic, but what I'm actually doing is mentally tallying the closest place I can get a pregnancy test.

"We did, we did," I tell her reassuringly, nodding. "But it's not foolproof. We'll just...let's get you a pickle and peanut butter sandwich and a test, okay?"

"Rodion." Her voice is a whisper.

She looks so small, so fragile, it twists something deep in my chest. "We need to find out," she finally says, shaking.

"We do. But listen." I pull her into me. Her fear is palpable. "What if I can't do this? What if I—"

"What if you're not alone?" I finish. "What if the two of us are together?"

Holding my gaze, her eyes shimmer, her fear still palpable. "Together."

I nod. "Wait here," I say, stepping away after seeing the notification on my phone.

It's time.

"Rodion, what are you doing?"

"You'll see."

I slip outside, ignoring the snow biting at me. The driver meets me at the gate, and I take the small bundle he's holding. It squirms in my hands, the softest little growl followed by a squeak. I can't help but smirk. Feisty little thing.

Perfect.

"Behave," I whisper, handing the driver a tip before I turn to the house. I take a deep breath and place another order before I go in.

My heart swells. Our little family might be growing in more ways than one...

When I step back into the warmth of the kitchen, Ember's perched on a stool. The moment she sees me, her brows knit. "Rodion... what did you do?"

"Ordered pregnancy tests."

"*Rodion...*" her voice trails off in a whisper as I set the bundle down at her feet, the blanket falling and revealing the sweetest little creature wobbling on tiny legs with big, fluffy paws promising he'll grow to be big and strong enough to protect my girl in my absence.

Ember's hands fly to her mouth. "A puppy."

"I may have, uh...hacked into those folders of yours, and when I saw you have equal amounts of puppy videos with the book ones... well..."

Her gaze darts between me and the dog, her face unreadable for a split second before she melts.

"He's yours...ours." I reach down and pat his little head. When he turns and gives me an affectionate lick, not gonna lie... I melt a little, too.

She scoops the little guy up and he nuzzles her neck.

"I can't believe this," she says, kissing the top of his head.

I stand watching, my arms crossed on my chest. "You need someone to look over you when I'm not here. He might not be ferocious yet, but I'll train him."

"Is that right?" she asks, her eyes shining at me as her voice drops. "Thank you."

I bend and kiss her cheek. "And I love you. What are you naming him?"

"Oh my gosh… it has to be a book boyfriend name, of course. Rhett? No, no, Darcy. Maybe…Jasper? Romeo?"

"Bratvbloodline too much?"

When she laughs, I cup her face in both my hands. "Look how far you've come. You don't have to do anything alone anymore. Do you hear me? Not now. Not ever."

She lets out a shaky breath.

I smile at her. "I ordered peanut butter, too."

"And pickles?" she asks hopefully.

"And pickles.'

By the time the tests arrived, she's happily perched on my lap, eating her second sandwich and showing me her latest video, taken at a bookstore here in Moscow. The puppy is passed out.

And by the time the positive test sits in her palm, she's calm. Her eyes shine at me.

"A baby."

I smirk. "Semyon can't even get a wife and now look. Motherfucker better get his shit together."

"Rodion!" But she's laughing. "Be nice."

I lean in. "I will. I'll get you anything you need, little queen. More peanut butter? Pillows? Pickles?"

She lets out a sigh and lays her head on my shoulder. "I don't need anything, not really." I hold her to me, staring at the little test that will change our lives forever. "I already have everything I need."

I kiss her cheek.

So do I.

THE END

BONUS EPILOGUE

WANT TO READ MORE OF RODION AND EMBER'S STORY? SCAN THE QR CODE BELOW TO GET THE FREE BONUS EPILOGUE FOR *UNLEASHED: A DARK FORCED MARRIAGE BRATVA ROMANCE*!

PREVIEW
UNVEILED: A DARK ARRANGED MARRIAGE BRATVA ROMANCE

CHAPTER ONE

SEMYON

I shake my head and exit the warehouse, the relentless bite of a Moscow winter hitting me. I pull my coat tighter and check my watch. I wasn't planning on delivering an ass-kicking right before the huge benefit my brother's hosting, but here we are.

It was a problem I had to handle, and I couldn't let it slide. Behind me, I hear the telltale sounds of my brother Rodion cleaning up the mess I left—the heavy scrape of a body being dragged across the floor, the dull thump of a weapon hitting the ground, and his unmistakable carefree whistling. Like one of the fucking seven dwarves.

Only my brother would whistle while running the clean-up crew.

But he's impeccable, reliable, and takes pride in what he does.

My phone buzzes, the ringtone unmistakably Rafail's.

"Where the fuck are you?"

"Took longer than I thought." My jaw tightens as I start the engine. The dickhead had more fight in him than I expected, and I wouldn't let Rodion intervene.

Sliding into the driver's seat, I flip down the mirror to check myself. My hands are clean, my suit is immaculate, and not a speck of blood mars the fabric.

"How'd it go?"

"As good as can be expected. The job's done." I blow out a breath and glance at the time. "Got ten minutes to show up fashionably late."

"Good." There's a pause. Too long. I know immediately something's wrong. He didn't call to make sure I handled a job. Rafail knows better than that.

"Rafail. What is it?"

My older brother and I are tight. He became our legal guardian after our parents' deaths, and he's ruled the family with a tight fist ever since. I sit at his right hand. We don't waste words or time explaining things to each other.

"I've got bad news."

In the background, I hear Polina, his wife, murmuring in her low, soothing voice. She whispers something in Russian, and Rafail mutters back before speaking to me again.

I grit my teeth. I hate showing up late to anything. I plug the address into the GPS and throw the car into reverse. Rodion will get himself there.

When Rafail doesn't tell me right away, my patience begins to wane. "Yeah? You wanna tell me, or do you and Polina need to have a little pillow talk first?"

"Semyon," Rafail says warningly.

I pull the car into drive and ease onto the road before gunning the engine.

"I just kicked someone's teeth in while making sure I didn't get any blood on this fucking white shirt, Rafail. Patience? Fresh out."

I press my lips together. Nothing short of full allegiance to my family would drag me out to an event full of Bratva vultures—enemies and allies alike. But tonight is important. Tonight, I have massive plans that will affect all of us.

I hadn't intended to punish one of our men, but somebody had to do it. Rodion would've been happy to handle it, but I lost my patience.

It happens.

Rafail sighs heavily on the other end of the line. "Your buddy was sighted on a plane heading to Costa Rica twelve hours ago. He's disappeared."

I grip the wheel tighter and exhale slowly. Rodion would have punched the dashboard by now. Rafail would be seeing red. But I've learned to stay calm when everything is falling apart.

No one knows what you'll do next if you don't show your hand.

"Is that right?" My voice drops, cold and venomous. I glance at the GPS. Ten minutes out. "So I'm boarding a plane to Costa Rica tonight." I'm already mentally combing the streets.

"No. I wanted to talk to you first."

"What's there to talk about? Borzov was supposed to give us the details on the shipment and the harbor security leak. That was literally all he fucking had to keep him off our shitlist. And now you're telling me he's gone? Vanished with the shipment?"

Sometimes, as a kid, you think you can tell how people will turn out. I thought I knew him. Borzov and I were as close as two brothers could be, unrelated by blood. We spent every afternoon by the creek in Zalivka, the city outside of Moscow where we both grew up, throwing rocks, climbing trees, swearing that nothing would ever come between us.

As teens, we bought each other condoms and borrowed each other's weapons. We shot by the creek until Rafail caught us and kicked both our asses. We didn't stop—we just got more discreet.

I should've seen it coming.

I shoot Borzov a text, watching the message hang before failing to deliver.

After all these years, after everything we've been through, he fucking *betrayed* me. All of us.

As if his family can fucking afford it.

"We don't know if he's dead or if he betrayed us. We don't know if he was taken or if he left on his own. What we do know—and Polina's confirmed it—is this: The Romanovs are circling. If we don't secure this family now…"

"It's war," I finish with a sigh.

Motherfucker.

Rafail married Polina, the Romanov sister, after a series of events that could've demolished our entire empire. Mikhail Romanov made us a deal: provide critical intel, and he'd allow their marriage—and forgive our trespasses.

"How do you propose we secure the family if we don't even know where he is and you don't want me to go to Costa Rica?"

Rafail exhales sharply. "I don't know. I can't fucking think straight—not with Mikhail breathing down my neck. And *he's* breathing down my neck because Novak's breathing down *his*."

I hear him cover the mouthpiece of his phone, his voice lowering as he speaks to Polina. I can imagine her, torn as always—tight with her family but fiercely loyal to Rafail. Concerned for both our wellbeing and theirs.

When he gets back on the line, his tone is tight. "Polina says she can buy us time. Mikhail's furious, but she knows his wife and is close with her brothers. She'll talk to them, explain the situation. But our timing sucks."

It does.

We're already in debt to two of the most powerful Bratva groups: the Romanovs in America and the Morozov family in Moscow. If we falter for even a moment, we're finished.

We can't take another risk. Not again.

Rafail's voice dropped, just loud enough for me to catch, likely trying not to wake a sleeping baby. "I've given everything to keep us together. Don't make me watch it fall apart now." His words were a rare crack in the iron. For a moment, I'm not just his second-in-command—I'm still his kid brother, watching him bow under the weight of responsibility.

When my parents died, Rafail was barely an adult himself, holding us together with sheer willpower and a string of desperate decisions. He's seen us through every struggle since then, and I won't let him bear this burden alone.

"I've got this," I promise him, even though I have no idea how I'm going to fix it.

"How?"

I shake my head. "I don't know. But I promise you, I will not let this happen. I'll do anything it takes."

He exhales again, the sound heavy with frustration, before continuing.

"Anything?"

A prickle of cold awareness slides down my spine at the shift in his tone. It's the voice I've learned to mimic myself—the cold, calculating tone that signals danger and demands attention.

"Yes?"

"Anya will be there tonight."

He doesn't need to say her name. I know exactly who he's talking about.

Anya Borzova. Elizar Borozov's younger sister.

The girl who used to chase fireflies by the creek, her laughter making me smile when the world seemed dim and hopeless. The girl who would look at me like I hung the moon, with such wide and trusting eyes it would make my heart ache. She'd blush furiously and run whenever she caught my gaze.

I watched her grow from a shy, freckle-faced kid into a headstrong woman with too much light, too much innocence for this world. I kept her at a distance.

I *had* to.

She was off limits.

I knew the world we lived in and I knew how easily I'd corrupt her. In my mind, if she was still my best friend's little sister, she would stay untouchable—*safe*.

If I could just pretend—if I could freeze her in time, hold her in my memory as the innocent kid who loved books more than people and dreamed of worlds bigger than ours— maybe she'd stay untouched by this life.

By me.

I play dumb. I need to buy time.

"Who?" I force the question out, playing dumb. I want to

hear him say her name. I need to hear the words. Make them real.

"You know exactly who. Anya's... an option."

She could never be a fucking option.

I curse under my breath, gripping the wheel tighter.

But I don't tell my brother no. I'm not allowed to and live to tell about it. Bratva law is unchangeable and I don't challenge the law.

"Is she even legal?" I ask, shaking my head. For fuck's sake. The last time I saw her, she was traipsing off on scholarship to college, aiming to get her degree. Her family couldn't afford anything more, but she was determined. Always determined.

I've always had a soft spot for her. But now? Now, she's... collateral.

If Rafail is thinking what I think he is...

"Be specific, brother." My voice is ice, my back rigid as I watch the needle on the speedometer creep up.

"We go to her father and make a proposition."

Why did we ever let them negotiate with us to begin with? They aren't Bratva, they don't know the risk they took...

Rafail continues. "...we forgive the debt owed to us in exchange for his daughter's hand in marriage. And you, brother, take her home."

No.

I shake my head, grateful he can't see me right now. Rafail held us together when our parents died, barely an adult himself.

Now, every mistake feels like a betrayal of that sacrifice, a weight I can't afford to drop. It wasn't just our lives he was trying to save—it was our family, our name, our future.

And now that rests on my shoulders. Marriage will strengthen our family. We can't afford a misstep.

Not another one.

I'm silent for long moments, unable to respond.

Anya. Beautiful, headstrong, willful, and brilliant. I remember her at five years old, sitting in the corner of her room with her freckled nose wrinkled in concentration, reading book after book while ignoring her chores. When she wasn't risking her neck down by the stupid fucking creek, she was dreaming too big for her world.

"I can arrange a marriage with her father in the blink of an eye," Rafail continues. "He has nothing to stop us from claiming her as collateral, and you know it. It means your world gets turned upside down, though, Semyon."

Marry her.

"She's a fucking child."

"She was when you knew her. I promise you," Rafail says in a low voice. "She isn't now."

A sharp thrum of blood pulses through me as I grip the wheel tighter, my teeth clenched.

"You mean to tell me..." I pause, breathing in through my nose to calm my temper, when realization dawns on me, "she's all grown up, her brother's fucked us over—and who knows who else in the process—and she's at that fucking ball, *alone?* Dressed in God-knows-what? Vulnerable and single?"

"That's *exactly* what I'm telling you."

"Call her father," I snap.

An idea forms, one that just might work... at least at first...

"And Rafail?"

"Yeah?"

"Swear him to secrecy. He tells no one... not even Anya."

I hang up and gun the engine.

WANT TO FIND OUT WHAT HAPPENS NEXT? ORDER YOUR COPY OF "UNVEILED: A DARK FORCED MARRIAGE BRATVA ROMANCE" BY SCANNING THE QR CODE BELOW.

Fueled by dark chocolate and even darker coffee, USA Today bestselling author Jane Henry writes what she loves to read – character-driven, unputdownable romance featuring dominant alpha males and the powerful heroines who bring them to their knees. She's believed in the power of love and romance since Belle won over the beast, and finally decided to write love stories of her own.

Scan the QR Code below to receive Jane's Newsletter & be notified of upcoming new releases & special offers!

Be sure to visit me at www.janehenryromance.com, too!

www.ingramcontent.com/pod-product-compliance
Lightning Source LLC
Chambersburg PA
CBHW060613300726
48975CB00005B/1554